Chris asked – 'no pressure of course' – when the time would be right for us to have sex. Just a ballpark figure.

Thought for a second then told him around three hundred and seventy-five days.

He seemed really startled at first, then depressed. I asked him what was wrong and he said, 'Nothing.' Then he said it just seemed *very* specific and *very, very* long. About five seconds later he'd worked out the implications and said that any day when we made love would be totally and completely romantic and it didn't have to be Valentine's day, but I told him that the first time we did it had to be perfect, as it was not just the first time we made love to each other, but also the first time either of us had ever done it at all. Obviously no other date but the most romantic day in the year could possibly be right.

Chris said, 'Er, right.'

Praise for *My Desperate Love Diary*:

'Heartfelt but at the same time fantastically funny, this is a must read' MIZZ

'A feel-good summer read' SUN

'Very funny . . . the reader is drawn directly into Kelly Ann's World' WRITERS' NEWS

Also by Liz Rettig

My Desperate Love Diary

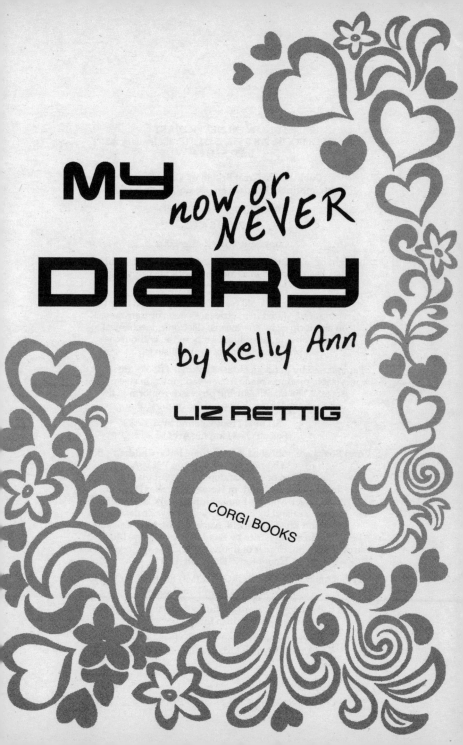

MY now or NEVER DIARY

by kelly Ann

LIZ RETTIG

CORGI BOOKS

MY NOW OR NEVER DIARY
A CORGI BOOK: 978 0 552 55334 6 (From January 2007)
0 552 55334 4

Published in Great Britain by Corgi Books,
an imprint of Random House Children's Books

This edition published 2006

3 5 7 9 10 8 6 4 2

Set in 11/16pt Palatino by
Falcon Oast Graphic Art Ltd

Corgi Books are published by Random House Children's Books,
61–63 Uxbridge Road, London W5 5SA,
a division of The Random House Group Ltd,
in Australia by Random House Australia (Pty) Ltd,
20 Alfred Street, Milsons Point, Sydney, NSW 2061, Australia,
in New Zealand by Random House New Zealand Ltd,
18 Poland Road, Glenfield, Auckland 10, New Zealand
and in South Africa by Random House (Pty) Ltd,
Isle of Houghton, Corner of Boundary & Carse O'Gowrie Roads,
Houghton 2198, South Africa

THE RANDOM HOUSE GROUP LIMITED REG. NO. 954009
www.kidsatrandomhouse.co.uk

A CIP catalogue record for this book is available from
the British Library.

Printed and bound in Great Britain by
Cox & Wyman Ltd, Reading, Berkshire

For Eileen Clarke

With special thanks to Kelly Cauldwell, Annie Eaton
and Guy Rose

Also Liz Marshall for her corpse's feet story

And John Doherty, paratrooper, poet, and international
sales person

WEDNESDAY JANUARY 3RD

The worst thing about having a boyfriend is that I can't get away with tatty uncoordinated knickers and bras now that someone might see them even if I'm not knocked down and have to go to hospital. Have checked through my underwear drawer, and apart from a bra-and-thong set that my friend Stephanie bought me last year I have absolutely nothing decent (or indecent) to wear.

I suppose there's no rush as I have secretly decided not to have sex with my boyfriend Chris until Valentine's day so that everything will be totally romantic and absolutely perfect when we do it for the first time. Still, if I buy now I can get something cheap in the sales and it's not as though underwear goes off or anything.

Made straight for the town centre and bought a gorgeous strawberry-pink silk bra with matching lacy pants, then spotted another teal-blue satin set with broderie anglaise trim and bought that too. Of course, nothing I wanted was actually *in* the sale (must remember to read the small print – i.e. *up to* 50 per cent off on *selected* items) so the whole lot cost £40 and totally cleaned me out of cash but I reckon it's worth it. Especially as both bras were a B cup and I fitted them. Well, I will do with the help of a smidgeon of tissue paper.

Stephanie and my other best friend Liz came over tonight and I showed them what I'd bought. Liz said the underwear was really nice and she was glad I was finally making practical and psychological preparations to lose my virginity but what would I do about the toilet paper I normally stuffed into my bra if things got really passionate with Chris?

Stephanie, however, seemed a bit doubtful about my purchases. She said that guys (the heterosexual ones anyway) weren't really into pretty pastel underwear and preferred black or scarlet balcony bras, possibly made from nylon or perhaps leather, with matching butterfly thongs.

This was typical of Stephanie. She isn't exactly the most romantic person in the world. When her boyfriend Dave first told her he loved her she just said, 'Yeah, right . . . whatever.' Stephanie denies she's unromantic, pointing out that she sometimes likes to shag by candlelight, but I don't think that counts.

Told Stephanie that perhaps the type of boys she'd dated in the past were like that but that Chris was different. He was intelligent, sensitive and special.

Stephanie said, 'Bollocks.'

Chris and I are finished. I hate him and never want to see him again as long as I live. Stephanie is right. All guys are revolting, sex-obsessed scum (although she likes them like that).

Went over to Chris's tonight. We were snogging for a while in his room, then he said he had a present for me and handed me a small soft parcel. From the size and feel of it I thought at first it must be an embroidered hanky and wondered at him buying me such a Great-aunt Winnie type of gift, but when I opened it I was horrified then furious.

It was an underwear set from God's knows where – probably one of those mail order only places, as it was totally disgusting. The bra was made of black see-through nylon decorated with scarlet concentric circles radiating out from the nipple area. The pants, if you can call them that, were even worse and consisted of a tiny fragment of satin in the shape of a heart, complete with glitter and fake fur around the border, connected to what looked like three pieces of black dental floss. Gross!

Couldn't believe Chris could have bought such a tacky and repulsive thing and told him so. What did he think I was – some sort of cheap slut? Well, he had another think coming.

But Chris was unrepentant. He said he hadn't meant to offend me and saw absolutely nothing wrong with his present. He said – get this – that I should be flattered and that most girls hadn't the figure to wear something like that.

Told him that what most girls didn't have were boyfriends with no taste and even less respect and that I was going home right then and I'd show this disgusting underwear set to my dad who would be so incensed he'd probably shoot him and Chris wasn't to bother walking home with me as I'd rather be raped and murdered on the way back than spend another second in his company.

Chris said he might be more worried if my dad owned a gun but anyway I shouldn't go home on my own, it was late.

Chris's dad is a detective in the police force, and I suppose because of some of the stories his dad has told him, Chris seems to imagine that any girl left walking unescorted at night for even a nanosecond is liable to be attacked. Have tried to reason with Chris before and tell him that statistically it is young males who are most likely to be the victims of violence but he doesn't listen, just says, fine, *I* can protect *him* then.

Argued with him again about it but he still insisted on walking back with me, which made me even madder. I hurried along with Chris trotting miserably beside me. Kept telling him to sod off and leave me alone but he ignored me. Then I spotted a policeman so went right up and said, 'This person is bothering me, Officer.'

Turned out that the policeman was a friend of Chris's dad and knew Chris. He just said, 'Girlfriend trouble, I suppose, Chris. You should take my advice and steer clear of women, son, they're nothing but trouble. God knows, I wish I had.'

Was utterly furious with the policeman. Thought this was typical of the cronyism and sexism that were all too prevalent in the force and told him so.

But the policeman just laughed and said to Chris that he had 'a right one here' and that he didn't envy him. Then he said he'd walk me home and for Chris to tell his dad he was asking after him.

FRIDAY JANUARY 5TH

Stephanie and Liz came over tonight. Told them about the underwear set and how mad I was with Chris but they just thought it was a scream. Stephanie demanded to see the outfit, then insisted on putting it on and strutting around the room, mimicking my voice and saying, 'Oh Chris, you're not like other boys. You're *so* intelligent, sensitive and special.'

Hilarious.

SATURDAY JANUARY 6TH

Have calmed down a bit about Chris's present but am still mad that I've probably wasted £40, unless of course I get a gay boyfriend and what's the point in that?

Both Stephanie and Liz are meeting their boyfriends tonight and I was quite missing Chris so texted him to say I wasn't mad at him any more but he didn't reply. Called him instead but he is still furious with me for reporting him to the police and won't speak to me, far less meet up.

In the end Liz said I could come with her and her boyfriend Julian for pizza. It wasn't as though they'd just started going out or anything so I wouldn't be in the way and she promised not to snog in front of me.

Julian is Stephanie's big brother. He's really nice and a total genius with computers but can't be arsed getting a job. He's going to have to though as his dad, despite being rich, says he won't give him any more money. Julian has pleaded with his mum to make his dad relent but even though she's divorced from Julian's dad, so probably doesn't like him much, she has taken his dad's side.

Tonight Liz said she was on a diet so would only have one slice of the pizza. Yeah, right. Julian, of course, did what all boyfriends have to do after such a statement and pleaded with Liz to eat some more, assuring her that she was perfect just as she was, practically wasting away in fact, and that he didn't want her to faint for lack of nutrients. He told her (while eyeing her DD breasts) that she mustn't lose a single ounce.

Liz quickly relented and tucked into five slices of pizza followed by chocolate fudge cake.

Liz *is* slightly plump but she's blonde and busty so loads of guys fancy her. Well, they fancy her until she starts doing all her psychology rubbish on them, which usually means asking them loads of nosy questions and then telling them how they came to be the weak, pathetic creatures they are today. Only Julian, who never takes any insults seriously, can put up with her.

I do envy Liz her big boobs and blonde hair. Or I did until Chris made me feel like I was totally gorgeous anyway, even though I'm brunette and will probably never have guys drooling over my cleavage unless I go for implants.

Really missed Chris tonight. Why, oh why do guys never call you when you want them to?

SUNDAY JANUARY 7TH

Chris still won't speak to me. Wish he didn't always take such a long time to get over an argument. Have known Chris for ages and we've been friends since the beginning of primary school, although I didn't fancy him then of course. Once, when he was ten, he fell out with me for five weeks just because I burst his football with a pair of scissors when he wouldn't let me be striker in a game he'd organized with his pals. He still goes on about it sometimes, even now.

He said it had been difficult enough persuading the

others to let a girl play at all and that I was better suited to goalkeeping anyway. He added that playing the rest of the game with a busted ball wasn't much fun and that, yes, he knew I'd later offered him my ball but it wasn't a proper football and moreover it was pink. What had colour got to do with anything? Oh, give him a break.

MONDAY JANUARY 8TH

First day back at school. Everyone was expecting me and Chris to be all loved up since we'd only just started going out together but Chris barely looked at me, never mind spoke to me.

Ms Conner, our English teacher, *is* really all loved up though. She imagines her affair with religious education teacher Mr Dunn is a total secret. *As if.* Of course absolutely everyone in the school knows about it, from the staff (except Miss McElwee, who's too old and past it to notice anything) down to the lowliest first year.

Don't know what she sees in Mr Dunn. Ms Conner is really brainy and interested in loads of intellectual stuff like Culture and Philosophy whereas Mr Dunn is only interested in motorbikes, martial arts and getting pissed. It's amazing that he ever got to be a teacher, but I suppose since no one wants to teach RE they just have to take what they can get even if it's a tattooed moron like Mr Dunn. But what on earth can he and Ms

Conner have in common? What would they talk about?

Mentioned this to Stephanie but she just shrugged and muttered something about who says they needed to talk anyway?

Gross.

Ms Conner is still spouting all the feminist rubbish that she did last year after her husband left her for his secretary, but she now qualifies it by saying that there are some exceptional individuals who rise above the limitations of their gender, culture and time. She also says that this year, as well as studying mainstream feminist literature we would also be exploring women's powerful potential for sensual and sexual expression. Thus she will be adding D. H. Lawrence, Durrell and Chaucer to our reading list.

Don't know about exploring women's potential – it was mainly the boys who scrambled eagerly to the front for details of the extended reading list.

One piece of definite good news though is that Mr Simmons has been promoted to principal maths teacher. He is no longer our register teacher and we have a new, young (and quite sexy) register teacher who couldn't tell a forged parent's note if a five-year-old wrote it. Fantastic!

Shelly said she was really sorry to hear that Chris and I had split up. Told her not to worry, that we hadn't really split, and that it was just a temporary fall-out. I said that Chris could be stubborn at times but I thought he was looking really miserable now and I'd probably go talk to him and make it up today.

But Shelly advised me not to approach him first. After all, she said, if Chris really cared for me he'd make the first move. I shouldn't humble myself by going to him. Then she said not to worry – so far she hadn't seen him and Linda together again but she'd keep an eye out for me and let me know if anything was going on.

Shelly has become a really good friend to me. It's great that she is taking the trouble to keep tabs on things for me but I think she worries too much about the Linda thing: Chris and Linda finished ages ago and he never even mentions her now. Still, I suppose you can't be too careful, and anyway, since Shelly lives right across from Linda it will be no trouble for her to check on what's going on.

Shelly goes out with Gerry, a guy I'd fancied all last year for some stupid reason and who I used to just call G (that was his real initial, a double-bluff intended to fool Mum just in case) in my diary. Don't know how I could have been so daft really. I mean Gerry *is* very good looking but he's a total tosser and forever trying to hit on every fanciable girl he meets. No wonder Shelly is so paranoid about cheating.

FRIDAY JANUARY 12TH

Despite Shelly's advice I gave in and made the first move at getting back together. Passed Chris a note during maths today saying: '*Sorry about the police.*'

Chris passed it back with '*Sorry about the glitter and fur underwear*' written underneath. Unfortunately Mr Simmons spotted the note and demanded I hand it over to him. His eyes bulged a bit when he read it, though all he said was that he didn't know or want to know what this was all about but it certainly had nothing to do with the calculus exercise he'd just set me and didn't I realize the Prelims start next week. Then he gave me a punishment exercise consisting of a 1000-word essay on the importance of maths education, which I thought was a bit over the top for just one small note.

Chris arranged to meet me after school to 'talk things over'. We agreed that he would never buy me underwear again. Even if I was down to my very last pair of knickers and begged him on my knees. I agreed never to report him to the police again. Not even if I discovered he was a serial murderer and international terrorist. Chris also said he'd do the Simmons essay for me.

It was so good spending almost the whole weekend with Chris, even though we are both so broke (partly due to underwear purchases) that we had to make do with watching MTV and playing Monopoly (I always beat Chris at this so it's my game of choice with him).

I've always enjoyed Chris's company, so I don't know why it took me so long to realize just how gorgeous he is too. I didn't even think of him as boyfriend material until nearly the end of last year. Maybe it was because I was so used to thinking of him as a pal.

Chris, though, has fancied me for ages. Asked him tonight when he first knew his feelings for me were more than just friendly, and he said when I was twelve and he stopped being really annoyed when I cheated at Monopoly as soon as he started winning, just so long as the game lasted longer and he could spend more time with me.

Told Chris that I didn't cheat at Monopoly – although, OK, admittedly I sometimes liked to change the rules halfway through to make the game more interesting.

He said, 'Yeah, right,' that was the definition of cheating if you asked him, but he wasn't really annoyed. Can't see Chris and me arguing about anything ever again – we're just so happy together. There isn't anyone or anything that could ever keep us apart.

Well, except for exams, that is. Chris said we wouldn't

be able to see each other next week as we would need to study for the Prelims.

Am dreading these – I've got really behind with my work. Also suddenly remembered all the carry-on last year: everyone now knows, from an informer teacher, just what teachers get up to when invigilating exams. Apparently while exams are nerve-racking for us pupils they are a total bore for invigilators, who make up stupid games to amuse themselves. One is called Chicken: two invigilators walk towards each other down the same aisle and the first one to step aside is 'chicken' and loses. This has occasionally led to head-on collisions, with both invigilators utterly determined to win: things turned ugly when two really dogged players had to be taken to Accident & Emergency suffering from concussion after a long Geography Advanced Higher exam.

As if the Chicken competition wasn't bad enough, there's worse – at least from us pupils' point of view. A particularly nasty game involves invigilators standing beside the desk of the ugliest pupil they can find. The ugly pupil candidates are then compared and scored by an independent non-competing invigilator and the one who had spotted the ugliest is the winner.

It is difficult to believe just how childish and nasty supposedly responsible adults can be – and most invigilators are teachers or ex-teachers. Sometimes I think that teachers don't actually like pupils at all, although I suppose they must do to work with us. Stephanie disagrees. She says all teachers hate teenagers, if not when they started out, at least before the end of their first term in the job. You can't blame them really. Think how we wind up new, young teachers and take the piss out of old, past-it teachers and constantly annoy in-between teachers.

Hmmm. I suppose we do give them a hard time on occasion, but as I said to Stephanie, teachers are supposed to be role models for us. They should be able to rise above all that petty stuff and instead of looking for revenge, lead by example.

Stephanie said, 'Bollocks.'

TUESDAY JANUARY 16TH

Shelly says that there is no way her boyfriend Gerry could go without seeing her for a day, never mind a week, no matter what was going on. Of course Gerry was just too mad for her to let anything come between them. Chris was very sensible to say he had to study this week and he was no doubt quite right but her Gerry was just too crazy about her to be sensible.

WEDNESDAY JANUARY 17TH

English exam today. Wasn't too bad.

THURSDAY JANUARY 18TH

Maths today. Don't ask.

I don't have anything tomorrow but Chris has physics. Am really glad I don't do physics. It's like maths only worse but Chris likes it – I suppose because he likes maths. In fact he and Ian have been fast-tracked to the Advanced Higher and do different stuff from us in maths.

Pleaded with Chris to let me come over and see him tonight. Said I wouldn't stay long and anyway I wouldn't be any bother, I'd just bring my French along and we could study alongside one another.

After a bit more persuasion or 'nagging', as he called it, he agreed. Neither of us actually got much work done though. Chris complained he couldn't concentrate on physics while I was sitting on his knee and trying to snog him all the time so he soon abandoned any attempt at serious study. However, having proved to myself that I could definitely distract him from his revision, I decided I'd better go home and get some work done despite Chris's pleas for me to stay and keep him company as his concentration was shot anyway.

FRIDAY JANUARY 19TH

Attempted to study today. However, my sister Angela was trying but failing to cope with her new baby, which was screaming blue murder most of the time. Used to call Angela MNP – short for Miss No Personality – but since becoming a mum she *has* developed a personality. Unfortunately it's a moany, miserable one. Wish her fiancé Graham hadn't been sent to Manchester to work for the year – not that I'd ever liked that boring geek but at least she'd have someone to moan to other than me.

I decided to escape to the library, but just as I was ready to go Angela pushed her bawling brat into my arms and told me to take it, she couldn't stand it any more. Then she put on her coat and fled.

So much for all her pregnancy fantasies about her and the baby lying listening to Bach and Mozart while gazing into each other's eyes and blissfully bonding.

Mum and Dad were at work – Dad was at the garage as usual and Mum has just started as an assistant under-manageress at the local supermarket (i.e. she gets to stock the shelves as well as check out shopping, wash the floors and lock up) – so there was no one else to give the thing to. In fact I hardly see my dad any more because he's always working, trying to pay for Angela's wedding in December. Her fiancé Graham's parents have offered to help but Dad is too proud to take anything from that 'stuck-up fur coat and nae knickers' couple, although that's not exactly what he said to them.

Will probably also see less of Mum now too as she's decided to study Spanish with the Open University. It's a kind of long-distance course done by post and Internet.

Mum says she now accepts she's getting older and her body is going 'to rack and ruin' so she's going to concentrate on developing her mind.

Am pleased Mum at last seems to be coming to terms with her age. It was awful last year when she freaked out after she turned forty and learned she was going to become a granny. I still cringe when I remember how she started wearing my clothes, then ran off with a twenty-two-year-old Spanish waiter she'd met on holiday.

Since I wanted to encourage Mum to accept the fact she's getting old, I didn't tell her that according to my friend Liz the brain deteriorates with age as well and that millions of Mum's brain cells are dying off every day. Liz says the memory is the first to go. It will start with Mum not recalling whether she's put on conditioner after she's shampooed her hair and end up with her not remembering who I am and – here's the good news – whether she promised to buy me an iPod for Christmas.

Anyway, it looked like I was stuck with Angela's baby for the afternoon so had to walk up and down with it while practising my French vocabulary. Noticed that it seemed to like the sound of the French words so put on a French tape, then propped it up on a cushion in the corner of the sofa. It's not my fault if it ends up with no friends because it grows up only talking French and no one can understand it. After all, Angela is supposed to be the one teaching it how to talk. Warmed a bottle of baby milk for it then, using another cushion and a thick book, managed to manoeuvre things so that it could get fed without me having to hold it.

It fell asleep mid bottle so I could get back to studying again, but oddly found myself gazing at its face and stroking its cheek. Then, even though it was sleeping and I didn't have to soothe it, I picked it up and held it close to me. Put my face next to its, and discovered that when not smelling of pee (or worse) babies do smell nice, a sort of sweet milk and Johnson's baby talc combination.

The doorbell rang so rushed to answer it, still holding the baby before another ring woke it up. It was Chris. He said he'd called me but had got no answer and guessed Angela's baby was making a racket again. He looked a bit surprised and concerned that I was walking about cradling a baby so I told him not to worry and assured him that I wasn't getting broody, perish the thought.

Chris took the baby from me and laid it in its carry cot beside the sofa. Then he kissed me and said he wasn't worried. He said the last time someone had a baby in my state was at least two thousand years ago in Bethlehem so he felt pretty confident we were safe.

Noticed how cold Chris's face was when we kissed, which wasn't surprising – though it hadn't snowed yet, it was Baltic outside. I suggested we sit close to the fire so he could warm up. Told him I didn't want my boyfriend dying of hypothermia. Especially as we'd only been going out a few weeks and I hadn't had time to get fed up with him yet.

Chris laughed but then started talking about the symptoms and treatment of hypothermia. He is really interested in medical stuff as he is dead keen to be a doctor one day, so at first I thought he was up for a serious discussion when he told me that the symptoms of hypothermia included disorientation, confusion and loss of balance. But when he staggered and fell onto the sofa, pulling me down on top of him, and then said the best treatment was very close bodily contact followed by sex, I reckoned he was acting it.

Yeah, right. Told him that I wasn't daft and knew from survival programmes that woolly hats, warm drinks and aluminium foil wraps were what was really recommended but Chris said those were optional extras and swore blind that sex was the most efficient way to increase body temperature. He said if I wanted to be wrapped in aluminium foil and wear a woolly hat at the same time that would be OK by him.

The thought of this made me giggle, which woke the baby, so I made Chris walk about with it while I revised my French as it was his fault, sort of, that it woke up.

Angela came back about an hour later but said she was knackered and went off to her room without even looking at her baby. Chris suggested we go and get a burger and Coke so we had to shove the baby in its pram and take it with us. Chris also said I had to stop calling him it. The baby's name was Danny.

Actually the baby's name is Graham Daniel – he was

named after his dad – but we all preferred Danny so only Graham calls him 'Graham' now and he's hardly here because of his work in Manchester.

Met almost everyone I knew on route to the café, all of whom thought they were the first to say stuff like 'Christ, that was quick work!' and 'Heard of speed-dating but this is ridiculous!'

Hilarious.

MONDAY 22ND JANUARY

French today. Didn't do too badly despite bloody awful night last night.

Was wakened as usual by the baby bawling its head off. Put my head under the pillow and tried to block it out but then heard another wailing sound which turned out to be Angela sobbing.

Brilliant. Now I had the two of them creating a bloody racket. Mum and Dad as per usual were sleeping through the whole commotion, probably because Mum now always sleeps with ear plugs in (she'd been through the sleepless nights stuff twice already with us and what thanks had she got for it?) and absolutely nothing ever wakes up Dad until morning.

Finally got up and marched into her room. Couldn't believe what a dump it was. Angela used to be so neat; now the place was littered with baby paraphernalia and didn't look much better than my friend Liz's room, which hasn't been tidied since, well, ever really. Angela was sitting in a chair wearing a nightie stained with baby drool and holding her head in her hands. Meanwhile the baby was screaming blue murder in its cot.

I picked it up and told Angela to get some sleep. She sobbed, 'Thanks, Kelly Ann,' then crawled into bed. Took the baby next door with me and walked up and down shoogling it for a bit until it had stopped crying. It wasn't asleep but it did give a wide toothless yawn which looked really cute.

It's funny really how a baby can look cute with no hair or teeth. I mean no one else does. OK, I suppose some guys do look good with a crew cut which is nearly bald, and some actors and even actresses looked fantastic totally bald, but none of them would look great if they didn't have teeth.

Decided not to risk waking Angela up again by taking the baby back into her room so just took it to bed with me.

Taking the baby to bed proved a mistake: when I woke up my bed smelled faintly but definitely of pee. No wonder – its nappy was heavy and saturated. Took it to Angela's room but she was asleep and looked so knackered, with horrible dark circles under her eyes, that I didn't have the heart to wake her. Mum and Dad had already left for work, so though I'd sworn blind I would never change a nappy, it looked like I would have to. Peeked inside while holding my nose just to make sure it wasn't anything worse than pee – there are limits to sisterly concern – then having checked, fetched another nappy and undid the sodden one.

Vile thing peed in my face. That's it, I am never having a baby, but if I do it's going to be a girl.

Fed it anyway and popped it back in its cot before showering and putting all my bedclothes in the washing machine. Was fifteen minutes late for French but managed to finish on time.

Chris says my sister isn't well. He says she's depressed and should see a doctor but he doesn't know Angela like I do. She's never exactly been the most fun person to be around so it's no surprise she's turned into a miserable pain who could moan for Scotland. It would be impossible to tell whether she was really depressed or just being her normal self. Unless doctors have Fun Person pills I don't see how they could help.

WEDNESDAY JANUARY 24TH

Another bloody awful night when I had to take the baby again. Wish my sister would get her act together and start looking after it like she's supposed to.

Am absolutely determined never to have a baby. Have heard lots of horror stories about condoms splitting so I've decided to go on the pill as well just to make totally and completely sure I don't get pregnant when I eventually do it with Chris. (It's what Dad would call 'belt and braces' if I ever told him about it, perish the thought.) However, am not quite sure how to go about this. I know I'll have to ask a doctor and Liz says they can't tell my mum about it, but what will I say? Even if I go to Dr Curtis, the woman doctor at our practice, it will be so embarrassing basically admitting that I'm going to have sex.

Stephanie says I'm mad but if I feel that way about it I could just say I've got irregular periods as they prescribe the pill for that as well, but I don't have irregular periods and I'm sure they'd know I was lying.

Liz says that I could tell them I'm suicidally depressed about my spots and that I need the pill for that. Now she tells me! Maybe Liz is wrong and there is a God after all. A contraceptive pill that also gets rid of spots. Will fix up an appointment straight after I finish these Prelims.

MONDAY JANUARY 29TH

When I rang the surgery the nosy receptionist asked what it was about. Told her it was personal, private and confidential. Cheeky thing said if it's head lice I didn't need to see the doctor and could get the treatment free at the pharmacist.

Told her quite snootily that I would require to see my

general practitioner, thanks, and that, yes, it was urgent (Stephanie has told me I have to be on it for two weeks before Valentine's day).

TUESDAY JANUARY 30TH

Don't believe it. The one day I really want to have spots and I've practically none. Just one tiny spot on my chin. I can hardly say I'm ready to top myself over that. Thought about painting some fake ones on but I suppose with all that training and experience the doctor will probably be able to tell. I'll just have to tell her the real reason I want a prescription.

Sat in the doctor's waiting room trying to work up that courage to go in. Told myself this was stupid. I was practically an adult, after all. I was over the legal age for sex and no one could stop me doing it if I wanted to. I had as much right as anyone else to get the pill and I'd absolutely no reason to be embarrassed about it. I would just have to be totally calm, sophisticated and assertive; just as Liz had advised me.

It was my turn. Went into the room marked DR CURTIS. She smiled pleasantly at me, told me to take a seat then asked, 'How can I help you, Kelly Ann?'

I blurted out, 'I want to have sex.'

Dr Curtis raised her eyebrows but said calmly, 'Not right now, I presume, Kelly Ann. I hope you don't mean right at this very moment in my consulting room.'

I ploughed on. 'You can't stop me. I am absolutely determined to do it. I really, really want it.'

Dr Curtis smiled at me and I felt my face flush scarlet as I realized I must have sounded totally mental, like some mad nymphomaniac. She was probably going to refer me to a psychiatric institution, where I would be sectioned and forced to spend the whole of the rest of my life in a padded room eating mushy food with plastic cutlery.

However, she just took my blood pressure then printed out a prescription for the pill along with instructions for using it. As I was leaving she said, 'Your boyfriend is a very lucky lad, Kelly Ann, to have such an *enthusiastic, indeed positively eager* partner.'

WEDNESDAY JANUARY 31ST

Am mortified by my stupid carry-on at the doctor's. Liz and Stephanie nearly wet themselves laughing when I told them. Stephanie says I'm mad. She says everyone is totally cool about contraception now. It's seen as just a normal bit of shopping. Responsible too.

Even so, didn't want to go to the local chemist, where everyone would know me, so took the bus into Argyle Street after school and went to Boots there.

Handed over my prescription to the pharmacist and

resisted the urge to say it was for my spots or period problems. She just took it without any fuss. She didn't even give me a disapproving look, never mind ask any nosy questions or make remarks like 'A bit young to be having sex, aren't you,' and 'does your mum know?'

Feeling quite grown up and sophisticated now, I decided to have a look at the condoms displayed on the shelves nearby while I was waiting for my prescription. Have never bought condoms before, of course, or taken a close interest in them really, so was amazed that there seemed to be so many different types – though none of them said what colour they were. Was determined not to get green ones like Gerry had bought last year when I almost but didn't have sex with him. Feeling really cool and confident, I decided to ask the assistant nearby, who happened to be a guy not much older than me.

Picked up a packet at random and asked him if he knew what colour they were. He seemed a bit surprised but muttered something about their being normal colour, he supposed.

But was he absolutely sure? Had he used these ones himself? Could we take one out to look at it?

He flushed and muttered no, he didn't think we could do that. He seemed really uncomfortable and I felt a bit sorry for him. Obviously, unlike me, he hadn't got over the immature, silly stage of being embarrassed about stuff like this. I would show him by my example how totally grown up and sophisticated a young person should be.

I asked him which ones he used so I could be sure of the colour. He seemed totally taken aback by my frank and businesslike approach but managed to wave a hand in the general direction of one type, which I collected and showed to him just to make sure I'd got the right ones. So he was sure these were the ones he used, was he? And he could vouch for the fact that they were definitely not green?

He nodded mutely.

I turned the packet over and read out the blurb to him: 'It says here that they are ultra fine and super sensitive. Also that they give maximum pleasure for both her and him.' Could he confirm that? Would he recommend them? The assistant spluttered some strangled comment, which I took to mean something along the lines of: they were OK, considering. Would have questioned him further but my name was being called as my prescription was ready. In my new resolution of openness I paid for the condoms then told the assistant I would have to go as my contraceptive pills were ready for picking up.

It was marvellous to be free of all my stupid, immature inhibitions about talking about contraceptives and I strode confidently towards the exit, only to be met by the assistant, who asked for my phone number.

What a sleazer. I mean what kind of total slut did he think I was? And stupid as well. Like he really wanted my number for market research. Yeah, right. Market research my arse.

* * *

Have just taken my first pill. Only 13 more to go, then it will be V day!!

THURSDAY FEBRUARY 1ST

Chatted with Shelly at lunch time today. She always seems so friendly and genuinely interested in what I do these days. Ended up telling her about going on the pill but she seemed really concerned for me. She told me that taking the pill was very dangerous. She said loads of girls had died of taking the pill after blood clots had stopped their hearts or brains. But she said not to worry – maybe I'd be one of the lucky ones and perhaps survive, and anyway, it would be so worth while just to make Chris happy. She added that she was really impressed with the risks and sacrifices I'd make for love.

Stephanie says Shelly talks rubbish. She says not to trust that stupid slapper, who in any case has been on the pill since third year. Then she told me the pill would push me up at least another bra cup size.

Well, that's it decided. Chance of instant death versus

possibility of fitting into a C cup. No contest. I'm staying on the pill.

But if I'm dead, the size of my breasts probably wouldn't be much consolation. Am undecided again. Wish I could ask Chris – he usually knows about this kind of thing since he's constantly reading all this medical stuff, but I still want to keep my Valentine's plans a secret.

Had the great idea of asking him about it but pretending I really wanted the information for 'a friend'.

Told him I had 'a friend' who had just gone on the pill and was really worried about dying of a blood clot but I, er, she was excited about maybe growing bigger breasts.

Chris said my friend should really ask her GP but his understanding was that modern contraceptive pills had a very low risk of thromboembolism but were not associated with significant breast tissue development so she shouldn't worry too much about heart attacks or strokes but hadn't much chance of fitting a double D cup either.

Then he said that he was sure her boyfriend would be totally OK about using condoms, which were very safe in any case, and probably thought her breasts were absolutely perfect anyway.

Didn't really know whether to be relieved or

depressed by that but on balance have decided to stick with it.

Now that almost everything was in place for Valentine's day, decided to make a definite arrangement to spend the night with Chris then. Reckoned there should be no problem. Chris's mum and dad got married on Valentine's day and they do the same thing every anniversary. To start with they go to the Italian café where they first met as teenagers, then they have dinner and stay the night at the same hotel (although taken over by a different group) where they spent their wedding night. This would give Chris and me the whole night together once I'd told my parents I was staying at Stephanie's on Valentine's.

But got a nasty surprise from Chris. He said it was his parents' silver wedding anniversary, and instead of their usual routine, all their relatives and friends were invited to a dinner dance party. He said he'd really like me to come along.

Bollocks. This means it will be another year before the perfect time for Chris and me to have sex comes again. Oh well.

SUNDAY FEBRUARY 4TH

Was snogging with Chris tonight but had to push him away as he was getting too excited about things.

Chris asked – 'no pressure of course' – when the time would be right for us to have sex. Just a ballpark figure.

Thought for a second then told him around three hundred and seventy-five days.

He seemed really startled at first, then depressed. I asked him what was wrong and he said, 'Nothing.' Then he said it just seemed *very* specific and *very, very* long. About five seconds later he'd worked out the implications and said that any day when we made love would be totally and completely romantic and it didn't have to be Valentine's day, but I told him that the first time we did it had to be perfect, as it was not just the first time we made love to each other, but also the first time either of us had ever done it at all. Obviously no other date but the most romantic day in the year could possibly be right.

Chris said, 'Er, right.'

MONDAY FEBRUARY 5TH

Am totally furious and disgusted. Chris has confessed it would not be his first time 'actually'. He says he's really sorry that he didn't 'wait for me', as I'd put it, but the way

I'd been acting over the last few years he thought he'd have needed Viagra by the time I'd shown any interest in him.

Chris says I'm being too judgemental. He says it doesn't matter what happened in the past and he really, really didn't want to talk about it. All I needed to know was that he'd been 'careful'. And couldn't we just drop the whole subject now?

Spent the rest of the afternoon scowling at Chris and also Linda. I suppose if I was ever to do it with Chris I would have this odd connection with Linda and I didn't like it. That is, I suppose it was Linda.

TUESDAY FEBRUARY 6TH

On further questioning or 'relentless interrogation', as Chris called it, he has told me his first time was with a Swedish girl he met while on holiday in France with his parents when he was fifteen. She was with her parents in the same hotel and also fifteen. And yes, of course she was blonde, he'd already told me she was Swedish, but no, she didn't have large breasts and could we please, please not talk about this any more? Right, if I really wanted to know, he was crap – well, the first time anyway. Well, of course there were other times – it was a two-week holiday – and, yes, it got better but that was definitely, definitely all he was going to say.

I was furious but at least it wasn't Linda, which was a relief. However, I berated him about being too young for sex and it being totally immoral.

He said they were a bit young and he'd expected just a snog, but she suggested sex and it's not as if he was going to say no thanks. Why not? Oh, for God's sake.

Told him there were very good reasons not to engage in underage sex. It was totally illegal for a start and he, being a policeman's son, should have more respect for the law.

Chris said yeah, right, he'd been tortured by guilt for ages. It was just that he was undecided whether to confess at the local police station or contact Interpol as the 'crime' was perpetrated abroad. Then he just refused to say anything else.

WEDNESDAY FEBRUARY 7TH

Stephanie says I'm bonkers. She says why would I want Chris to be a virgin, it would be like getting driving lessons from another learner.

Stephanie is learning to drive just now. She has had ten lessons, each one with a different instructor as no one will take her twice. During her first lesson she got two speeding tickets. On the second the instructor told her that he wouldn't be getting into a car with her again but for future reference she was supposed to drive on the left-hand side of the road at all times. Even when she spotted her favourite shops on the right-hand side. Stephanie justified this to us by saying it was Ted Baker and they were having a sale. You can't hesitate.

Anyway, she'll be sitting her test this Saturday and she's confident of passing. She says she's going to wear her stilettos with a short skirt, stay-up stockings and plunge top. She plans to accidentally on purpose rub her hand along her instructor's thigh every time she changes gear and make sure he gets an eye full of cleavage whenever she checks her rear view. She says he'll be so flustered he won't notice any tiny little errors she might make.

THURSDAY FEBRUARY 8TH

Chris says it's not that important who his first girlfriend was. What was really important was that he wanted me to be his last. If he could have me he never wanted anyone else ever and that was how he felt.

Thought this was quite a nice thing to say so am talking to him again. Anyway, at least he hasn't done it with Linda, who I'd have to see at school every day.

FRIDAY FEBRUARY 9TH

It just occurred to me that he might have done it with Linda as well. Asked him outright but he flatly, totally refused to say anything. He said it was none of my business and he absolutely refused to discuss it. Ever.

SATURDAY FEBRUARY 10TH

Stephanie failed her driving test. Her examiner was a woman.

TUESDAY FEBRUARY 13TH

It's so nice to definitely know absolutely guaranteed that I am going to get a valentine, but a bit unexciting too.

VALENTINE'S DAY

Don't believe it! Got three valentines - one from Chris and two others. Think Stephanie must be right and boys fancy girls who've already proved they can get a boyfriend. Only problem was I didn't know which one was from Chris – everyone had signed it 'Guess Who?'

and he must have disguised his writing as I didn't recognize any of them. Met up with Stephanie before start of registration and she just advised me to 'wing it' by thanking Chris for 'the lovely card'.

Did as she said but Chris looked at me strangely for a moment then asked if I liked the design and whether I thought the verse was particularly appropriate for us.

I said, 'Yeah, absolutely.'

But then he asked what I particularly liked about it. Thinking fast I said, 'Oh everything. Absolutely everything.'

He said that was great. He'd always known I was talented but had no idea my abilities included predicting the future. Then he took a card and a boxed chocolate teddy bear from his school bag and said, 'Happy Valentine's.' He also gave me an amethyst ring in the shape of a heart which was really nice.

Stephanie said she wasn't to blame and nine times out of ten her advice works. Besides, she said no guy ever dumped a girl for being too popular with other guys. It was as likely as a blonde dying her hair brown. Trust her, this would just keep Chris 'on his toes' and stop him taking me for granted.

Seemed she was right: though Chris sulked for a bit and questioned me, he snapped out of it by the afternoon and I'll be going to his parents' do tonight.

Mr Dunn came into our English class today, supposedly

to borrow a red pen. Ms Conner and he acted all super-formal with each other: Mr Dunn was sorry to disturb Ms Conner but could he borrow a red pen please.

Ms Conner said it was no bother at all. She handed him the pen with a smile and asked if there was anything else he needed or wanted.

Not right then. A bit later perhaps. Although now that he came to think of it, there were some ideas he wanted to discuss with her. Maybe he could run these past her at the break. Just quickly. It was so important that the English and RE departments worked closely together.

Ms Conner said she'd be delighted to accommodate him. Any time. It would be her pleasure.

Honestly, this was *so* annoying. I mean just who did they think they were fooling? Only last week they were caught snogging in the walk-in RE store cupboard by a second year looking for a Bible to do his 'Christians in Ancient Rome' history project. The story had gone all round the school and they knew it. Wish they'd stop this stupid charade.

Wasn't much looking forward to Chris's parents' do but actually had a great time. We had dinner in this really nice hotel and then there was a ceilidh thing where everyone did these old-fashioned and complicated country dances with stupid names like Strip the Willow, Dashing White Sergeant and the Gay Gordons.

Fortunately I learned how to do these in PE in second

year so felt quite confident getting up with Chris. *Un*fortunately I remembered too late that there were more girls than boys in the class and the teacher had teamed me with another girl so I ended up learning the boys' steps. This led to a bit of confusion when I tried to do stuff like make Chris twirl under my arm, particularly as he is at least six inches taller than me even with high heels on. Well, that is, I mean even with *me* wearing high heels.

Still, it was a good laugh if not the totally romantic and special Valentine's I'd hoped for.

THURSDAY FEBRUARY 15TH

Have discovered the identities of my three mystery valentines. One was from Fraser, a primary school boy who lives across from us. His mum rang to say he'd developed an awful crush on me and to ignore the text message he'd sent inviting me to go for a cycle ride in the park followed by an ice-cream. She said if he was outside my house now to tell him to get home for his tea or he's grounded for the rest of the week.

The second card was from my Aunt Kate (who'd disguised her handwriting). She says I always get so upset about never getting a valentine so she thought she'd cheer me up. However, Mum had now told her Chris and I were going out, so Aunt Kate says just to ignore it.

The third is from the underwear shop where I'd wasted £40. I got a second card from them today saying they were my 'mystery admirer' as I was such a valued customer. They told me they were having a fantastic post-Valentine's sale where there would be up to 50 per cent off on selected items.

It was a bit depressing not to be as fantastically popular with boys as I'd thought (unless you count Fraser, and obviously I don't). However, when I called Liz to moan about it I ended up saying nothing as she was really upset.

Her boyfriend Julian has told her he'll be leaving for New York at the end of the month. He says if he works for one year for a software security firm there he'll make enough money to do nothing for the rest of his life, which is his dearest ambition – well, that and the overthrow of capitalism but one out of two wasn't bad. He says he loves her and he'll be back for her when this is all over.

FRIDAY FEBRUARY 16TH

Stephanie's boyfriend Dave has told her that he will be going to the slums of Sri Lanka and then on to impoverished villages in Gambia as part of his gap year.

Stephanie is pretending to be cool about it all: 'There's loads more fit, muscular fish in the sea.' She also said anyway, it was about time she tried out her pulling techniques again, they might be getting a bit rusty, but Liz and I know she's pretty gutted.

Like all Stephanie's previous boyfriends Dave has a body to die for but unlike them he's intelligent and from a wealthy, upper-class family.

This caused a problem at one time. Not the fit body but the other stuff – Stephanie usually prefers 'a bit of rough', as she puts it. However, Dave won her over by promising never to act in a remotely intelligent way in front of her, or give up lager for sherry, or ask her to wear pearls.

He says he loves her and has asked her to be faithful to him until he gets back in October. Of course, he didn't mean sexually faithful but he *has* asked her not to do stuff like holding hands with anyone else while watching romantic films or listening to soppy music while snogging. All that love stuff. Stephanie has promised.

I asked Stephanie why Dave chose to go to all these impoverished regions when his family are loaded. If I were him I'd want to travel to luxurious exotic places and live in five-star hotels. She said for rich people poverty is *interesting* and nearly all of them slum it at some time, sort of like an adventure holiday. But she said she thought since Dave has already spent over six months living in a high rise in a sink estate in Glasgow, that would be enough poverty for anyone.

SATURDAY FEBRUARY 17TH

It will be odd to be the only one of the three of us with a boyfriend. Makes a change from being the only one without. Still, at least their boyfriends have told them that they love them; Chris has never said that to me.

Stephanie says I should just ask him but I couldn't do that. I mean what if he said no? It would be just too humiliating.

Liz says if I told Chris that I loved him he'd be sure to say it back out of politeness. But what if he didn't? What if he just said, 'Oh right, thanks,' or worse, what Stephanie had said to Dave: 'Whatever'? It was too risky.

Instead went over to Chris's tonight with my *100 Perfect Love Songs* CD, which I hoped might inspire him to romantic declarations. Some hope. After ten minutes he said, Christ, this music was awful, like slowly drowning in treacle after having overdosed with saccharine. Couldn't we put something decent on?

SUNDAY FEBRUARY 18TH

This time decided to try a love film on DVD. It was about a girl who gets leukaemia but doesn't tell her boyfriend so as not to upset him. Anyway, he never tells her he loves her until she's lying on her deathbed in a coma and he's clutching her and kissing her but it's too late.

Chris seemed mostly bored by the film and complained about the ludicrous plot and 'God-awful acting' until it got to the deathbed scene, at which point he started laughing out loud. When I asked what was so funny – and some doctor he'd be, laughing at terminally ill patients – he said real illness was no joke but this film was hilarious. Imagine someone who'd been in a coma for days still managing to put on eye shadow, lip gloss and blusher then waking up for a few seconds to murmur 'Goodbye, my one true love' before copping it. Give him a break.

TUESDAY FEBRUARY 20TH

Went over to Chris's to watch the football. Normally I like watching football but this time I couldn't concentrate on the match as I was absolutely determined to find out whether he loved me or not. Eventually just blurted out, 'Do you love me?'

Chris said, 'Yes. Look at that, Kelly Ann! That was never a foul. The guy took a dive!'

Was absolutely furious with Chris. He had just ruined what should be the most romantic, important declaration of a girl's life. How could he do this to me?

I said what did he mean 'yes' – what was 'yes' supposed to mean?

Chris tore his eyes off the screen long enough to ask in

a supposedly puzzled way, what did I mean what was 'yes' supposed to mean? What did it usually mean? Then, turning back to the screen, he continued, 'I don't believe it. The ref's awarded a penalty. I mean, is he totally blind or just in the pay of the opposition or what? If they get a goal with that, Kelly Ann, it's nothing short of robbery. A bloody travesty of justice. This sort of thing makes a mockery of the game.'

That was it. I was leaving and told him not to bother walking me home. Obviously football was the only important thing in his life and I meant nothing to him.

Chris walked me home anyway, all the time protesting that he didn't know what he'd said or done wrong. Of course he loved me. He'd just said so, hadn't he?

Yeah, right.

But he kept insisting that he really, really didn't know why I was pissed off with him. Obviously he loved me. I knew that anyway. Eventually told him just as we got back to my place that if he didn't know why I was upset then there was no point in telling him.

Chris said that was the most stupid, illogical thing he'd ever heard. How was he supposed to fix things if he hadn't a clue what was wrong? I told him this was nothing to do with logic and he said I could say that again and stomped off.

Haven't spoken to Chris all week. Stephanie says all guys are scum but thinks I'm being a bit hard on Chris, though Liz supports me absolutely. She says that he has been grossly insensitive to my feelings, emotions and aspirations.

Since I won't speak to him, Chris has pleaded with me by text, email and voice message but I refused to forgive him. He even sent Gary, his best pal, to appeal on his behalf. That was a joke. Gary just asked me to get back with Chris, 'for God's sake', as everyone is fed up with Chris's bad temper since I fell out with him. He then went on to say that he didn't know why I was pissed off with Chris. What was wrong with watching football? Didn't I like football anyway? Honestly, girls were all so moody and difficult. A bloody nightmare to deal with.

Despite Gary's touching speech I told him to shove it.

In the end Liz offered Chris and me couples counselling. She says our first session will be free but our problems are so deeply ingrained and complex that we may need at least six months of counselling – two or three sessions a week, depending on the progress we make. She says that she can offer us special bulk-rate deals but she'll discuss that with us later.

Chris is so desperate to get back with me he has reluctantly agreed, in principle, to one session anyway.

* * *

Liz hadn't bothered to tidy her room for our counselling session except for her discarded underwear, which instead of being strewn haphazardly across the floor as usual had been crushed into a small heap and jammed under a pile of magazines on her chest of drawers.

Liz started by saying that she intended to be an unbiased neutral facilitator in our discussions. It was not her role to advise, far less dictate to us what we should do or say; instead, with her assistance, we would explore our feelings about relationships openly and honestly. She would help us bring to the surface underlying conflicts, fears or emotions and we would work through them together. She cautioned that couples counselling was not a simple cure-all. Some relationships were simply doomed to failure and it was not her role to try to save a dead relationship but rather, in that case, to help the couple navigate a new path to successful, fulfilled independence.

Chris interrupted to say that he didn't want to navigate a path to successful fulfilled independence. He wanted us to stay together and that was why he'd agreed to this stupid session in the first place. If all Liz was going to do was try and split us up then she could stuff it.

Liz rounded on him. She told him that mutually agreed ground rules would have to be established right away and the first of these was absolutely no inter-ruptions when she was talking. Then she added that she was beginning to understand already some of the problems Chris must be causing in our relationship. 'Does Chris often interrupt you, Kelly Ann? Do you feel that your views and opinions aren't valued by him, thus leading to feelings of inadequacy and ultimately worthlessness?'

I said, 'Er, well, not really, I mean maybe—'

'Don't try to protect him, Kelly Ann,' interrupted Liz.

Then she went on to explain that I was displaying the classic signs of someone involved in an abusive relationship but told me that here in this therapy room I could be completely honest and unafraid.

Chris nearly went mental at that, standing up and shouting at me and Liz. Just *what* was Liz accusing him of? What did she mean *abusive*? He'd never *ever* hurt me in his life. Not even when I deliberately stabbed his hand with a compass in third year just because he'd said he liked my curly hair. And how was he to know I'd spent two hours trying to blow-dry it straight. And don't think he didn't know it wasn't an accident. He wasn't stupid. Liz had better take back what she said or he was out of there right now. Abusive his arse.

But Liz was beaming at him. This was excellent. Already the therapy session was releasing pent-up anger and aggression. Then she turned to me and said did I find Chris's temper caused problems in the relationship? Did I find his frequent irrational outbursts intimidating at all? Never mind – we would work on that.

Chris shouted at her, *'I am not bad-tempered!'* Then, realizing how he must have sounded, added, 'That's it, I'm not saying another word.'

But Liz leaped on this too. By refusing to talk to us he was now displaying 'passive aggression', which could be even more destructive to relationships than direct honest aggression. 'Oh yes,' she said gleefully, 'there is so much more work to be done.'

Totally exasperated now Chris told her that, OK, he gave in. He was an abusive bad-tempered passive-aggressive and absolutely everything was completely his fault. Although what, by the way, had happened to her promises to be an 'unbiased neutral facilitator'? Never mind – he accepted it all. All he wanted, absolutely *all* he wanted, was to know how to fix things so I would talk to him again and he could get the hell out.

Liz tormented him for a while longer, telling him there were no 'quick fixes', that psychotherapy was not about simplistic solutions to complex human problems; rather it was a voyage of self-discovery.

But then she said, 'Look, you idiot, you can't just say yes when a girl asks you if you love her or not, then talk about the football. This is the most important romantic moment of a girl's life and you have to do it properly. You have to say how much you love her, how deep your love is. Show how much you long for her. You have to be totally romantic so she can tell all her friends about it, every detail—'

Chris interrupted incredulously, 'Tell all her friends? Every detail?'

'Of course,' Liz replied. That was the best bit of it. When Julian told her he loved her, she told everyone. Every detail. The tone of his voice, the look in his eyes, how mad for her he was. Everything. In fact she got Julian to put it on a website – www.julianlovesliz.com. Had he happened to see it at all?

Chris looked horrified. A website? Was this what I wanted?

Well, no, not a website but, yeah, something a bit more romantic than just a yes. Of course now that he's had to be told it was all spoiled anyway.

Chris said that right, that was it, we were both certifiably insane and he was going.

As he made for the door Liz called after him, 'Same time next week then?'

Chris told her she must be joking. He said he'd rather have every tooth extracted without anaesthetic. He said he'd prefer to have his toenails ripped out with pliers. He said it would be better to have electrodes attached to his— Well, never mind that but this was definitely the last therapy session he would ever attend in his life. Than he left.

Liz said brightly, 'I think that went very well.'

Chris visited my house tonight. He'd brought a piece of A4 paper from which he read aloud. He said he loved me very much. He said he loved me even though the first day we met I borrowed his radio control car and never gave it back. He said he loved me despite the fact I always cheated at Monopoly and always *tried* to cheat at chess, except that he remembered where every piece should be even when I tried to move them when he wasn't looking or accidentally on purpose tipped the whole board over when I knew it was nearly checkmate.

He said he loved me despite my having a temper like my mother's and all the emotional control of a toddler who'd just lost its dummy. He said I was the most beautiful, fun, totally frustrating and exasperating girl he'd ever known. He said he loved me so much it hurt sometimes and that he'd die for me if he had to. Now did I love him?

I said, 'Yes.'

He said did he have to put all this on a website for me? And I said, 'No.'

But I emailed all my friends about it. Every single detail.

SUNDAY FEBRUARY 25TH

Stephanie hosted a farewell party for Dave and her brother Julian tonight. Didn't see her all evening as she spent the entire time shagging Dave noisily in her upstairs bedroom. Dave emerged a couple of times, wearing just a pair of blue jeans, to ask for something to drink. The first time Chris handed him a beer but Dave shook his head – 'definitely no alcohol' – and got some sport isotonic Lucozade from the fridge before staggering back upstairs again.

Liz was upset about Julian going even though she spouted stuff about how this would be good for their relationship and it was healthy not to be too co-dependent. We all cheered up, though, when as a goodbye present Julian gave each of us perfect fake IDs he'd knocked up on his computer. We got two each. One gave our ages as eighteen so that we could get into pubs and clubs, and the other said we were fifteen so we could get half fares on the buses and trains.

Everyone wished Julian good luck in his software security job.

THURSDAY MARCH 1ST

Was chatting to Liz and Stephanie during registration today. As usual the conversation turned to when I was going to go all the way with Chris. Stephanie says all guys are scum of course, but Chris isn't all that bad and I shouldn't keep him waiting for a whole year for sex – it would drive him mental. Besides, why waste time holding onto my virginity when I could be having fun? She says I should just get on with it.

Liz says that losing my virginity is an important Rite of Passage. She says she could give me counselling to help me make my decision but maybe I should just get on with it and she could counsel me afterwards, when of course she would have to know every single detail of what we'd done.

Maybe they're right.

Ayesha had obviously overheard us talking because she interrupted to tell us we were all daft.

Ayesha is a drop-dead gorgeous Asian girl, with thick, straight black hair and a figure to die for. Although her parents come from Pakistan originally, her Glasgow accent is stronger than mine, which I find odd somehow though I suppose I shouldn't. Nearly all the boys fancy Ayesha but she seems totally uninterested in anyone and just wants to become a fabulously wealthy lawyer with a huge house and servants.

She's OK but has definite opinions on just about everything, which she insists on sharing with you whether you want to hear them or not. Usually not.

Like now, for instance, but it didn't stop her droning on. She told us that white girls all drop their knickers far too quickly, then we end up bawling our eyes out when some useless tosser doesn't ring us. Well, except for Stephanie, that is – at least she wasn't a hopeless romantic like the rest of us.

Although we made it quite plain to her that we weren't interested in hearing any more of her views, Ayesha ploughed on regardless. She said that Asian guys get nothing, not so much as a kiss, until they've signed a marriage contract and promised to be nice to all the girl's family. And that means *all*, the entire family, even the great-aunt who keeps taking her teeth out to clean them during dinner and the second cousin's toddler who thinks it's a laugh to pee on people's DVD collections.

Told Ayesha to can it but asked her if her great-aunt really takes her teeth out at the table to clean them and said that was gross. Ayesha said yes, she did, but at least Asian families looked after their old people (unlike us, who shoved them in homes).

However, her best friend Yasmin interrupted at this point and said we shouldn't listen to this rubbish from Ayesha. She told us that Ayesha had hidden her great-aunt's false teeth because she was grossed out about her cleaning them at dinner. The poor old woman had to exist on mushy pulp for a week.

We were still talking about Ayesha's great-aunt when Imran sauntered over to us, gave Ayesha a dazzling smile and asked what we were all gossiping about.

Ayesha gave him a withering look, told him we didn't 'gossip', we discussed important stuff like society and geopolitics, so he wouldn't be able to understand or follow any conversation of ours. The bell for the end of registration went, so she walked away haughtily from Imran – although her dignified exit was spoiled when she tripped over a bag someone had left in the aisle and landed on her arse. Imran put out his hand to help her up but she slapped it away, hauled herself up and stomped off.

Imran walked with me along the corridor to maths, questioning me, as usual, about Ayesha. What had we been talking about and had Ayesha mentioned him at all?

Er, not much, and no, not really.

Imran looks like a Bollywood star and has had loads of girlfriends, though none of them Asian. He always says he would like to have an Asian girlfriend but their dads won't let them out. He also complains that in any case Asian girls give you nothing, not so much as a kiss, unless you sign a marriage contract and promise to be nice to all their family. He says he'd be willing to do that for Ayesha but she can't be bothered with him.

Imran is really mad about her. He writes her soppy poetry and buys her stuff like chocolates and jewellery but she just laughs at his poetry, tells him she's on a diet so can't eat the chocolates and gives the jewellery to her friends. Yasmin and I have both got very nice earrings that way, but Chris made me give them back to Imran.

Have told Chris I can't understand why Imran bothers. Ayesha is nice looking and she's a good laugh as a friend, but she can be so moody and difficult sometimes she'd be a nightmare to go out with.

He just said it's amazing what some guys will put up with if they're in love.

SATURDAY MARCH 3RD

It's Chris's birthday on Wednesday. This time his parents haven't organized anything special for him, which is surprising as they usually make a big deal of it. In fact both of them will be out as his dad is working a four until midnight shift on that day and his mum is meeting her pals straight from work and won't be back until eleven at the earliest.

Feel quite sorry for him really. It's a shame that they can't be arsed to organize a proper celebration. I'd like to get him a fantastic present to make up for it but am completely broke as usual this month, especially as it's Mum's birthday next week, so have only got him the CD he asked for. Wonder what I could do to make his seventeenth birthday really special.

MONDAY MARCH 5TH

Stephanie has suggested a fantastic birthday present I can give Chris.

TUESDAY MARCH 6TH

It's decided then. Am going to have sex with Chris on his birthday so it will be like a best ever, huge birthday present.

WEDNESDAY MARCH 7TH

Met Chris just outside maths. Said 'Happy birthday' and gave him a kiss, then handed him his birthday card. He kissed me back to thank me for the card so I kissed him again to thank him for the kiss and, although we don't usually do this sort of thing in public, it turned into a bit of a snog really, because it was his birthday after all. Mr Simmons came along just then and told me to leave Chris alone for God's sake as he was Mr Simmons's only hope for a distinction this year and he didn't want me ruining Chris's concentration.

We went in, sat down and then got out our maths stuff. I don't sit with Chris in maths as he's taking the Advanced Higher and most of the time doesn't do the same work as us. However, I was able to see his face when he read the message in the card. It said that he could unwrap his special surprise birthday present later . . . *me*. Also said, 'Let's celebrate Valentine's day tonight.'

Chris passed a note over saying did this mean what he hoped it meant?

I passed a note back saying, 'Yes.'

This morning Mr Simmons started by giving us all, even Ian and Chris, a short fifteen-minute test on logs. Everyone was really surprised when Chris got nearly every question wrong. Even I got a better mark than him. Mr Simmons glared at me accusingly but Chris didn't seem bothered by his crap marks at all.

Chris also failed his physics test and scored an own goal when he played football in the afternoon. Was beginning to think it would have been better to have given him the card after school as Stephanie suggested.

At four o'clock I was hurrying out so I could get home and make myself ready when Chris caught up with me and asked where I was going. Told him I was going home to get dressed up for tonight. But Chris put his arm round my waist and said why bother getting dressed just to get undressed again? It was a waste of time. He wanted me to come home with him right then.

Suppose that was logical enough. Thought about it. At least I had matching underwear on, even if it was pink and not red like I'd planned. Also, at Stephanie's suggestion, I had put on the black hold-up stockings this morning, which were supposed to make me feel 'like a sensual, sexual being' all day and so get me in the mood for the evening. All they really made me feel, however, was absolutely freezing. My legs were covered in goose-bumps and I really missed my warm thick black tights. Still, I supposed they *did* look better.

Decided, OK, I'd go home with Chris, which is probably just as well as he had already steered me in the direction of his place and we were nearly there.

He opened the front door, took my bag from me and threw it in the hall along with his own. Then he picked me up and carried me in, 'bride over the threshold' style. He set me down, and as soon as we'd taken our blazers off he started kissing me while at the same time frantically unbuttoning and peeling off my blouse. Maybe Stephanie was right and months of snogging but nothing much else had been making Chris a bit frustrated (or, as she put it, bonkers for a proper bonk). But at this rate we'd be having sex in the hall, which I didn't think would be very romantic and told him so.

He disagreed about it not being romantic but took my hand and led me into the living room anyway, where he lit the gas log fire, before closing the blinds and putting on some music. I asked for a drink and he went into the kitchen while I stood by the fire to get warm.

He came back with a single glass of red wine. He said he didn't want alcohol interfering with his 'performance' and I was reminded of Chris's drive to be good at absolutely everything he did. Was not sure whether this made me feel excited or anxious really. Maybe a bit of both.

He handed me the wine and I took a sip of it. It tasted really nice as he'd mixed it with lemonade the way I like, even though he always says it's a terrible way to drink wine. Then I kissed him, and when he started to undo the zip of my skirt I didn't stop him like I used to when our snogging got a bit serious. However, when my skirt fell to the floor I felt a bit nervous (there was no going back now) so I took another gulp of wine to calm me down.

Chris said he liked the stockings and he expected they were Stephanie's idea. He said to tell Stephanie thanks from him, then he began tracing his fingers round the bare skin above the lace tops, which felt so nice I spilled some of the wine down my front so Chris licked it off, which felt very, very nice . . . mmmmm. Began to think Stephanie was right and I should have got round to this much earlier. Chris took the wineglass from me and placed it on the mantelpiece, then I put my arms around him and we kissed and I was so excited and happy and hardly nervous at all any more. I kicked off my shoes, which made me a lot shorter than Chris so it seemed natural and more comfortable for us lie on the rug in front of the fire.

By this time I was feeling absolutely fantastic, which was why I was really annoyed when the doorbell rang. Chris whispered to me to ignore it as it was probably just someone selling something and they would soon go away if we didn't answer.

He was wrong. The ringing stopped but whoever it was started hammering really loudly on the door like they were the police or something. In fact, next moment someone shouted at the door, 'Open up. Police!'

My God, what had we done? Surely it wasn't illegal for us to have sex. We were both over sixteen. It was maybe immoral or something but not actually a crime. I was sure of it. And yet the police were definitely after us. Or perhaps just me. Maybe someone had told them I'd just been drinking wine and they'd come to arrest me for that. It seems a bit OTT though, and how did they know? Chris had shut the blinds. But I felt terrified and guilty anyway.

Chris told me not to be daft. He said it was most likely one or two of his dad's colleagues having a laugh. They were always playing this kind of practical joke and he was sick of it. He turned off the music but told me to stay there and not move, especially not to get dressed. He would go and get rid of whoever it was and be back in ten seconds flat.

He went out to the hall. Despite Chris's instructions I got up and peeked out at what was going on from behind the open living-room door. Sure enough, there were two policemen in full uniform standing on the step. Behind them I could make out not just a regular police car but a large van. Were they going to arrest us? Surely they wouldn't need a whole van just for us. One of them asked Chris his name and what school he went to in a very officious, severe-sounding voice. Then the other one asked him what his date of birth was. Chris told him, then the policemen took off their caps, put on stupid party hats and started singing, 'Happy Birthday to You'.

Then, *Oh. My. God.* Chris's mum and dad plus aunts, uncles and cousins, also wearing stupid party hats, were streaming up the garden path, having got out of the police van parked outside, chorusing *'Happy birthday, dear Christopher . . .'*

No, this just could *not* be happening. A surprise family birthday party. They were all pressing their way in and I had no time to get dressed. Anyway, my blouse was in the hall. In a total panic I ran into the kitchen, shut the door and stood with my back pressed against it. Was just in time as I heard them all happy birthdaying their way into the living room about a nanosecond after I'd shut the kitchen door.

Then, total horrors, I heard Chris's mum say she'd just get his birthday cake which she'd hidden in the kitchen. He hadn't discovered it, had he, and ruined his surprise?

Knew I had no chance of keeping the door shut as it opens inwards, and anyway, Chris's mum is taller and heavier than me. I ran to the door to the garden but then thought if I went outside I'd probably be arrested for indecent exposure or something and get my picture in the papers, which might have been worse – I wasn't sure.

I turned round, looking for somewhere to hide, but of course it was too late. Chris's mum was in the kitchen, staring at me. She was silent for a moment but then seemed to recover and said, 'Hi, Kelly Ann.'

I just stood there, totally motionless and dumbstruck. I mean what do you do or say when you're standing in your boyfriend's mum's kitchen dressed only in your bra, knickers and hold-up stockings and she says 'Hi'?

It was like the nightmares I used to get where I'd turn up for school and discover too late that I'd forgotten to get dressed, but this, in a way, was worse. Nowhere in my naked nightmares had I ever imagined myself in this position: totally obviously about two minutes away from having sex with someone and then having to make conversation with his mother! The stockings were the worst bit. Somehow they seemed so *lewd*, like I was a total prostitute or something who'd gate-crashed a wholesome family afternoon gathering.

But Chris's mum prattled on anyway, I suppose in

some sort of futile attempt to relieve the tension. Wasn't I a bit cold in that outfit? How was school going? How had I got on in my Prelims? Was I feeling confident about the Highers?

The door opened and Chris came in carrying my skirt and shoes but no blouse. He put my skirt on the chair beside me and dropped my shoes by my feet but still I couldn't move or speak. He then started to take off his shirt and I stared at him with renewed horror. Was Chris so desperate for sex he intended to strip off and do it here in the kitchen in front of his mother?

But he just put his shirt on me, guiding my arms into the overlong sleeves like he was dressing a toddler. He whispered to me not to worry, things weren't as bad as I thought and hugged me.

Slowly I felt some feeling and movement return to my body. I held Chris's shirt closed with one hand and was stepping into my skirt with the other, when Chris's dad came in. Fantastic. If there is anything worse than being half naked in the kitchen with your boyfriend's mum it has to be being half naked in the kitchen with your boyfriend's mum and dad.

Chris's dad quickly took in the situation and said, 'Sorry, son. I told your mother this surprise birthday party was a stupid idea but she wouldn't listen.' Then, looking at my face, which despite the cold in the kitchen must by this time have been scarlet, he said, 'Aw, don't be embarrassed, Kelly Ann, love. Things could be a lot worse. I mean this isn't nearly as bad as when I came home early from work last year and found Chris and Linda actually shagging on the carpet. Is it, Chris?'

Chris swore at his dad and said he couldn't believe he'd just said that. Chris's mum swore at her husband and said she couldn't believe he'd just said that. Chris's dad swore at himself and said he couldn't believe he'd just said that.

But he had. So then I didn't feel just totally embarrassed, I felt humiliated and cheap too. Clearly I was just one of the many girls Chris brought home to shag on the living-room floor. It's probably a pretty common occurrence for Chris's parents, practically falling over half-naked girls that he is constantly inviting home for sex. Must be one of the hazards of having a teenage son who's a total sex maniac.

I finished putting on my skirt but the bloody zip snagged and wouldn't go up. Slapped away Chris's hand when he tried to help me. I buttoned up the shirt. Realized when I got to the end that I was two buttons askew and that the shirt looked totally stupid anyway as it reached below the hem of my skirt, but looking stupid was better than half naked, on balance. Lastly I put on my shoes and said that I would be going home. Told Chris that if he tried to follow me I would stab him through the heart with his mum's cake knife and did he understand me. He said that he did.

THURSDAY MARCH 8TH

Woke today to an awful hangover and was too sick to go to school. Instead, spent the whole morning throwing up in the toilet while listening to Angela's baby crying its head off. Why can't she look after it properly?

Had phoned Stephanie last night to tell her about the disaster and she rushed right over with a bottle of vodka. Liz had been in the bath when I called but came over an hour later to see what was going on. At first she went on at Stephanie for plying me with alcohol. Liz said that alcohol was a dangerous prop and that emotional and psychological crises were far better handled by facing up to problems with the assistance of a skilled therapist. She said that the use of chemical depressants was a foolish and ultimately self-defeating distraction to coping with life problems.

But when Stephanie told her what had happened to me, Liz rounded on her again. Why had she brought only *one* bottle?

Chris had phoned and texted me almost all night but I wouldn't speak to him. Eventually Stephanie used my phone to send him this text message back: U R DMPD KA.

Chris visited me at lunch time today anyway on the pretext of returning my blouse and blazer. Angela let him in. I was lying face down on my bed with the duvet pulled up over my head and a basin beside me on the floor (just in case) when he came in.

He started trying to apologize to me again about the embarrassment with his parents and the Linda thing, but I refused to dignify his pathetic excuses with a reply or even to acknowledge his presence by bothering to raise my head from underneath the duvet to look at him.

Despite this he persisted for a while, but then he must have spotted the empty vodka bottle in my bin and the basin because he told me (still speaking to my inert covered form) that I should know by now that I couldn't handle spirits, then proceeded to give me a lecture about females and excessive alcohol consumption.

He droned on about our livers and blood volume being smaller and something about our hormones and fat-to-muscle ratio being contra indicators. Obviously he'd never seen my mum and Aunt Kate having a session, although come to think of it, *his* mum had downed at least eight double vodkas at her anniversary do and looked absolutely none the worse for it. Mind you, Chris's mum is a nurse and my mum says all nurses can drink for Scotland. She's got a nerve to talk though.

Anyway, I couldn't make any of these points to Chris as I was too weak and ill to talk, but I did manage to stick two fingers out from under my duvet in a rude gesture, then fortunately Angela yelled up to him to come and feed the baby while she had a shower, after which, thank God, he went back to school.

FRIDAY MARCH 9TH

Chris tried to make up with me again today, telling me he had never lied to me about Linda, he just hadn't told me the whole truth. Yeah, right.

He also said that the 'incident' in the kitchen wasn't as bad as I was making out and his parents were totally OK about it.

Told him that it was all right for him to talk. He hadn't been the one standing in bra, knickers and hold-up stockings in his parents' kitchen after all.

Chris had no answer for that one.

SATURDAY MARCH 10TH

Stephanie said maybe I shouldn't be so mad at Chris. She said it wasn't his fault his stupid parents had organized a totally stupid party. She said two previous 'proper girlfriends' weren't that bad and she doubted whether his parents were constantly tripping over a succession of naked girls in the house or they would probably be a lot more pissed off with him than they were. Trust her, she knew about this.

Mum's birthday. She wasn't as bad as she was last year, when she hit forty, so only cried in her room for a couple of hours before getting very drunk by 11 o'clock in the morning and moaning that it was only nine years now until she was fifty. Less than a decade. Bloody single digits until she would be getting insulting cards with stupid messages like 'What a scunner, half a hunner!'

All this didn't please Aunt Kate, who will be fifty next year. Or Uncle Jack, who is fifty-one.

I'd bought Mum some 1980s CDs – a suggestion from Aunt Kate – but soon wished I hadn't. Mum put one on to 'cheer herself up' and at first it seemed to be working but then they all got up and danced around the living room, bums swaying, arms and legs flailing about. It was *so* embarrassing. Why don't they realize people of their age just should *not* dance? I quickly closed the blinds so at least the neighbours wouldn't see them, then went to the kitchen to get the birthday cake and candles. Surely that would stop them.

It worked and they started behaving like normal adults again, just sitting around eating and talking about the past, so I was able to relax again but not for long. Next thing I knew Mum and Dad were having one of their stupid arguments and trying to involve me in it.

'Tell your father anyone who doesn't like the Eurythmics knows sod all about music.'

'Tell your mother it's a free country and everyone is entitled to their own opinions. Anyway, I didn't say I didn't like the Eurythmics, I just think Queen are better. That's all.'

'Tell your father if he thinks Queen are better than the Eurythmics his taste is in his arse.'

On and on. Aunt Kate tried to calm things down, saying, 'We'll all just agree to differ then.' That's a laugh. Mum has never agreed to differ in her life and I couldn't see her starting now.

Decided to leave them all to it and escaped to Shelly's. She was just so nice to me and seemed really interested in me and how I was feeling. Ended up pouring my heart out to her about Chris's birthday and how he must have had sex with Linda. She was so sympathetic.

But then she said that Chris has always had a really bad reputation with girls and she thought I knew that. She said Chris was 'a player', which means he sleeps around with loads of girls at the same time. Well, not exactly at the same time but nearly.

Told Shelly she must be mistaken. That couldn't be Chris. I'd known him for years, after all.

But then she said how well had I really known him? I hadn't known what he'd got up to with Linda, for example, had I? Maybe there were other things I didn't know.

Chris came into my French class today (he dropped French last year) carrying a piece of paper and telling Mrs Valentine that the deputy head Mr Smith wanted to see me in his office straight away.

Mrs Valentine beamed at Chris (Why do all the teachers like Chris? Obviously they don't know what he's really like) and, without even looking at the piece of paper, nodded for me to go.

I sat where I was, folded my arms and told her I wasn't going anywhere. Had she actually checked that *supposed* note from Mr Smith?

But Mrs Valentine got really mad at me. She told me *of course* she'd checked the note and she hoped I wasn't questioning her professionalism. She said I'd better go right now or she would be referring me to Mr Smith for outright defiance.

I stormed out, fuming. Once in the corridor I turned on Chris. How could he do this to me? What did he think he was playing at?

Chris said that, yeah, he knew how much I loved double French and how disappointing it would be to miss a minute of it but what was he supposed to do when I refused to talk to him alone?

He found an empty maths classroom and we sat down. He asked me when I was going to 'snap out of it' – he was getting fed up waiting for me to stop 'sulking'.

I hate it when Chris talks down to me like that as though I'm some moronic three-year-old. Told him I'd had enough of him. That I was on to him now. That I knew he was a total player and we were finished.

'A *player*?' Chris said incredulously.

'Yes, it's a person who—'

Chris interrupted to say he knew what a player was. For example, Gerry, whom I'd fancied all of last year practically, was a player but he himself wasn't and never had been. It just wasn't his thing.

Felt myself redden at the mention of Gerry. It was true I had been completely mad about him for ages. I even used to do his homework for him in the hope he'd notice me and maybe ask me for a date out of gratitude. And when I think about the stupid love poems I wrote about him! Oh God. Eventually he did ask me out, but of course all he did was pressure me for sex all the time while still trying to pull other girls.

How could I have been such an idiot? Thankfully I am much more mature and sorted now. There was no way I was ever going to be that stupid over any guy ever again. Not Gerry. And not Chris either. Told Chris that I wasn't convinced, that I'd heard all about him and he couldn't fool me any more.

Chris tried some more to protest his innocence, begging me to trust him, but finally he gave up and said that OK, he admitted it. He was a player. In fact he confessed that he'd had sex with almost everyone at the school, male and female alike. Including the staff. He reminded me how I'd always complained that all the teachers seemed to like him. Well, here was the real reason. It wasn't that he got good marks in their subjects; the truth was he was sleeping with them all. He'd enjoyed a particularly intense and satisfying affair with old Miss McElwee, the home economics teacher who's due to retire next year. Did I know she was a player too? Oh yes, and another thing – he might as well get it all off his chest – at weekends he worked as a rent boy, hanging round game shops hoping to be picked up by wealthy businessmen.

By this time I couldn't help giggling, and Chris had taken my hands in his. He said that he was prepared to give it all up for me. Well, everything except Miss McElwee. There was just something irresistible about her. Maybe her cooking. What did I say?

Told him that OK, I believed him about not being a player but I couldn't go out with him any more. At least not while his parents were alive. I was too embarrassed.

Chris said, 'Please don't do this, Kelly Ann. Please don't make me wish my parents dead.' Then he asked me to 'be reasonable'. He said his mum was a nurse and his dad had worked in Vice for ten years. We couldn't possibly do anything that would really shock them. He said his parents liked me and were just sorry they'd embarrassed me.

Finally I agreed to make up but was determined never

to try to have sex in anyone's parents' house again. I was going back to my original Valentine's day plan and it would have to be in a hotel.

Chris said OK, then he kissed me and I kissed him back and it was so good to be close again. In fact we snogged for quite a while and it felt really nice until we were interrupted by Mr Simmons barging in.

He said shouldn't we be in a class somewhere? Then, turning to me, he said he thought he'd already asked me to leave Chris alone until after his maths exams.

How come it's always my fault? He never blames Chris.

Then Mr Simmons said he'd had enough of mixed schools. He was going to look for a transfer to a single sex school and he didn't care whether it was run by fanatical Jesuits or the ruddy Taliban as long as it was single sex, it was OK by him.

I was surprised at this really as I thought Mr Simmons was happy teaching here and said so, but Mr Simmons said yeah, he was so happy he could spit and to clear off, the pair of us.

I went back to French after that. Mrs Valentine asked what Mr Smith had wanted to see me about. Hadn't thought about this so just blurted out the first thing that came into my head. 'Spitting.'

'Spitting?!' said Mrs Valentine, aghast.

'Er, yes. Um, spitting in the corridor. He says I've to stop it.'

FRIDAY MARCH 16TH

I think Danny might have slept right through the night yesterday – so for once I needn't have got up and see to him as I usually do when Angela can't get him back to sleep.

However, I woke at three o'clock in the morning anyway and found myself straining to hear if Danny was crying. When I heard nothing, instead of falling gratefully back to sleep like a normal, sensible sleep-derived person, I started to worry that maybe Danny was quiet because he was dead. A victim of cot death maybe.

There was nothing for it but to get up and check. Crept into Angela's room, leaving the door open and the hall light on. Peered into Danny's cot, but in the dim light couldn't be sure whether his chest was moving up and down. Nor could I hear any snuffly breathing noises.

Poked his chest with my finger to check he was still alive, which he proved by waking up and bawling angrily. Couldn't blame him really.

I picked him up and hurried into my own room, where I quickly soothed him to sleep again. Danny looks gorgeous, especially when he's sleeping. Don't know why Angela doesn't seem to like him. She seems scared of him, as though he were the Devil's spawn or something instead of a cute baby. If I were Danny's mum I'd love him. Well, I do love him actually. Someone has to.

Graham came up to see Angela today. He's meant to come every other weekend but usually doesn't because he's supposedly had to work – actually he probably can't be arsed because Angela is always moaning at him about how tired and fed up she is. Can't say I blame him for not coming. If she isn't moaning his face off she's crying or sulking. As usual I've offered to look after Danny so they can go out, but Angela just said she wanted to sleep. Graham isn't much good at taking care of a baby because he isn't used to it, so in the end I just took Danny off to Chris's.

Showed Chris how Danny giggles when I make funny faces at him now. *So cute.* Then I suggested we go to Mothercare and buy those really nice stripy socks I'd seen last week.

Chris said, 'I thought we'd planned to watch the football at Ian's then go see a movie, Kelly Ann. Shouldn't Graham and your sister be spending some time with Danny now? He's their baby, after all.'

Got mad at Chris then. So he didn't like my Danny? He didn't want to spend any time with us? Fine by me. Obviously his friend Ian was so much more important. Clearly Danny would just have to go barefoot and probably catch pneumonia and die – young babies were so vulnerable to cold – but hey, never mind all that, at least he and Ian would have a fun afternoon.

Chris started to yammer on about pneumonia being a bacterial infection unrelated to cold but trailed off when he saw my face. Would those be the orange and yellow striped socks or the blue and green? Right, we'd better be going before they sold out.

After we got back Chris helped me feed Danny and put on his new socks. Noticed how gentle and kind Chris is with him and couldn't help thinking what a nice dad he would make for my Danny. Better than Graham anyway, who's almost never here.

THURSDAY MARCH 22ND

Fantastic news! Chris has passed his driving test. He turned up at school in his mum's car (even though he only lives about five minutes' walk away) and parked in the school car park along with the teachers. We went for a drive at lunch time and had a sandwich at Subway, where we didn't have to wait for nearly an hour because of hordes of annoying school kids. Chris also told me that his mum plans to buy a new car so this one can be his.

Imagine! Not only do I have a gorgeous boyfriend, I have a boyfriend with a car so I'll always get to sit in the front seat. How cool is that?

Stephanie was a bit annoyed at first. She says she

doesn't mind Chris being good at useless stuff like maths
and physics but driving is different. And anyway, he had
an unfair advantage as he'd been given a 'crash course'
by his uncle, who trains police drivers. Besides, what did
Chris need to drive for anyway? When would he ever
need to check out the latest fashions at out-of-town
shopping centres and designer label direct stores? Hmm,
good point. Stephanie has persuaded Chris to take her
shopping after school almost every evening next week so
has stopped moaning. Chris looked a bit glum though
and has told me he's just realized there's a downside to
driving.

FRIDAY MARCH 23RD

*He's not the only one to realize there's a downside to
his driving.* Shelly says that now Chris has a car loads more
girls will fancy him so I'll have to fight off the
competition. Honestly, she didn't want to alarm me, but
so many relationships have broken up as soon as the guy
gets a car it wasn't true. I'd have to be extra careful and
make sure I was always as perfect as possible if there was
to be any hope of my hanging onto Chris. As a friend she
had to tell me that my hair was a bit frizzy today, and did
I want to borrow her concealer for those spots on my
forehead?

Suppose she's right – I know lots of girls do fancy even

quite ugly guys if they have cars, but the prospect of always having to look perfect was depressing.

SATURDAY MARCH 24TH

Made a special effort to look fantastic for Chris today, but all he said was why was I wearing high heels, a short skirt and sleeveless top just to watch him play football? The ground was really muddy and it was cold today. Did I want to borrow his sweater?

He wasn't kidding. My nice shoes sank right into the mud, covering my toes and ankles with muck, and since I'd declined his offer of the shapeless sweater, I shivered in the chilly wind. By the end of the match I was so bad tempered I told him to stuff it – I didn't care how many other girls fancied him, they were welcome to him; he was an arrogant tosser and see if I cared. And no, I didn't want him to drive me home, I would walk, thanks all the same. Just because he drove a car didn't mean I had to be nice to him, and don't think that it did because it didn't. In fact I positively enjoyed walking. It was healthier and better for the environment. Cars just polluted the atmosphere and caused global warming which threatened our whole future.

Chris said, 'Fine.'

I squelched off, my feet sinking deeper into the sodden ground with each step, so that twice I strode out leaving my shoe embedded in the mud. Just to complete the misery, it started to bucket down. So when Chris stopped the car beside me, opened the door and said, 'Car sharing cuts down pollution, you know, Kelly Ann,' I gave in and got in the car.

On the journey Chris asked what was wrong with me. Was I premenstrual or what? He really didn't understand what was upsetting me this time. What had driving a car got to do with anything – it just meant we could get to more places more easily. He wished he knew who or what gave me these stupid ideas.

He seemed sincerely puzzled and I realized then that owning a car would make no difference to Chris and how he felt about me. It was nice of Shelly to be concerned about me, of course, and obviously I value her advice but she needn't have worried. However, told Chris not to ask personal, patronizing questions, he wasn't a doctor yet and could I borrow his sweater, please, I was freezing.

SUNDAY MARCH 25TH

Chris rang this morning. He said now that word has got round that he's got a car he didn't think he'd have time to see me any more. Honestly, he's been inundated with offers from so many girls desperate to go out with him. He's already knocked Britney back twice and she's gutted but when Christina and Jennifer cried down the phone and begged to see him he didn't have the heart to turn them down. However, he might be able to spare me an hour this evening – he'd just check his diary.

Hilarious.

SUNDƏY APRIL 1ST

Liz rang this morning. We chatted for a bit, then she asked me if I'd heard about the new topical treatment for breasts which is meant to make them grow like marrows. She says it's dead easy to make, anyone can do it – it's just a paste made from porridge, milk and baby oil. You're supposed to apply it to the breasts and leave it on for as long as possible. Apparently after just a month of this treatment some women have gone up two cup sizes. Everyone is talking about it. Although no one knows how it really works, an article in the *Lancet* (which Liz said is a magazine that's only allowed to print totally true stuff about medical research done by complete geniuses) has suggested that it might be due to the lactates in the milk combined with the complex carbohydrates in the porridge stimulating local oestrogen hormone pro-duction, which leads to an increase in breast tissue development.

Sounded fantastic. As soon as I got off the phone I made some up and was just smearing the disgusting gunge on my left breast when I realized what date it was.

Washed the stuff off then phoned Liz back and told her that of course I hadn't been fooled for a moment by her ridiculous story but to tell Chris from me he was in trouble – it was just *so* obvious who had provided her with all the medical jargon for her stupid trick.

Liz confessed right away and said that in fact Chris was with her at the moment and wanted to know if I'd cooled the porridge down before applying it as he'd been a bit worried about me burning myself.

Told her of course I'd cooled the porridge down, I wasn't stupid.

Heard Chris and Liz laughing on the other end of the phone and realized that I'd as good as admitted to being conned. Bollocks.

MONDAY APRIL 2ND

Mum has turned into a real swot with this Open University stuff. Practically as soon as she gets home from work she'll spread her books and notes on the kitchen table and start working. I wouldn't mind so much but she mutters to herself all the time while studying, and she's also taken to speaking to us in Spanish even though she knows no one can understand a word.

Am sure sometimes it's rude, insulting stuff she's saying – often she cackles to herself afterwards. It's hard to believe just how immature parents can be.

I *have* now picked up the meaning of a few words and phrases in Spanish though, such as 'nada' and 'mañana', as these are the usual replies to 'What's for dinner, Mum, and when are you making it?'

It's got so bad I've had to learn to cook or I'd have starved. Dad was very wary of my efforts at first because of the fiasco last year, when I cooked a dinner for boring Graham and his awful parents. It *was* a bit of a disaster: the canned steak-and-kidney pie blew up in the oven (I forgot to take the lid off) and the pudding was so sticky and chewy that it gummed people's jaws shut and dislodged Graham's mum's false teeth.

Still, I'm much better at cooking now, which is just as well: neither Mum nor Dad seem to have any time these days and Angela can't be arsed to do anything. Especially not look after her baby properly.

TUESDAY APRIL 3RD

Angela is getting even moanier. Sometimes she just lies in her bed or on the sofa and spends whole days just moping about in her pyjamas without ever getting dressed or washing her hair. Mum has been on her case a bit to pull herself together but she's been too busy with work and her new job and Open University stuff to take much notice. Dad can't understand why Angela is so fed up as he thought she was dead keen to have this baby, but says right enough, a new baby is very tiring and maybe she needs a break.

That's a laugh, her needing a break. Every day after school she begs me to take care of Danny while she sleeps or watches telly. Also almost every time Danny wakes during the night she ignores him and I have to get up and see to him. I really do love Danny but I'm getting totally knackered by the whole thing.

Angela has pleaded with me not to tell anyone about how I'm always taking care of him – she can't face everyone knowing what a rubbish mum she is. Suppose I can understand that. It must be dead embarrassing to admit you're useless at looking after babies after having boasted all through your pregnancy about how you were going to be such a perfect mother and do everything so much better than anyone else.

Chris is getting fed up with the situation too as I almost always bring Danny with me on dates. Tonight I took Danny with me to his house, where we planned to watch a movie. Unfortunately Danny was in a grizzly mood and we didn't get a chance to see even half of it. Chris got annoyed and started on about how we needed time together without always having a baby around.

He said he wasn't a 'baby hater' and yes, Danny *was* very cute but he wasn't Danny's dad and he'd like to see me by myself occasionally. Also he'd like to talk about something other than baby care for a change. And while he was on the subject, shopping had never been his idea of a good time, but going shopping with me in Mothercare had to be the absolute pits. He just couldn't understand why I drooled over baby socks and mittens; they were not cute, just small. He insisted that my sister wasn't well and needed to see a doctor and get help. He said we should speak to my mum and dad about it.

Told Chris he was talking rubbish and that he'd better not tell on Angela or he was dead meat. She might be a moany bore but she was my sister and there was no way I was going to tell on her.

Chris said that I should grow up – 'telling on her', for God's sake – and that I'd hardly changed since primary. I told Chris he was an arrogant know-it-all bore who obviously hated children as well as me and my entire family. Also informed him firmly that I wasn't prepared to stay in a place where my Danny wasn't welcome and we'd be going then.

WEDNESDAY APRIL 4TH

Went to Stephanie's with Danny after school. She looked at him warily. I asked her to hold him while I went to the toilet. When I returned she was holding Danny at arm's length and said, 'Quick, take him from me, he's just drooled on my Ted Baker top.'

Don't think Stephanie is too keen to have him round again.

THURSDAY APRIL 5TH

Took Danny to Liz's after school. Liz said she hadn't yet reached that stage of psychosocial development which involved losing interest in MTV and make-up while gaining an interest in teething and nappies.

Don't think Liz is too keen to have Danny round again either. Maybe Chris is more patient than I'd realized.

Am still annoyed with Chris though and won't talk to him.

FRIDAY APRIL 6TH

Liz has offered Chris, Danny and me 'family therapy'. Chris said he'd rather be boiled in oil, thanks all the same. So she suggested another couples counselling session. After all, he could say what he liked about the last one, but in the end it had worked.

Chris said the only thing he'd enjoy less than a couples counselling session run by Liz was being slowly castrated.

MONDAY APRIL 9TH

Chris has agreed to one session in principle but he wanted it over at his house so that it wasn't an 'away match', and if it was anything like the last one he would throw us both out right away.

Liz said OK and that we'd come over straight after school. Talked to Liz about it at lunch time and said that I really wasn't mad at Chris any more and I could understand him being fed up always having Danny around. But Liz said we should have the session anyway and use the opportunity to wind Chris up for a laugh.

I said OK.

Back at Chris's place after school, we settled down in the living room since his parents were out at work, then Liz kicked off by saying, 'All right, Chris, let's just hear from you first. What is your take on the current problems in your relationship with Kelly Ann? Please feel free to speak openly and sincerely to us without fear of judgement or criticism. It's our aim in this therapy session to treat each other at all times with unconditional positive regard so that we can talk with absolute total honesty about everything and anything, no matter how shameful or depraved it may be.'

Chris asked what unconditional positive regard was supposed to mean, but Liz just tutted, said she didn't have time to explain the finer points of psychology to someone as ignorant of the subject as he clearly was, and would he just answer the question.

Chris said fine, right, then we would 'crack on'. He told us that he was fed up with practically being a dad to Angela's baby without, he added jokingly, having any of the fun dads normally had before becoming fathers.

Liz said, so he wanted to sleep with my sister then? She added that he shouldn't be ashamed of admitting to any feelings, no matter how totally immoral and disgusting they were, and that he wouldn't be judged within the parameters of this therapy session.

'Bloody should be ashamed,' I said. 'What a perve.'

Chris spluttered that God, no, of course he didn't want to sleep with my sister – what he meant was that he'd like to have sex with me. That wasn't a crime, was it?

Of course it wasn't, Liz soothed. It was entirely natural and normal that he should want to have sex with me. It was also totally understandable too that since he wasn't getting any he would be frustrated, angry and resentful, which was probably why he wanted to hurt me by rejecting our baby.

Chris said angrily that yeah, he was a bit frustrated but he wasn't angry or resentful, nor did he want to hurt me and anyway Danny wasn't 'our baby', which was the whole bloody point he was bloody well trying to make.

Liz said we would deal with Chris's 'anger issues' later but that right now we should explore his relationship with me further. She assumed then that he wanted to have sex with me and that he wasn't interested in anybody else.

Yes.

And that he never so much as thought about having sex with other girls?

Er, no.

Stephanie, for example. Be honest now – honesty was so important to a successful therapy session and therefore to the resolution of his problems with me. He *never* thought *even fleetingly* about having sex with Stephanie?

Chris said this was a totally unfair question. He said that *everyone* thought about having sex with Stephanie. You couldn't *not* think about having sex with Stephanie. She practically *invited* you to think about having sex with her.

Liz shook her head and tutted disapprovingly at Chris. This was typical of males, trying to avoid blame by projecting their sordid desires onto girls, but we'd discuss Chris's pathetic defence mechanisms later. Right now we should move on.

Chris muttered something which sounded a lot like 'sordid desires?' and 'so much for unconditional positive regard' but just said, 'Yeah, let's get this thing over with, for God's sake.'

Liz went on to say she had been talking to me earlier and I'd told her that I believed he wasn't satisfied with me. That I was a disappointment to him, in fact, and that he wished I could be different. Wasn't that right, Kelly

Ann? I nodded yes and dabbed my eyes as though trying to hold back tears.

Chris said that this was rubbish, that he loved me and didn't want to change anything about me, that I was perfect just as I was. He simply wanted to see a bit more of me and a bit less of Danny, that was all.

So, Liz went on, he never wished I was a little more like Stephanie?

God, no.

Not even slightly less inhibited, a little more wanton perhaps, at least with him? He never wished that I was the type of girl who couldn't go a week, never mind months, without asking him, begging him even, for sex?

Chris smiled at the thought and said, 'OK, maybe slightly more wanton.'

And he never wished that my breasts were larger?

No.

He didn't like large breasts? Like hers, for instance? Didn't he like her breasts?

Chris said warily, 'Erm, yes, they are, er, very nice.'

Now, he was to be honest with us. If he could have Kelly Ann just as she was but maybe a bit more wanton and with slightly larger breasts, wouldn't he like that?

He supposed so, yes.

So Kelly Ann must be an awful disappointment to him then. She supposed that was why he constantly fantasized about at least one of my best friends and maybe my sister. No wonder I was so hurt and upset that I didn't want to see him any more.

By this time Chris had just put his head in his hands and started groaning. We decided to take pity on him and quit winding him up, especially as neither of us could stop giggling.

Chris said very funny – the pair of us were totally hilarious, he didn't think, and he hoped we'd enjoyed ourselves.

Oh, we had. Anyway, I sat beside Chris on the sofa and kissed him on the cheek. Liz sat on the other side and kissed him too. I promised to see him tomorrow without Danny to watch the DVD we hadn't managed to see last time, so in the end Chris didn't go into a sulk. But he did refuse Liz's 'totally genuine' offer of psychosexual counselling, saying he'd rather go twelve rounds with a world heavyweight boxing champion than spend five minutes being counselled by Liz.

TUESDAY APRIL 10TH

Stephanie, Liz and I spotted Chris and Gary coming through the school gates this morning. We walked up to them, Stephanie in the middle, to say hi. Stephanie smiled at Chris and said she'd heard he'd been thinking *fondly* about her. In fact, she'd heard he'd been thinking *very fondly* about her. Then she blew him a pouty kiss and laughed.

*   *   *

Went round to Chris's straight after school today. His parents were both working late shifts and wouldn't be home until after ten so we had the place to ourselves. Not that we were going to have sex or anything. Chris knows I am determined to wait until next Valentine's, and besides, I'd be too nervous to do anything at his parents' house now in case they came back unexpectedly. Still, it would nice to have a bit of privacy for a change. Chris put the movie on and we settled down on the couch to watch it.

Unfortunately Danny had been really restless the night before, waking me up three times, so I was knackered. The last thing I remembered was seeing the opening credits. The next thing I knew, Chris was waking me up gently, saying it was ten o'clock and time for me to go home.

It couldn't have been much fun just watching me sleep for six hours but he didn't say anything, just walked me home and kissed me goodnight. God, hope I hadn't snored.

WEDNESDAY APRIL 11TH

Easter holidays. Liz and Stephanie are going to New York to see Julian. He is paying for Liz's ticket and they'll stay with him. Can't help being jealous – New York is just the coolest city ever. Have never been there but have seen it in so many films and TV programmes I feel like I know the place. But there is no way Mum and Dad can afford for me to go. Every last penny is going towards Angela's wedding. Not that she's grateful. She won't even discuss arrangements with Mum; just says Mum and I can decide what's happening.

Unfortunately just about the only thing she *has* decided on is my bridesmaid dress and it's a fright. It is orange and made of stiff satin material, which flattens my chest but (incredibly!) manages to make my tummy look big. If that wasn't bad enough, it also has puff sleeves and hundreds of little daisies scattered all over. Have tried to protest about it but Mum says it's my sister's wedding and her wishes come first.

SaTURDaY APRIL 14TH

Mum has heard there's a sale on in Frasers today so she's going to look for an outfit for the wedding. Angela couldn't be bothered to go with her so I volunteered. Was furious when Mum said there was no way she wanted me with her as my taste was in my arse; just look at that awful bridesmaid dress I'd chosen. She said she'd be going with Aunt Kate.

The pair of them didn't get back until after seven but the trip had been a success. Mum tried on her dress/suit thing and even Dad said she looked nice. But when she told him that was great as with 25 per cent off it had only cost £700, I thought Dad was going to faint.

When he'd recovered enough to speak he told her she'd have to take it back, it was daylight bloody robbery and what was the thing made of – twenty-quid notes?

But Mum was having none of it. The sales assistant in Frasers had told her that a mature beauty like Mum required the finest quality garments. Then Aunt Kate pointed out to Dad that the bride's mum would have to wear something expensive enough to make sure none of the guests would be wearing the same outfit.

Had been feeling a bit sorry for Dad but was gob-smacked when he said in a genuinely puzzled tone, what did it matter if someone else was wearing the same outfit as long as it was nice?

Aunt Kate opened her mouth as though to reply but shut it again. As she said later, the chasm of understanding had been too vast to bridge.

In the end, of course, Mum will be keeping the suit plus matching shoes (£125), hat (£75) and bag (£50). Dad will work more overtime.

EASTER: APRIL 15TH

Dad is working today even though it's Easter Sunday, and mum is visiting Great-aunt Winnie, who's just come *out of hospital after a hip operation.* Was supposed to go with Chris for a drive in the country but offered to stay and babysit Danny so that my sister could go out with Graham, who is up for Easter.

Shouldn't have bothered. When they got back about five in the afternoon she went straight to bed without looking at Danny or talking to Graham.

Graham said she hadn't eaten any of the lunch they'd ordered even though there was nothing wrong with it, then she'd cried all the way through a film that was supposed to be a side-splitting comedy.

Chris, who'd stayed in with me, told Graham that he thought Angela might have post-natal depression and that he should insist she sees a doctor. Graham says he's mentioned making an appointment but she won't listen.

Told Chris we should really get a baby seat for his car, then we'd be able to get out more, but he says definitely not. No way. Over his dead body.

TUESDAY APRIL 17TH

Had promised Chris that we'd drive up to Loch Lomond and go for a picnic as it's a gorgeous sunny morning and the forecast is good all day, but when I told my sister she went mental. She just sat in the corner of the living room in her pyjamas screaming and threatening to top herself if I left her alone with Danny today. Meanwhile Danny was wailing in his cot and she hadn't even changed his nappy.

Obviously there was no way I could go to Loch Lomond but I didn't want Chris moaning at me about how I'm always looking after Danny. Called him and said I wouldn't be going out today as I wasn't well, and OK, if he must know I'd got cramp but not to ask any more cheeky personal questions. He wasn't a doctor yet.

Chris came over anyway, ringing the bell then hammering on the door like the police, so I was forced to answer. He took one look at Angela, who was still sitting in the corner in her night stuff bawling, and said right, that was it. He threw a coat at her, told her to put it on, then marched her out in her bare feet to his car. He told me to bring Danny and her shoes and sit in the back: we were going to her doctor's.

I was totally embarrassed turning up at the surgery with my sister still in her pyjamas, but Angela didn't seem to be aware of it and Chris said he didn't care if she was starkers just so long as she got seen by a doctor. He told me to ring Mum and Dad and tell them they had to come home. As we waited he also advised me that next time I lied about being ill, I should make it a bit more believable. Most girls didn't have periods every week.

The doctor has said that Angela has post-natal

depression, which means that she is more than just a bit fed up after having a baby but totally miserable and hopeless. She said that my sister is a really bad case and she was considering a period of hospitalization, but we would try antidepressants first – although they would take a while to work and she would need a lot of support in the meantime.

Mum and Dad feel really guilty about not paying enough attention to Angela recently. After they got home early from work they told her how sorry they were and later suggested she go off to bed for a rest even though it was still early afternoon. When she'd gone, they thanked Chris for taking her to the doctor's and then Mum talked to us about what would happen now. Mum said she would take some time off work to look after Angela. Meanwhile I would help take care of Danny. It was about time I helped out more with him. When Chris heard Mum say this he mimed pointing a gun at his foot and firing but all he said was, maybe he would buy a baby seat for the car after all.

FRIDAY APRIL 20TH

Got an email from Liz. She says New York is fantastic and definitely the place for her in the future. Everyone who's anyone (and even if they're not) has a therapist and they're paid a fortune. Same with lawyers – tell Ayesha.

New Yorkers are really open, friendly and not stuck up at all, although she wishes they'd stop prodding her breasts, saying 'Great job!' and asking who her surgeon was. Loads of people have invited them to their apartments for meals and stuff, which is very nice of them, although Julian says you have to be careful not to get drunk beforehand and turn up at the wrong address or you might get shot.

Not that getting drunk is easy. You have to be twenty-one and they're really strict about it. Most teenagers in New York just have to make do with stuff like with marijuana or cocaine. My mum wouldn't like it there either. You're not allowed to smoke anywhere and it's rumoured they're going to introduce the death penalty for illicit lighting up in toilets.

But the food in New York! Huge bagels, doughnuts, hot dogs, burgers. And everything is so cheap. The food is to die for.

Saturday April 21st

Got an email from Stephanie. It said, 'So many shops, so little time.'

MONDaY APRIL 23RD

Back at school but not for long. We'll soon be off on study leave.

Mr Dunn came into our English class today to borrow the TV and video. As he was wheeling it out, Ms Conner smiled at him and asked him if there was anything else he might require, because if there was anything, anything at all, she'd be happy to oblige him. It would be her pleasure.

Mr Dunn said, God no, he was knackered. He was going to shove on a video about lions eating Christians for his first-year class so he could sleep while they watched. Then he hurried out with a hunted look.

Mr Dunn is always falling asleep in classes these days – not just on Mondays like last year, when he was hung over from a weekend's drinking. There is a nasty rumour going round it's due to Ms Conner's constant sexual demands, but Gerry of all people defended her. He said he didn't believe she could stop talking long enough to shag anyone but his pal Johnny disagreed. He says she probably talks right through the whole thing, giving instructions, then grades Mr Dunn afterwards. Probably 'F minus and must try harder' – she was a really strict marker.

Told the pair of them to shut it. The thought of teachers like Ms Conner having sex is almost as bad as parents. It's just *so* wrong.

THURSDAY APRIL 26TH

Saw Chris talking to Linda at break today and got annoyed. Have told him before that I don't want him having anything more to do with her but Chris just says that I should 'grow up' and that he won't be told by me who he should and shouldn't talk to. He says I really have to get over my stupid jealousy and trust him.

He's got a nerve talking about 'stupid jealousy'. Reminded him how furious he'd been just because Gerry sat beside me in assembly last week and offered me one of his mints.

But Chris refused to back down, saying that was completely different as Gerry (or 'that tight tosser') never offered anything, not even a mint, for free, and I should stay away from him.

FRIDAY APRIL 27TH

Last day of school before the exams so we finished early. Was still annoyed with Chris about Linda and refused to meet up with him after school. Instead, went to the pub with Liz and Stephanie using our fake IDs. We'd no sooner ordered three vodka and Cokes when practically the entire staff of our school except for Miss McElwee piled in and chased us out. Just our luck. Couldn't help noticing that our untouched drinks were quickly taken care of by three of the female teachers, who had the cheek to raise their glasses to us and shout 'Cheers, girls' as we made for the door.

On our way out met Gerry and his friends plus some guys from the Catholic school about to go in, and warned them about the staff invasion. Gerry said thanks, then suggested we all just buy some booze from the off-licence and take it to the park. It was a nice day and we could get drunk cheaper that way. Liz said sarcastically, 'So classy,' and told them she wasn't going anywhere with them, but Stephanie fancied one of the guys from St Kentigern's so in the end we agreed to go.

Was disappointed Shelly wasn't there as I'd wanted to moan to her about Chris and Linda, but Gerry said she'd gone shopping with her pals. After about five minutes in the park Stephanie had gone off with the guy from St Kentigern's and later Liz left to get something to eat, she was famished, so it was just me, Gerry and three of his pals sitting on the bench drinking cider. Well, when I say sitting on the bench, there wasn't room for four of us so I sat on Gerry's knee, which probably didn't look good when Chris, Ian and Gary wandered by.

I stood up and tried to explain things to Chris but my voice had gone all slurry and in any case he wouldn't listen to me. Instead he swore at Gerry, hauled him off the bench and threatened to beat him up.

Gerry's friends were useless, just drunkenly egging both of them on, but Ian and Gary dragged Chris off

Gerry and eventually calmed him down, telling him Gerry wasn't worth the hassle, and besides, it wasn't as though he was snogging me or anything. In the end Chris just told Gerry to stay away from me in future and we left.

Walked back with Chris but I was really annoyed at him embarrassing me like that and said so. Told him that he should grow up, that I wouldn't be told by him who I should and shouldn't talk to, and that he really would have to get over his stupid jealousy and trust me. Well, that's what I meant to say. What came out sounded something like Gezzy was my fwend and why didn't Chris truss me?

Later, when I'd sobered up at Chris's house, he said he did trust me but he didn't trust Gerry, who by the way had been almost completely sober while plying me with alcohol, and to stay away from him.

Told Chris that I could take care of myself, thanks all the same, that I knew exactly what I was doing and didn't need his interference – then I asked him to pass me the basin, I was going to be sick again.

MONDAY APRIL 30TH

Chris has said we can't see much of each other until the exams are over as we really need to study. He said he'd text me every morning and call me every night. He told me he loved me and couldn't wait for all this to be over, then he kissed me, explained that the log of 0.1 was minus one, and said yes, he'd tutor me before my maths exam.

Shelly called. She said wasn't it fantastic our being on study leave now? She and Gerry were going to use the opportunity to spend loads more time together. She would be over at his place tomorrow. It would be fantastic having the place to themselves as his parents would be at work. What did Chris and I plan to do?

Shelly is my friend so I don't know why I lied to her and said, 'Oh, same actually.' I suppose I didn't want her to think that Chris cared more about passing exams than he did about me. Which isn't true. Definitely not.

TUESDAY MAY 1ST

9:00 text from Chris: Luv u
9:10 text from Chris: Miss u 2
9:15 text from Chris: Yeah stll luv u
9:20 text from Chris: Yeah stll stdyg
9:22 text from Chris: KA, stop txting!

THURSDAY MAY 3RD

Am so stressed with this studying thing. Why, oh why didn't I do more work during the year? Well, OK, part of the reason I didn't was that I'd already decided that I wanted to be an actress so exam results wouldn't be too important. However, when I mentioned this to Mum last month she said actress her arse and I'd better work at school or I'd end up a failure, stuck in a life of boredom and drudgery like her. Dad wasn't quite as blunt but said

I'd best get an education too just in case things didn't work out.

Don't know why my parents won't take my ambitions seriously and have more faith in me, but when I mentioned this to Chris he wasn't very supportive. He reminded me that at various times I'd wanted to be a ballerina, a striker for AC Milan, a poet, and, oh yes, a mechanical digger operator. You couldn't blame my mum and dad for being a bit sceptical about this latest idea of mine.

Thanks a bunch, Chris. I mean what's the point of having a boyfriend if all he does is agree with your parents, for God's sake? And besides, I'm not the only person to change my mind about careers. Right up until the end of second year Chris wanted to be a fighter pilot in the RAF. He dropped this ambition in third year shortly after his granddad died and decided on medicine instead. I used to tease him that he wanted to become a doctor so he could pull lots of nurses, but actually Chris was gutted about his granddad as they were pretty close, and apparently if his illness had been caught earlier, he'd have survived. I suppose that's really what made Chris change his mind, although he never talks about it. Anyway, you can't get two careers much more different than fighter pilot and doctor, yet everyone takes Chris seriously but not me.

Whatever the reason for my not studying earlier, the only thing I've any hope of doing well in now is English.

Will probably fail everything else and I can't see my parents supporting me while I seek fame and fortune as an actress.

Have moaned about it to everyone, even Danny, who just gurgles and waves his fists about. Mum's response wasn't any more useful. Just got the usual spiel about how I could only do my best and that's all anyone could ask for, and besides, she was sure I'd do fine and would I find the TV control so that she could see if *EastEnders* had started – oh, and bring her fags over.

This time I screamed at Mum: What if my best wasn't good enough? What if I failed miserably and ruined my whole life? How could she watch TV when my entire future was at stake? Then I stormed off to my room, sobbing and banging doors behind me.

FRIDAY MAY 4TH

Called Chris and begged him to see me over the weekend but he said no, he had to study. Shelly rang right after my call to Chris so I ended up telling her about it. She said if Chris really loved me he'd do what I asked but Liz said to ignore her, that Chris was certifiably crazy about me but just needed to do well to get into medicine, that's all.

THURSDAY MAY 10TH

Shelly called today. She just chatted for a while but then she said she expected Chris had told me he'd been to see Linda twice this week at her house. No? Really? That was odd – he'd spent hours there so she'd have thought he'd at least have mentioned it. Never mind, she was sure he'd had his reasons. Best not to bring it up with him. If there was one thing guys hated – trust her on this one – it was a suspicious nagging girlfriend. In any case I wasn't to worry, as she would keep an eye on things for me and let me know if anything serious was going on.

Called Liz and Stephanie. Neither of them like Shelly even though she's been really nice to me this year, so they both said not to listen to her. But they did agree about not mentioning it to Chris, who hates me going on about Linda.

SUNDAY MAY 13TH

Shelly called today and asked me to go round and see her right away. It was important. When I got there she ushered me in, told me to sit on the sofa by the window, then sat next to me and embarrassed me a bit by taking my hand in hers. She said she was very sorry to be the one to break the news but she was sure there was some- thing going on between Linda and Chris and felt it was only right that I should know. They were in Linda's house right now and had been there for ages. Look, there was his car parked in her driveway. It was best not to go over there right then: I shouldn't confront them at her place. Best to wait until he came out, then I could speak to him.

Shook Shelly's hand off and stood up. I bloody would go over there and find out what was going on, but Shelly said, 'Wait, Kelly Ann, look, there they are.'

I looked out the window in the direction Shelly had pointed and saw them. Chris and Linda were walking down the path towards his car hand in hand. He walked round and opened the door for her, but before she got in she kind of leaned against him. Chris put one arm around her waist and started stroking her hair with the other hand. Then he drew her closer to him in a kind of bear hug and kissed the top of her head. They stayed like that for a moment before drawing apart again, then Linda reached up, kissed him lightly on the mouth and got into the car.

I watched in horrified fascination. At first I just couldn't believe what I'd seen. This had to be an awful nightmare and I'd wake up soon. Surely Chris would never do this to me. But no, I hadn't dreamed it, this was real. My boyfriend was cheating on me.

Chris and Linda were both in the car now and starting to reverse out when I was suddenly overcome with a murderous rage. I turned away from the window and started to run for the door, hoping to get Chris before he drove off, drag him out of the car and beat him to a bloody pulp, but Shelly caught hold of me by the shoulders and held me back, saying, 'Don't do it, Kelly Ann. You have to keep your dignity or you'll regret it.'

I hesitated for a moment, but then thought dignity my arse and ran out. Too late, he'd already gone.

Not knowing what else to do, I returned to Shelly's. Some of my rage was draining away, only to be replaced by worse feelings.

I slumped back down on the sofa, put my head in my hands and rocked slowly back and forth, all the while trying to block out the images of Chris and Linda I'd just seen. In a way I'd rather have caught them having full sex than witnessed that awful tender and affectionate scene. He must really care for her to touch her like that. I wasn't surprised or even that mad with Linda. She'd never been a particular friend of mine and I knew she'd always fancied Chris. She didn't owe me any loyalty, but Chris did and it really hurt.

Later I shrugged off Shelly's offer to stay and talk things over with her. I really needed to be alone. Practically ran back home, tears streaming down my face. I raced up to my bedroom before anyone could see me, flung myself on my bed and cried some more. Eventually, totally cried out, I tried to think what to do. I suppose I should have gone over and confronted Chris but I didn't feel ready. I was afraid I'd just totally humiliate myself by bawling my eyes out, and I was determined never to let him know how much he'd managed to hurt me.

Thought of calling Liz or Stephanie, but telling them about it would just make it seem so much more real and final, and I wasn't ready for that yet. Besides, when I was this upset the person I always went to was Chris. Now Chris had betrayed me and I'd lost him for ever. That's the problem with dating your best friend; when it ends you lose everything.

MONDAY MAY 14TH

English exam this morning. Only my first and most important Higher. Didn't sleep for ages the night before. When I woke up I thought for a moment that yesterday had been some kind of nightmare but no such luck. A text message from Shelly saying how sorry she was for me confirmed the bloody worst. Another text message from Chris said, 'Good luck in English. Luv u' and set me off crying again.

Couldn't let everyone see me all red eyed like this so decided to go late to the exam. And yes, I know you need every bloody second in an English exam even if you can write at the speed of light, but what else could I do?

Arrived ten minutes late (just before they stop you getting in) and was seated at the back of the hall. Started to read the exam questions but the print kept blurring, then teardrops made damp blobs on the paper so even though it was less than half an hour since the start of the exam and I wasn't supposed to, I left.

I knew I'd done a terrible thing and probably ruined my entire future but I couldn't have stayed there. I ran out of the school and started to walk home, but then I changed my mind and headed for Dad's garage.

When I was little I used to love going on Saturdays to watch my dad and the other car mechanics working in the garage, but my mum stopped it when I started saying things like where the **** is my Barbie doll and what ******* has stolen my crayons, and sent me to ballet lessons instead. Not that my dad ever talked like that in front of me but the others found it hard to watch their language all the time when I was there.

Today I recognized Tommy, who is supposed to be retired but according to my dad comes in almost every day to 'help out'. Didn't recognize the young guy, but since he looked as though he didn't have a clue what he was doing I guessed he was the latest 'training for work' candidate. Couldn't see my dad until Tommy pointed me to a car and I found him working underneath it. He took one look at my face, then slid out saying, 'What's the matter, love?' He wiped his hands on a rag then took me to the office, where we could talk 'in private' – although given that most of the walls were made of glass it wasn't really all that private.

I told Dad that Chris had cheated on me so we were finished and that I'd walked out of my English Higher.

Then I started to cry again. Dad said, 'Jesus, Kelly Ann.' He hugged me, which left engine oil stains on my blouse and face, but I didn't care. It was just a relief to admit to someone how unhappy I was. But then Dad started taking off his overalls and saying that he would just go and have 'a word with young Chris' and that he didn't care if he was sitting an English exam. Why should Chris be allowed to sit his English exam in peace when I was this upset?

Managed to persuade Dad that I needed him here with me so he calmed down a bit and hugged me some more. Around eleven o'clock Tommy and the training for work guy called Pete came in with mugs of tea and a plate of chocolate digestives. When I told Tommy about Chris he just said, 'Och, hen, ye should know by noo that all young lads are wee shites. Ye'd be better aff jist sticking wi' yer faither, so ye wid.'

Pete offered to take me out to cheer me up but Dad just glared at him and he shut up. Still, I was starting to feel a bit better and offered to go make some more tea. When I came back they'd hidden the poster of the girl playing tennis with no knickers on.

Spent the rest of the day watching them fix cars just like I used to. Tommy let me put on overalls and do some routine stuff like replacing spark plugs and brake pads under his supervision. Found it oddly soothing. Maybe I could become a car mechanic. You didn't need Higher English for that.

Later I asked Dad not to tell Mum or Angela what had

happened yet – just couldn't face it – and went over to Liz's.

After Liz got over the shock of Chris's betrayal she was brilliant. She said what I really needed now was peer therapy and set about contacting my support group. Soon I was getting text messages, emails and phone calls from loads of other girls whose boyfriends had cheated on them. Although I was still devastated about Chris of course, it felt really good to be part of a kind of sisterhood of two-timed girlfriends. I especially liked the tales of revenge exacted by some of the girls on their cheating ex-boyfriends and planned to use some of their ideas in the future. Oh yes, I was beginning to feel much, much better.

However, was a bit annoyed with Stephanie, who came along later. Instead of the 'guys are all scum and what did I expect' comments I'd, well . . . expected, she said had I spoken to Chris about this? I hadn't? Didn't he at least deserve a chance to defend himself? It wasn't as though I'd caught him actually shagging, after all. There might be a perfectly innocent explanation.

Innocent my arse. I mean, why would I want to speak to a two-timing cheating liar like him?

WEDNESDAY MAY 16TH

French exam today. Wasn't too bad. At lunch time loads of girls, most of whom I don't normally speak to, came up and told me how sorry they were I'd been cheated on, and said what a tosser Chris was but it was his loss. Then they gave me their own stories about their two-timing ex-boyfriends. Was really shocked when Madeleine, a drop-dead-gorgeous sixth year, told me it had happened to her. Madeleine is tall with waist-length straight blonde hair, blue eyes and a flawless complexion. She already models part time and is probably going to do it full time once she leaves school. She told me her ex had two-timed her with, and later dumped her for, a small dumpy brunette with crooked teeth and glasses. He'd said he really liked her. It had been so humiliating. Obviously, since there was no competition looks-wise, it meant there was something wrong with Madeleine's personality, and what can you do about that?

Never thought I could feel sorry for someone who looked like Madeleine but I did.

Chris has phoned and texted me loads of times but I've ignored him. Angela told me he came round to the house when I was out and why wasn't she to tell him where I was? Was there something wrong? Didn't want to bother her with it all as though the pills seem to be working and she's getting better, she's still a bit fragile so just told her it was 'nothing I can't handle', which is true, I hope.

FRIDAY MAY 18TH

Everyone was out this afternoon as Aunt Kate had volunteered to take Angela and Danny so I could get some peace. It was a beautiful day (why, oh why is it always sunny when you have to revise?) so after a while I decided to take a break from studying. I put on the 'I Will Survive' CD – a present from one of my fellow Victims of Cheaters Support Group – and was sitting by my open bedroom window listening to the music and idly looking out at the quiet street when I saw Chris walking up to my door. My group had warned me this might happen. Chris was obviously going to try and crawl back to me, pleading for forgiveness and begging me to take him back, but I had to be strong and show him the door. After all, once a cheater, always a cheater.

So I turned away from the window, grabbed a round hairbrush, which I pretended was a mike, and sang along loudly to the number, ignoring Chris's persistent ringing and later battering on the door.

Put the same song on again and was really getting into it when, turning round, was gobsmacked to see Chris scrambling through the open window.

Screamed at him that he'd no right to be in my room and that he'd better not have broken the drainpipes climbing up, then looked out to check they were OK. Chris meanwhile had marched right in, turned off the music and was standing in front of my CD player with his arms folded saying the drainpipes were fine and nice of me to worry about him breaking his neck climbing up to see me.

Was annoyed at Chris for forcing his way in. Still, I suppose it would be good to see him grovel. In fact it would be great to watch him completely humiliate himself, only for me to tell him to stuff it, he was total history, so I put on my most aggrieved but dignified and brave expression, and told him to say what he had to say then get lost.

Was really surprised as well as annoyed when he started on about what the hell I thought I was playing at – my explanation had better be bloody good or I was in deep trouble.

Was too taken aback by this unexpected attack to reply – hadn't much of a chance to anyway as he was ranting on about how he'd heard from just about everyone with the single bloody exception of me that we were finished. Some crap about how he'd cheated on me with Linda. And when he said everyone he meant *everyone*. He'd been called, texted, emailed about it. Total strangers he'd never met in his life had stopped him in the street and talked to him about it. It seemed that I'd told just about the entire population of the west of Scotland that our relationship was over – had it never occurred to me once, even bloody well once, to discuss this directly with him?

Had recovered from my initial surprise and now I was getting mad. This was typical of Chris, twisting things so that he looked hard done by when it was me who was the victim here. Put my hands over my ears and chanted, 'I'm so not listening to you. I'm so not listening.'

Chris grabbed my wrists, forced my arms down by my sides and said I bloody well would listen. I stomped on his toes and said I bloody wouldn't. Unfortunately I was barefooted so didn't cause him much grief but just seemed to annoy him. So was forced to put on a pathetic girly voice and say, 'Please let me go, Chris, you're hurting me.'

Idiot released me right away so I put my hands back over my ears again and chanted, 'Lying liar' – OK, I know this was childish but it was *so* much fun – 'pants on fire,' over and over again while Chris tried to talk to me.

Stopped chanting when he smashed his fist into my wardrobe door just behind me. Hitting the door was a really stupid thing to do as it not only made a large dent and crack in my door but must have hurt his hand lots, judging from the way he was shaking and rubbing it and swearing. It did demonstrate, however, that Chris's complaints about me were not part of an 'attack is the best form of defence' ploy: he was genuinely annoyed about something.

I decided that a change of tactics was needed so we agreed that I would listen to him for five minutes if he promised to leave afterwards without trashing the rest of my room.

Chris admitted that he had seen Linda a few times last

week and maybe (?!) he should have told me about it but didn't because of my 'stupid jealousy'. He said Linda had been upset about a problem she'd had and so he had hugged her and maybe he'd kissed her – he didn't remember – but he certainly hadn't snogged her, far less had sex with her. He refused to tell me what Linda's problem was about as she wanted it to remain private and confidential. Not that I'd understand the meaning of the words *private and confidential*, given how I'd discussed the details of our relationship with just about everyone on the planet except him.

Chris went on to say that he could do without this hassle from me just now as he really needed to concentrate on his exams. Medicine was so competitive. It was very important for his future that he focus entirely on getting the best results possible. Important for my future too.

Couldn't see why it should be important for my future and said so. Could hardly believe it when Chris replied that 'of course' I must know that he intended for us to get married. Not right away, naturally, but after he'd graduated and had made registrar in about seven or eight years' time.

Told Chris he'd a bloody nerve. At the very least he'd been seeing Linda behind my back, had just damaged my wardrobe, and now he'd delivered what must be the most unromantic proposal in the history of the universe. That's if it *was* a proposal as I hadn't actually heard a question in there. If he *was* asking, the answer by the way was 'no' and he could get stuffed. Told him that with an eight-year engagement – about half my lifetime – I'd die of boredom before I got to the altar. No doubt next he'd be talking about joint bloody pension plans.

Chris said OK, I didn't have to say I'd marry him. He hadn't meant to discuss that with me for a long time. But anyway, given that marriage to me was a long-term strategic objective for him, it wouldn't make sense for him to jeopardize this with short-term tactical or procedural errors such as two-timing me with Linda. So did I believe now that he hadn't cheated on me?

Only Chris could make a relationship sound like a military operation and I started to giggle. But yes, I did believe him.

Chris said he'd forgive me this once for 'being stupid' and did I have an ice pack – his hand was swelling up. Honestly, only a guy could punch a door and then call someone else stupid. Still, I got him some ice and kissed him and it felt so good to have him back again. Only problem was, what was I going to say at my Victims of Cheaters Support Group meeting tomorrow?

SATURDAY MAY 19TH

Liz 'facilitated' the group meeting at her place. She told the group that I'd some important news to share with them, but I couldn't bring myself to say Chris and I were back together, which seemed like such a betrayal, so just said how fantastic they all were. Will just have to keep our relationship secret, like I'm having an affair or something. Liz scowled at me but didn't give me away and has changed our group name to Survivors of Cheaters. She says that's more positive.

Did tell Shelly that Chris and me were OK now as I knew she'd be so pleased for me. At first she was sceptical but I managed to convince her that Chris really was telling the truth, I was sure of it, so she said that was great. She also said that I was such a nice person, so trusting and forgiving, and that Chris was very, very clever, wasn't he?

MONDAY MAY 21ST

Ms Conner nabbed me as I was coming out of the history exam and told me to come see her at the English base tomorrow lunch time. Obviously she must have heard about my walking out of English and was bound to be furious. Oh God. Don't know if I can stand her going on at me. Would rather spend an afternoon being questioned by the Spanish Inquisition than half an hour with Conner on a rant. Still, suppose I haven't any choice.

Ms Conner said that Chris had told her about my English exam. She said I wasn't to worry unduly as she intended to lodge an appeal for me in August. Of course, technically no appeal is allowed after a student has walked out of an examination. Those were the rules and Ms Conner believed that rules should be strictly applied – except of course when flexibility is required, and who better to judge such instances than an experienced and committed departmental principal teacher such as herself? She'd had occasion to argue this point with certain somewhat officious individuals (who shall remain nameless) in the past but they had soon come round to her point of view.

She added that she would be recommending I get an A grade, based on her assessment of my abilities. Of course, the examination authorities were not automatically obliged to accept her recommendations. In fact on one occasion – oh, about ten years ago – they did initially disallow an appeal lodged by her. She tapped her fingernails on the desk and her eyes narrowed at the memory. However, the incident was eventually resolved to Ms Conner's satisfaction, although not before several resignations had been tendered and some reputations ruined beyond repair. An unpleasant and in her view unnecessary business all round. Still, she didn't think we'd have any similar disagreeable occurrences in the future.

Then she ranted on at me for ages – about how I mustn't allow relationships with boys to impact on my academic or career ambitions and how I was betraying the very principles of feminism that had made my education possible. On and on, until fortunately Mr Dunn came in. Was there anything he wanted?

WEDNESDAY MAY 30TH

At long last the exams are over. It was a gorgeous day so Chris and I celebrated by driving down to Largs for the day. We bought ice-creams and walked along the pebbly beach. Chris told me that he intended to go to university this year if he could get into Glasgow to do medicine. He said most people don't get accepted from the fifth year but he was hopeful he would do well enough. He'd also got a summer job working as a hospital porter, partly for experience and partly for money. He said he'd need the money because he was sick of living at home and wanted to get a flat. Ian, Gary and he were looking at a place in Byres Road, which is where loads of students stay.

Couldn't see why Chris is sick of living at home. His parents think he's brilliant and treat him like a prince but Chris says that's part of the problem: as he's an only child, they take too much interest in what he does.

I'll be staying on for a sixth year as I'm not sure what I want to do yet – I don't think my results will be good enough for whatever it is, and my dad says I'm too young to go to university. It will be odd not to see Chris every day at school and I said so.

He said he'll miss me too but at least we could get some privacy from parents at his flat. Maybe I would like to stay over sometimes. We needn't have sex but at least we could sleep together. I said, 'Maybe.'

THURSDAY MAY 31ST

Stephanie says the 'we'll just sleep together' line is the oldest trick in the book. I said even I knew that and I'd no intention of just sleeping with him. Next Valentine's was too long to wait.

Stephanie said, 'At long bloody last. Hallelujah!'

saturday June 2nd

Just two more days until we go back to school. To be honest I'll be glad to get out of the house. Although Angela is getting better now, Danny still wants me all the time and cries until I take him. Love him to bits but he can get tiring.

Shelly called this evening. She said had I heard that Chris and Linda had been seen together at Linda's doctor's surgery recently? Didn't I think that was odd? Why would Chris be going to her doctor's with her?

It did seem odd, I suppose, but not if you really know Chris. Obviously the 'confidential problem' Linda had must have been some weird medical thing and it would be just like Chris to be interested in that. Or maybe she'd just asked for a lift to the surgery and he'd waited around so he could take her back home too. Chris was really kind and thoughtful like that.

SUNDAY JUNE 3RD

Got another phone call from Shelly. Even before she spoke I felt anxious. Somehow, whenever Shelly contacts me these days it leaves me feeling bad, but even so there was no way I was prepared for her bombshell. She said had I heard the news? Linda was pregnant. She won't tell anyone, even her parents, who the father is but almost everyone is assuming it's Chris because he was her last boyfriend – though some are saying it's not because the baby is due in November and they split up in December. She just thought she should let me know.

Felt a horrible twisting sensation in my stomach. It couldn't be true, could it? But no, I'd doubted Chris before and it had all been rubbish. Wasn't going to make the same mistake again. In fact I was going to phone him right then.

Called Chris. He said that yeah, he'd heard Linda was pregnant and he'd also heard the rumour about him being the father but like most rumours it was rubbish and no one who knew him well believed it. I wasn't worried about it, was I?

Told him of course I wasn't but when I hung up I couldn't help thinking about Linda. She'd always been crazy about Chris and she'd never had a boyfriend that anyone knew about since they'd split. If it wasn't Chris, who could it be? Linda wasn't a slapper who slept around. Decided to go see her.

Didn't know her phone number so went round to her place. Her mum answered the door and I noticed her eyes were red. She said that Linda wasn't there and had gone to stay with her gran in Edinburgh for a while. Then she said she expected I'd heard the news and had I any idea who the father was – Linda wouldn't speak to her. She hesitated, then said Linda had always been very fond of Chris, and I, er, wouldn't know anything about it, would I?

I shook my head and turned to go, only to find Linda's best friend Beth at my back. Linda's mum gave her the same message but also told her Linda would be in touch soon, then closed the door on us.

Beth turned to me in a fury, hissing that I'd some nerve coming here. It wasn't enough that I'd 'stolen' Chris from Linda last year; now I had to come and gloat that he'd dumped her for me again and this time she was pregnant with his baby.

I stared at her in horror. Linda had told her this? Chris was definitely the father?

Well, not exactly, but who else? Beth knew Chris had been seeing her, plus Linda had told her that the father had a steady girlfriend and had asked Linda to shut up about him. Everyone knew Linda would do anything for Chris. She wasn't even going to tell the Child Support Agency about him. She hoped I was happy now that I'd made sure Chris broke her heart again.

Happy! I put my hand over my mouth to stop myself being sick with rage and shame. Beth was going on at me some more so I was glad to see Shelly coming out of her house towards me. I couldn't take much more abuse. I felt bad enough without Beth rubbing it in some more. Shelly told Beth to shove off, put a hand round my shoulders and started to guide me to her house. She said I shouldn't worry about this Linda thing. After all, it was obvious Chris must prefer me to Linda if he was willing to dump her for me, especially now she's pregnant with his baby. As long as I had sex with Chris pretty soon he probably wouldn't change his mind about Linda.

I know Shelly was trying to be supportive but, bloody hell, she couldn't know me very well. Right now I wanted to murder Chris and I'd never, ever take him back after what he'd done to me and Linda. I went home, my rage increasing with every step. I avoided everyone by dashing straight up to my room. Dad called up to me to ask what was wrong but I didn't answer him. I couldn't trust myself to speak to anyone. Heard Mum tell Dad just to leave me alone, saying, 'She's probably in one of her moods,' which would normally have annoyed me but not this time. I needed time alone to try and deal with what Chris had done to me.

I didn't feel angry with Linda at all. She'd fallen for Chris just like I had. She'd believed his lies about caring for her, again just like me. Now she'd been betrayed. Snap. Shelly was right, Chris is very, very clever, but I for one wasn't going to be a gullible idiot any more. I would get my revenge.

MONDAY JUNE 4TH

Didn't see Chris until the start of third period as I was making my way along the corridor to maths. He was standing between Ian and Gary, waiting for a first-year class to file out. He spotted me too and smiled over for me to come and join him. I forced a smile onto my face until I got right up to him, then, *wham!* I punched him as hard as I could right in the eye saying, 'That's for Linda.' It was even more successful than I'd hoped as I was still wearing that stupid ring he'd bought me at Valentine's and it must have cut him because he was bent over clutching his eye in agony and blood was seeping through his fingers. Yes! Violence is so satisfying. It really is.

Was going to hit him again and Chris had stretched out his other hand to try to stop me when Mr Simmons came out to see what the commotion was about. He sent Chris to the medical room and me down to Mr Smith.

Knew I was in serious trouble – people are always sent to Smith when it's serious – but I didn't care. Mr Smith was in a meeting so I had to wait outside his office, which is right next to the head teacher's. Have sometimes wondered what our head teacher is for as he seems to do nothing except maybe grovel to important people like businessmen or politicians who occasionally visit our school. It's Smith who actually runs the place and deals with any problems, although there are times, like now, when I wish he didn't bother. The door to his office was slightly ajar and I could hear him arguing with staff – I recognized the voices of Mrs Brown, the senior biology teacher, Mrs Parker from guidance (nicknamed Mrs Nosy for obvious reasons – she honestly is the nosiest teacher in the school) and Mr Dunn, the so-called RE teacher.

Mr Smith was saying that Linda was the third pregnant teenager at the school this term and just what was this sex education course Mrs Brown had devised about? A how-to manual, was it? Or perhaps 'Sex for Complete Dummies in Five Easy Steps'?

Mrs Brown wasn't having any of this. She said she wasn't going to lie down and take this from Mr Smith, which made Mr Dunn laugh. She said her job was to give pupils the scientific facts, not to tell them whether to say yes or no to their spotty boyfriends and what to do if they couldn't be bothered to put on a condom. She said social issues like these were the responsibility of the guidance department, who are supposed to look after pupils' personal and social welfare.

Mrs Parker said she was 'sorry but' her job wasn't to impose any one version of an ever-shifting and diverse social code of acceptable conduct on her charges but to facilitate pupils' awareness of personal choices and help them to reach their own decisions based on their in-dividual needs as well as their unique environmental circumstances. She said she was not the moral gatekeeper of her students and that these issues were the province of the RE department.

Mr Dunn said did they know that the Aztecs sacrificed young virgins to their gods and that under Sharia law it was still legal in some countries to stone women for adultery?

Mr Smith seemed to lose patience at that. He pointed out that Mr Dunn's contribution to the debate, if disseminated, was liable to give mixed messages to the upper-school girls and they had all better come up with something more constructive in the very near future or they might just have to shut the school and open a maternity ward with crèche facilities.

If all else failed he would invite that woman from Georgia and her helpers from the CUMON (Celibacy Until Marriage or Nothing) society to talk to the pupils about abstinence again. They knew the woman he meant – the one none of the staff could stomach.

Mrs Brown said did he mean the woman who didn't believe in condoms, evolution or a spherical earth but did believe in 'right to life', the death penalty and guardian angels?

Yes, her, Mr Smith was *that* desperate so they'd all better get cracking on an alternative. He'd give them to the end of the week to come up with their proposals.

By the time I saw Mr Smith he was in a foul mood. He has suspended me for 'bullying' and I'm to report to his office tomorrow morning with one or preferably both of my parents.

* * *

Chris called round to see me tonight. I'd expected he might and told everyone not to let him in. Didn't tell them about the pregnancy thing or even Linda – just that we'd fallen out and I hated him now. Mum answered the door and shouted up to me that he was here. I shouted back to tell him to sod off but she yelled up for me to tell him to sod off myself, she was watching *EastEnders*. But she made him stand on the doorstep.

I came down from my room, meaning to slam the door on him, but he'd put his foot inside to prevent me. Noted with satisfaction that his left eye was swollen and discoloured. Yes, serves him right! He didn't mention his injury though, but instead started on at me about Linda. So this was what I thought of him, was it – that not only would he cheat on me but he'd dump his pregnant girlfriend, the mother of his own child, without so much as a thought? That was my opinion of him, was it, despite all the time I'd known him?

He sounded really sincerely angry and I *so* wanted to believe him, but I'd been here before and I didn't want to be fooled by him again. Asked him half sceptically, half hopefully, 'So I suppose you've no idea who the father is then?'

Chris looked away from me and said in a stiff voice, 'Er, no.'

And now I *knew* for absolute sure he was lying. He'd taken his foot from the door and so I slammed it shut on him.

TUESDAY JUNE 5TH

Arrived at Mr Smith's office with Dad, who'd had to take time off work when I knew he was very busy but he didn't complain or get on at me. In fact he tried to defend me by saying it was a bit daft accusing a slip of a lassie like me of bullying a big lad like Chris, but Mr Smith was adamant that he took bullying very seriously, whatever the size or gender of the pupil. He insisted as part of the anti-bullying policy that I would have to apologize personally to Chris, who would be down directly.

When Chris arrived (admittedly looking embarrassed and reluctant) I was pleased to note that his left eye was narrowed and even more swollen, with spectacular blue and yellow bruising.

Told Chris I was sorry I'd given him a black eye, I'd meant to give him two. Chris said apology accepted and my dad laughed but Mr Smith was not amused and has suspended me again. Dad said later, in an admiring tone, that it was some shiner I'd given Chris and that I got more like my mother every day.

WEDNESDAY JUNE 6TH

Mum went to Mr Smith's with me today. She went mental at me beforehand as she was furious at having to miss work, and consequently lose money, because her daughter had turned into 'a hooligan'. She says violence is no way to settle disputes and I should be ashamed of my unfeminine behaviour. She says I'll apologize to Chris today and do whatever else is necessary to get my arse back at that sodding school or she'd batter me up and down the house.

Apologized to Chris but – and OK, I know this is childish – kept my fingers crossed behind my back. Chris said as he was leaving Mr Smith's office, 'You can uncross your fingers now, Kelly Ann.'

THURSDAY JUNE 7TH

Back at school today with another warning from Mr Smith to behave myself. Ayesha came up to me during break. Given her usual contempt for brainless, gullible girls making idiots of themselves over useless boys, I expected a 'told you so' lecture about how stupid I'd been to trust a cheating, immoral guy, but she was really nice. She said she was shocked with the news about Chris and sorry I'd been betrayed like that. She told me she'd been to see Mr Smith during my suspension to argue that I had attacked Chris while the balance of my mind had been temporarily disturbed and so should be let off, but he'd refused to accept this defence and just told her to mind her own business and get back to her class. Then she offered me a Cadbury's Creme Egg which Imran had given her earlier. She hadn't intended to accept it but then she'd remembered it was one of my favourite sweets.

Honestly, when would Imran ever learn he'd as much chance of a getting a date with Ayesha as persuading the queen to go clubbing with him? Still, not my problem.

Ayesha went off to talk to Yasmin and I settled down to slowly relish my egg. I always eat them in a particular order. First I bite off the top (at the narrow end) and then I scoop out the white and yellow cream centre with my tongue. Lastly I demolish the thick chocolate shell. Mmmm. It didn't make up for a cheating boyfriend but it was very, very nice. Had just got to the chocolate shell stage when Imran interrupted me. For a horrible moment I thought he was going to demand I hand over the remainder of the egg and was about to explain to him that I'd already licked the inside of the chocolate but I needn't have worried. It was just the usual. He'd seen me talking to Ayesha. Had she happened to mention him at all? Honestly, if he wasn't male and therefore potentially a lying cheat I'd feel sorry for him.

Dad told me tonight that he'd heard all this stuff about Chris getting Linda pregnant and he didn't believe it. He said that all young lads were randy buggers of course and only after one thing but that if Chris had got Linda up the duff he'd have owned up to it.

Poor Dad. It's amazing really just how naïve and innocent parents can be. Probably when Dad was young, boys were more honourable and not the cynical nasty cheaters they are today. Just shook my head sadly, told him he didn't understand the ways of this modern amoral world, then went back to my task of deleting all Chris's emails and text messages from my computer and mobile.

Dad watched me for a while then said, 'Just remember you won't find it so easy to rub out your mistakes in real life.'

Told Dad the word he was looking for was 'delete', as in 'deleting unwanted messages', and he really should try to keep up with modern terminology.

Dad told me the word he was looking for was 'arse', as in I was about to make 'a total arse of things' because I wouldn't listen to good advice based on bloody years of experience but to suit myself.

FRIDAY JUNE 8TH

It's going to be a long weekend but at least I have my Survivors of Cheaters group to look forward to tomorrow.

SATURDAY JUNE 9TH

Meeting has been cancelled. One of them has got a new boyfriend, two of them have gone back to their cheating boyfriends (who've promised to be faithful from now on – yeah, right) and the other one is too upset to come.

Brilliant.

Liz tried to improvise by pinning a photograph of Chris to my door and inviting me to throw darts at it, but I thought that was really childish so instead drew an elongated Pinocchio nose on it in place of his real nose, and a pair of donkey ears. We decided to post it on the school notice board on Monday.

SUNDAY JUNE 10TH

Mum has announced that Angela and Graham will be going for a week's holiday starting Saturday June 16th. It will be good for them to spend time as a couple without having a baby around: Mum is going to work a four until ten pm shift that week so that she can look after Danny during the day and I can take care of him after school finishes. Dad will help out too of course when he gets back from work.

Yeah, right. Dad is always so knackered these days, working all hours to finance Angela's increasingly expensive wedding (the minus side of her recovery from post-natal depression has been a renewed and costly interest in her wedding plans). If he does manage to get back in time for dinner he usually falls asleep during it, sometimes ending up with his face covered in shepherd's pie, lasagne or whatever we happen to be eating.

Help out my arse.

MONDAY JUNE 11TH

Don't bloody believe it. Mrs Parker in personal and social development today says our class is 'privileged' to have been selected for a very exciting new pilot scheme. She says we've all to be given a robotic doll to look after for a week to teach us about the responsibility of parenthood and how looking after a baby isn't just about buying cute clothes from Mothercare and smiling at a happy gurgling infant but involves hard work, frustration and sleepless nights. The doll is programmed to cry and wet itself at all times of the day and night, just like a real baby, and will only stop crying if we give it a bottle, change it or cuddle it; we would have to figure out what would work when. She says it'll teach us the real cost of careless decisions abut sex.

Have pleaded with Mrs Parker that I already know about the hard work and sleepless nights of baby care. My sister's baby was nearly six months old now and I'd looked after him loads. Told her I'd be taking care of Danny all that week while Angela was away and to please not foist twins on me.

Also assured her I'd no intention of getting pregnant

ever, that I hated all guys and was never going to have sex with any of them. Told her that in the incredibly unlikely event of my agreeing to have sex with a boy I'd make sure he used a condom, I was on the pill, and that we didn't go all the way in any case, but she wouldn't listen. Just said this was the selected target pilot group and there were to be no exceptions. She said the scheme had the full approval, not to mention enthusiastic support, of Mr Smith and he'd take a very dim view of people trying to spoil things by opting out. She pointed out that I'd already been in trouble recently and that she wouldn't want have to add to this by reporting my uncooperative behaviour to Mr Smith.

Bollocks.

SUNDAY JUNE 17TH

Danny is teething again, judging by his flushed cheeks, drooling mouth and almost constant crying. Brilliant.

MONDAY JUNE 18TH

7:00 pm	Bathed, dressed, fed, burped, rocked and sang Danny to sleep.
7:30 pm	Sat down to dinner.
7:32 pm	Picked up and changed crying doll.

7:45 pm	Ate cold dinner.
9:30 pm	Danny woke. Gave him orange juice, rubbed Bonjela into gums for teething pain then walked up and down with him until he fell asleep.
10:30 pm	Went to bed.
10:31 pm	Doll woke.
10:32 pm	Danny woke because of doll's cries.
11:00 pm	Went to bed.
2:00 am	Danny woke. More Bonjela, more walking, more lullabies.
2:30 am	Danny asleep.
2:32 am	Doll crying.
2:32 am and 10 seconds	Doll's cries woke Danny.
3:00 am	Back to bed but too tense to sleep.
3:30 am	Doll woke; rubbed Bonjela on its gums by mistake. Sang lullabies to it anyway. Think lack of sleep is driving me mental.
5:00 am	Must have fallen asleep on chair with doll on my lap. Its nappy had leaked and wet me. Fortunately not real pee. I hope.
5:30 am	Danny woke. Dirty nappy, definitely real.
6:00 am	Danny still awake; very happy and wants to play peekaboo. Wonder if it's possible to actually die of tiredness and boredom. Looks like could find out this week.

6:15 am	Dad came into my room, took a giggling Danny from me, put him in his cot and said, 'Enough nonsense and off to sleep.' And Danny did. Very impressive – maybe men have their uses after all. Dad said, 'You too, love, you look knackered.' Then he left.
6:17 am	Doll cried.

TUESDAY JUNE 19TH

Totally shattered at school today but at least the dolls were put in a 'crèche' so got rid of it during school hours anyway. Mr Simmons gave me a punishment exercise for falling asleep in class. Thanks a bunch, Mr Simmons. All our pilot group looked knackered in fact, except for Ayesha. She'd had the doll looked after by two of her aunts, her grandmother and three second cousins. She defended not looking after the doll herself by saying that's how babies are looked after in her culture, by the whole family. She says we're all mad just leaving child care to desperately tired mums or strangers at nurseries.

Ayesha told us that her mum thought the school might have had the sense to give Ayesha an Asian-looking doll, but her Aunt Nadia is really taken with it. Her Aunt Nadia says it makes a change to have a wee girl with blue eyes and a complexion that really suits pink and has bought it some new outfits.

Stephanie is not pleased about losing her beauty sleep. She has contacted a nanny agency, told them it's urgent and will be interviewing this evening. She's going to defend her decision not to look after the doll by herself by saying that's how it's done in *her* culture.

WEDNESDAY JUNE 20TH

Liz has been allowed to hand her doll back. They accept, following a police and psychological report (the latter written by Liz), that she isn't capable of looking after a doll, never mind a baby.

She had got totally fed up with the doll and tried to drown it in the bath, hoping that this would mess up the electronics and stop it wailing, but the thing still worked. Next she stuffed it in a drawer, covering it with woolly jumpers in an effort to muffle the noise, but she could still hear it wailing. Finally, around midnight, and driven totally bonkers by this time, she went out into the garden in her pyjamas, dug a large hole in the vegetable patch and buried the doll. Then she went back to bed.

But not for long. Just ten minutes later the police came storming round. Some nosy neighbour had seen Liz and reported 'suspicious behaviour'. Liz told the police it was just a doll she'd buried but they made her dig it up again anyway while they watched. She said even though she'd told them it was just a doll they all nearly freaked out when she picked it up out of the earth and it started to cry.

FRIDAY JUNE 22ND

We were all really relieved at PSD today when it was time to hand our dolls back. Well, all of us except for Monica Cruthers, who'd grown really attached to hers and refused to hand it back. Mrs Parker offered to give her a picture of the doll to keep and even said Monica could write and ask about it, but Monica clutched onto 'Suzy', crying hysterically and refusing to be parted.

Mr Smith was called for and he insisted on her handing it over. It wasn't her baby, for God's sake – it was a doll and a very expensive one at that and she had to return the property to the school immediately.

Monica is a really mousy, shy girl normally – she's never had so much as a punishment exercise for bad behaviour in her life so we were all amazed when she stood up to Mr Smith and said she'd kill anyone who tried to take her baby from her.

Eventually someone got her boyfriend Peter, who's in the sixth year, to come and persuade her. He took her into a corner of the class, hugged her and whispered softly to her. Then he gently took the doll from her and carried it tenderly, like a real baby, over to Mrs Parker.

Mr Smith was impressed and said so. He asked what Peter had said to bring Monica to her senses. Peter shrugged modestly and said it had been easy. He'd just promised to give her a real baby. They'd make a start on it that night. Then he turned, blew Monica a kiss and said, 'Can't wait for tonight, darling.'

Mr Smith asked Mrs Parker if she knew the dialling code for Georgia. It was time – 'God help us' – to bring in the flat-earthers.

SUNDAY JUNE 24TH

Liz's birthday. Had been really looking forward to this but Julian flew in from New York yesterday to surprise her so she cancelled the all-you-can-eat pizza fest she'd been planning with us in favour of spending the whole weekend with Julian before he goes back.

Poor Liz. Obviously she is still naïve enough to believe that Julian truly loves her and that their happiness will last – when of course inevitably, since he's a guy (even if a bit of an odd one), it will all end in tears, deceit and betrayal. Didn't want to destroy her fleeting moment of happiness by pointing this out so just rang this afternoon to wish her a happy birthday and reassure her that I would always be there for her in times of need, even though she'd cancelled on me this weekend.

Liz said, 'OK, Kelly Ann, come on over. Julian has

brought so many doughnuts, bagels and Hershey's chocolates with him we'll never manage them all on our own anyway.'

Julian is such a great guy really. Maybe Liz will be lucky after all.

FRIDAY JUNE 29TH

Last day of school, and for some people really the last. At first period Ms Conner had sent me to Mr Smith's office with a note about expected pupil uptake of Advance Higher next year or some such, when half a dozen sixth years burst in, locked the door and told us we were being taken hostage.

This was all I needed. Every year at this time sixth years take one teacher and one pupil hostage and ransom them for charity. The staff have to pay for the teacher while the pupil is ransomed to other students. The 'hostages' are handed over to the person who made the biggest individual contribution for their release.

Mr Smith accepted his fate quite calmly but there was no way I was going to hang around all morning being a prisoner of these idiots and said so. They told me hostages didn't have options and to shut my face. I told them to shut their faces themselves and open the bloody door or I'd make them sorry.

Ended up being trussed up and blindfolded with their

school ties. This wasn't in any way traditional and I told them so. No hostages from previous years had been tied up and what did they think they were playing at?

They told me that hostages from previous years had entered into the spirit of the thing and had been pleased to do their bit for charity, especially one as worthy as the Sick Children's Hospital Fund. They said other hostages had not punched, kicked and scratched their charitable abductors and if I didn't stop complaining they'd gag me as well even though Mr Smith had told them not to on health and safety grounds.

For a laugh none of the staff would pay a penny towards the £200 set ransom for Mr Smith and he was therefore forced to write a cheque for the whole amount himself.

They had the £200 for me just after lunch time. Came as absolutely no surprise even before they took off my blindfolds when I was handed over to Chris as the biggest single contributor. They hadn't untied me and advised Chris not to as I was 'bloody vicious'. Then they added that of course Chris knew that already and said his left eye had healed really well – you could hardly see the scar now.

Chris *did* untie me but took his time over it, using the opportunity to talk to me about our split. He said I'd put two and two together and come up with twenty-two. He said that he would be proved to be innocent of everything and one day soon I'd see that. He asked me in the meantime not to do anything that would make it impossible for us to get back together.

Such as?

Well, falling for someone else.

Told him I'd think about it. Wasn't lying either – he'd given me a great idea. Even though at the moment I hated all guys and didn't want anything to do with any of them, if dating someone else would annoy or, better still, really hurt Chris, I'd do it. The only question was who and when. Well, the only *two* questions.

SUNDAY JULY 1ST

Called Gary and asked him to meet me at the Bean Scene. I fancied a hot chocolate and muffin and there was something I wanted to talk to him about. We took our order over to a table, then I sat close to him, smiled sexily and told him I'd always fancied him and did he want to go out with me?

Gary looked really uncomfortable. He told me that I was pretty and all that but he'd never seen me as a girlfriend, more just as Chris's girl.

So he didn't fancy me then?

Well, he'd never really thought about it. Of course he'd fantasized about having sex with me but he did that with most girls. The thing was, Chris was his best friend and it would be disloyal to date me. Besides, Chris would kill him.

Anyway, he wished the two of us would get back together as Chris was nearly always in a bad mood now and the thought of sharing a flat with him soon was turning into a bloody nightmare. He didn't think Chris had cheated on me with Linda and, more to the point, he was sure Chris hadn't got her pregnant. I could say what I liked about Chris but he wasn't stupid. He surely knew how to use a condom.

MONDAY JULY 2ND

Arranged to meet Ian. Told him I'd always fancied him and did he want to go out with me. Ian told me I was cute but, er, not really tall or, erm, big enough. I suppose he has a point: I'm only just over five feet two and Ian is six four as well as being built, as my dad says, 'like a brick shit-house'. In fact Ian brought about the end of my football career in third year when he fell on me during a game organized by Chris and bruised my ribs. Ian and Chris got into terrible trouble over it, which wasn't really fair as I'd deliberately fouled Ian to stop him getting the ball. I just hadn't expected him to fall on top of me instead of away. Anyway, Chris never let me play again and I refused to play in any girls' team so that was that.

Since then Ian has continued to grow and, now that I come to think of it, has often complained that he can't find a girlfriend because Glasgow girls are all midgets and he'd have to move to Holland one day where there were loads of tall girls.

Ian told me that if I were ten inches taller, a bit more sturdily built and wasn't the ex of his best friend he'd definitely think about dating me.

TUESDAY JULY 3RD

Stephanie got on at me today. What did I think I was doing trying to get off with Chris's friends? This was a really stupid and dangerous game to play.

She's got a nerve. What about the three Irish brothers she'd been dating?

That was different. They weren't the possessive, jealous types, none of them were in love with her, and besides, she was only seeing two of them now. It was all just a bit of fun. Chris was a much more serious guy. Honestly, what was she to do with me, I was a total idiot.

Liz agreed with her. She said instead of making passes at Chris's friends I should make a play for Gerry. If Chris got annoyed and knocked lumps out of Gerry we could all just enjoy it and he had it coming.

But I was horrified. Shelly was a friend and it wouldn't be right, even if it would really annoy Chris, whose dislike of Gerry seemed recently to have grown to outright hatred.

Liz said friend her arse – when was the last time Shelly had talked to me?

It was true. Shelly never answered my calls any more

and hadn't returned my last three texts. It seems that since Chris and I split she wanted nothing more to do with me.

Liz told me to wake up, Shelly had never liked me. Gary had told her just last week that Shelly had fancied Chris in the third year and she had never forgiven him for knocking her back. Add to that the fact that Gerry had dumped her for me last year and you could see why she hated me. Honestly, what was Liz to do with me? I was acting like a total idiot.

I couldn't believe this. For a start, Gary is always imagining girls fancy people they *so obviously* don't and I'd never heard anyone else mention Shelly wanting to go out with Chris. Certainly not Chris, and at that time we were friends, so he would probably have told me.

As for my going out with Gerry before, Shelly has told me she's totally cool about that now. We've even laughed about it.

No, Shelly has probably just been busy. Liz has never really got over her initial dislike of Shelly. Unlike me she's not mature enough to let go of childish earlier disputes. Wish Shelly wasn't so busy though. Now that I've lost Chris I really need the support of good genuine friends like her.

THURSDAY JULY 5TH

Fantastic news. Stephanie says her mum's boyfriend's sister has a timeshare apartment in Faliraki in Rhodes and we can use it for a week's holiday. Because her dad won't be taking her with him to Portugal when he goes with his girlfriend, he's agreed to pay the flights for Liz and me to join her on holiday there.

At long last a holiday without parents or teachers! Am so happy I could burst.

FRIDAY JULY 6TH

Dad says I can't go. I'm too young and anyway he's heard about the goings-on at these places: drunken parties and girls being assaulted. There was no way I was going.

Mum was totally cool about it and tried to reason with him. 'For God's sake let her go – at least then there'll be someone in this sodding family having a good time. There's no law against it, you know.'

But Dad wouldn't budge and Mum couldn't make him. It's so annoying. For years I'd wished that Dad would stand up to Mum and stop letting her boss him about so much. Now he has to go and do it at exactly the wrong time. Typical.

SATURDAY JULY 7TH

Dad said it didn't matter how much I begged him. His mind was made up. I wasn't going: that was that.

SUNDAY JULY 8TH

Of course he trusted me. But he didn't trust those lads in Faliraki. The answer was no. And that was final.

MONDAY JULY 9TH

No, he didn't want to ruin my whole life, and yes, he recognized that 'what with one thing and another' I hadn't had a 'proper' holiday in years, and of course he cared about me. He was just worried, that was all.

TUESDAY JULY 10TH

Finally!! Have convinced Dad that I would steer clear of any guys, never mind 'dodgy chancers', on holiday and that all I wanted was a bit of sunshine. And yes, of course Stephanie would give him our apartment address and phone number. Our apartment was in a nice, safe, totally respectable complex and everything would be fine, but yes, I'd call him every day and let him know the minute there was any problem – not that there would be one – and thanks, Dad, for trusting me – he was the greatest.

WEDNESDAY JULY 11TH

Liz and Stephanie are so pleased Dad has relented, especially as they've decided that the holiday will be the perfect opportunity for me to lose my virginity. They say loads of girls do it this way. A bit of sun, sea and sand will put me in the mood for sex, but the guy won't be able to boast about it to anyone I know back home afterwards. Plus there will be no chance of my getting attached to some unsuitable stranger just because he'd got a tan and bought me retsina as we'd never see each other again. Obviously I had to make sure that, pill or no pill, the guy used a condom but I knew that anyway. It was perfect. Trust them.

Wasn't too sure this was what I really wanted to do but at least didn't need to feel guilty about lying to Dad as I'd had my fingers crossed when I was promising him I'd have nothing to do with guys on holiday.

MONDAY JULY 16TH

Liz and I stayed the night at Stephanie's as we had a really early flight to catch next day. Before going off to bed I suggested we book a taxi but Stephanie said we wouldn't need one. Chris had offered to drive us and help with our luggage.

I was furious with Stephanie for going along with this. I'd told her before that I absolutely hated Chris now and wanted to see him as little as humanly possible.

But she said I should 'chill'. She said loads of guys cheat on their girlfriends and father illegitimate children all over the place. That didn't mean they couldn't be perfectly good chauffeurs and bag carriers.

TUESDAY JULY 17TH

Chris picked us up at three-thirty in the morning and I must admit he was quite useful, especially as Stephanie had five cases. Also he waited for an hour in the baggage check-in queue for us while we had something to eat and did our make-up.

When our flight was called Stephanie flung her arms round Chris and kissed him. Then she said, 'Thanks for everything.'

Liz just said a polite, 'Thank you.'

I didn't say anything but just turned to go. Chris asked

wasn't I going to say anything to him? Not even a 'thank you and goodbye'. After all, he had gone to quite a bit of effort on my behalf this morning.

I said, 'Oh yes, of course. I forgot. Thanks very much for coming along today and reminding me just what a tosser you are and how lucky I am to be rid of you. Now shove off.'

Chris said he was sorry I was taking that attitude, then held up a passport and waved it about for a bit before placing it in his inside jacket pocket. Chris said it had been dropped just five minutes earlier by a very careless girl. He said with the tight security at airports these days he doubted very much whether she would be able to sneak past airport officials without a passport.

Even in this private journal I cannot bear to record the grovelling I had to do to get that passport back. Stephanie said she would rather have performed an act of sexual degradation for Chris right there at the airport than grovel the way I had. I didn't pay much attention to that but when Liz agreed with her I knew it had been bad.

Stephanie said she didn't think she would be able to tell any guy that he was a god and say that she wasn't worthy to breathe the same air as him.

Liz said she would have drawn the line at getting down on her knees to beg.

But the worst part was when, after all the humiliation, Chris handed Liz's passport to her and told her she should be more careful with her things.

Was too stunned to protest when Chris kissed me and said to have a good holiday but be careful. Then he'd added that I'd looked really cute on my knees and he'd treasure the memory for ever.

Arrived at our apartment at around midday. It was fantastic, really spacious with a large veranda, and almost right on the beach. There was also an enormous communal swimming pool with diving boards which was surrounded by trees for shade.

Stephanie said this was a great place for me to lose my virginity.

We were too tired to unpack so we just put on our bikinis and headed for the pool. It was very hot so Liz and I spent most of the time dipping in and out of the water. Stephanie, however, immediately attached herself to the tanned and muscular Greek lifeguard. He was so taken with her that at one point an English woman had to come up to him and say, 'Er, excuse me, I'm terribly sorry to interrupt but I don't swim and I think my little boy is drowning.' It's amazing how polite the English can be.

In the evening Liz and I went into Faliraki town (Stephanie was seeing her lifeguard, Kostas.) Didn't like the Greek wine, which smelled and looked like pine disinfectant, but I suppose we were drinking really cheap stuff. Not as cheap as some of the girls partying in the town though. Honestly, they were so drunk and sluttish, flashing their breasts at everyone – even Liz and me – or rolling around on the pavement, totally pissed. They made Stephanie look positively reserved.

We were really tired so went back early. Kostas was finishing off painting Stephanie's toenails (a chore she hates), blowing on each nail in turn to help dry off the polish. When he had finished she dismissed him with a 'maybe she would see him tomorrow' and then started interrogating us. Had we met The One yet? What did we mean 'no'? We'd been here almost a full day. There were thousands of available guys on the island so surely we'd identified a likely candidate by now. We weren't looking for total perfection after all. Just some guy who wasn't too ugly that I'd throw up and not so drunk that he couldn't manage to take care of my 'virginity situation'. Honestly, what was she to do with us? It was like sending us to a beach to collect a bucket of sand and our coming back to say we couldn't find any.

WEDNESDAY JULY 18TH

Went to the pool this afternoon, where we met two English guys, Alan and Paul. They weren't tanned at all so we reckoned that, like us, they had just got here, although we later learned that they had been here nearly a week but had spent the whole time clubbing from night to dawn and sleeping during the day. This was the first time they'd seen daylight.

They had what Stephanie calls estuary English accents, which is the kind you hear on TV adverts and *EastEnders* all the time. She says it's really fashionable and quite sexy but Liz and I weren't really impressed. They had the cheek to tell Liz and me that they liked our accent. We told them that *they* were the ones with the accent, not us, but if they liked we could teach them how speak properly.

Then, since I've watched countless episodes of *EastEnders* because of Mum and can imitate the accent pretty well, I had some fun winding them up by exaggerating how they talked. 'Oi, wot you doin' 'ere then? A fort you lot 'olidayed in Saffend or Ibeefa or sumfin'?'

The one called Paul looked annoyed but Alan just laughed, said I was a cheeky tart then asked if it was true that all Scottish guys wore skirts and played the bagpipes and how would we like to get to know some 'proper' guys who wore trousers and wouldn't play bagpipes even if they knew how to?

Liz said was it true all English guys were either gay or Union Jack waving football thugs and to shove off.

But they were quite apologetic after that. In fact Alan said he'd seen *Braveheart* and he was sorry about how rubbish the English had been to Scottish people for ages. He said how about he and Paul take us out for a drink tonight to help make up for the centuries of English oppression.

We said, 'Maybe.'

* * *

I really liked Alan, who had dirty fair hair and nice blue eyes. He said he was twenty-one and worked as a car salesman so I said I was nineteen and a university student.

We went to a taverna where the local waiters did a Greek dance balancing bottles of wine on their heads. Alan and Paul tried to do the same with pints of beer but spilled them after about two seconds. Later a belly dancer with tassels on her bikini top jiggled her way round the tables. Then we were all invited to have a go.

Alan and Paul looked really funny thrusting their chests out and wiggling their hips suggestively, but it was Liz and I who won the prize – a bottle of ouzo and two melons – for the most authentic imitation. Although I think it was Liz's double D breasts that really did it.

When we got back to the apartment Alan kissed me and asked if he could see me again. It felt really odd to kiss someone other than Chris. Somehow I felt vaguely guilty, as if I was being unfaithful or something, although that's a laugh given that Chris had been *really* cheating on me and even getting people pregnant. I said, 'Maybe.'

Stephanie has decided that Alan is going to be 'The One'. She says he's perfect. London is just far enough away to make dating practically impossible afterwards and so there would be no emotional messiness after the holiday. She says English guys have an undeserved reputation of being rubbish at sex. She says they *do* drink a lot of lager but they are dead keen, really like girls (unless they've gone to certain public boarding schools) and have lots of stamina. You just had to stop them making jokes while doing it, particularly fart jokes, which could be very off-putting.

She is totally determined and Liz supports her. Liz says it will help me move on emotionally, socially and psychologically. Besides, it would really annoy Chris when he finds out. Even though we're not dating any more he'd be gutted – and anyway, remember how it felt kneeling at the airport.

That was it. Alan is definitely going to be The One.

THURSDAY JULY 19TH

Liz has decided *not to see* Paul again: she *quite fancies him but doesn't want to cheat on* Julian. Stephanie says she's mad – no guy was worth this kind of loyalty, especially not her brother – but Liz was determined, so that was that.

I went into Rhodes town with Alan in the morning as I wanted to shop in the market and see the old town but by eleven o'clock it was too hot to move. Alan bought two bottles of ice-cold water and poured one of them down my spine; the other he poured into his cap then put the cap on his head. This only cooled us down for about two minutes so we decided to quit the town and go to the water park.

Had a great time there and we were very careful to ensure we didn't burn between rides by slathering each other's bodies with suntan cream, which was quite a nice way to get to know each other. Alan asked if I had a boyfriend back home and I said no. Alan said Scottish guys must be a bit slow off the mark then.

I asked him if he had a girlfriend and he said hundreds, but none of them could roll their Rs like me.

Alan insisted on paying for everything, saying that he knew students were always broke, but I felt uncomfortable about it. He told me not to worry as his job selling new and used luxury cars paid pretty well. He had a real talent for it and earned a lot on commission. His friends all say he could sell sand in the Sahara, he was that persuasive. It must be true because, look, he'd managed to persuade me to go out with him even though I don't like English people and (despite what I'd told him earlier) am probably in love with some lucky bloke back home.

Told Alan I wasn't in love with anyone back home and that I was starting to like English people quite a lot actually.

Afterwards we went back to our compound and Alan asked me to have dinner with him tomorrow at a nice restaurant he knew on the beach and I said, 'Maybe.' Stephanie and Liz were waiting for me on my return and questioned me immediately. Had I done it with Alan yet?

Honestly, what was I supposed to do, have sex with him in the middle of town or during one of the water rides? Give me a break. But Stephanie was scathing: there were a million places on this island to have sex – miles of beaches for a start – and I was to stop making excuses and get on with it. Liz and Stephanie said they would be going out clubbing tomorrow so Alan and I would have the place to ourselves. They would ring to check up on my 'progress'. I had promised them, after all, and it was for my own good.

FRIDAY JULY 20TH

Stephanie decided I would wear a black strappy top with no bra and a wrap-around cream skirt. This did look nice, especially as I'd got a bit of a tan, but I wasn't keen on going without my Wonderbra. However, she was adamant and told me to sit by the air conditioning unit for ten minutes before Alan was due to pick me up. She was appalled that I'd only brought trainers or flat sandals with me. She insisted I borrow her gold sandals, which were only slightly too big for me and had six-inch stiletto heels. She also cautioned me that I mustn't confess to Alan I was sixteen and a virgin as, although this would turn some guys on, it would worry others and she thought he might be in the second group.

Alan came for me at seven. He said I looked gorgeous and, er, much taller. Started walking towards the restaurant, which Alan said was just ten minutes away and almost right on the beach. However, I soon found walking in Stephanie's shoes practically impossible. The instep was so high it threw my whole body forward and I would teeter uncomfortably for a few steps before losing my balance and have to be supported by Alan. Yet I'd seen Stephanie dance in the things and she swore these were one of the most comfortable pair of heels she had! In the end I had to take them off, but as the pavement was dusty and still hot, Alan offered to carry me fireman's-lift style the rest of the way.

Had expected him to set me down before we reached the restaurant but for a laugh he carried me inside and asked straight faced for a table for two, finally depositing me on my chair, which the waiter pulled back for me with a flourish and smile. It wasn't the dignified, sophisticated entrance I'd hoped for but at least the restaurant was lovely. The roof was made of vine leaves and there were candles as well as flowers on the tables – so romantic! We both ordered lamb, which was delicious, and red wine, which I didn't like, especially as I couldn't add lemonade to it in case it looked too unsophisticated for a nineteen-year-old.

We talked about football and Alan was surprised I knew so much about the English Premier League. Then we talked about cars and he was very surprised that I knew not just about different makes of car but also about maintenance and repair stuff – engine tuning, clutch replacements and wheel alignments.

He was well impressed with my knowledge of guy stuff and said if all Scottish girls were like me he was moving up there.

Stephanie texted me halfway through dinner to ask whether I'd done it yet. Ignored her. Liz called me just as we were finishing the lamb and asked me . . . you guessed it. Cut her off and switched off my mobile.

The thing was, I would have really enjoyed just chatting to Alan but there was this awful pressure to get this 'virginity problem', as Stephanie called it, sorted out and I couldn't bear the slagging I would get from both of them if I failed tonight. Problem was, apart from a quick kiss when he called round for me, he hadn't made any passes at me at all. Not so much as a hand on my knee. I supposed I would have to do it but realized that while I was used to fending off sexual advances I hadn't a clue how to make them.

As Alan was looking at the dessert menu I decided just to come right out with it. Would he like to have sex with me?

He said, 'Maybe.'

There was a horribly long pause as he continued to 'consider my offer', as he put it. Felt my cheeks burning with embarrassment. This was awful. Obviously Alan didn't actually fancy me and didn't know how to tell me. Clearly I'd mistaken his friendliness for genuine romantic interest and he'd just been wanting a bit of a chat or companionship. Maybe like he'd said in the beginning he just wanted to improve relations between England and Scotland and make up for the Highland Clearances and stuff like that.

But then he laughed and said OK, he'd thought about it and on balance he'd decided to give it a go.

Stephanie was right about English guys and their jokes. Hoped he wasn't planning to keep this up. He asked if I'd like dessert first but I told him I'd rather 'just get it over with'.

He said, 'Bloody hell, Kelly Ann, it isn't as though we're married or anything. You don't have to lie back and think of England or whatever it is Scottish girls think about when they're having a duty shag.'

But I convinced him it was just that I was so 'up for it' tonight, I didn't want to waste any time, so he paid the bill quickly, leaving a large tip, and we left.

When we got back we went into my bedroom, which I'd tidied in preparation. Alan kissed the back of my hand – for a laugh presumably – before kissing me on the mouth and pulling me down onto the bed. Felt nervous but at least there was no chance of anyone's parents interrupting us.

He caressed my breasts over the material of my top,

which felt quite nice, then he stroked and kissed my thighs, which felt very nice. Maybe losing my virginity with Alan wasn't going to be the uncomfortable 'let's get it over with' ordeal I'd imagined.

Just then the phone next to the bed rang. Stephanie. Had I done it yet? For God's sake! Slammed the phone down.

Alan asked if there was a problem – not a jealous boyfriend, or worse, husband, was it?

I shook my head and whispered to him just to carry on doing what he'd been doing when the phone bloody well rang again. Honestly, how could Liz or Stephanie expect me to have sex if they kept ringing me constantly? Alan asked if I wanted him to get rid of whoever it was. Yes please. He lay down on the bed, pulled me on top of him, motioning me to unbutton his shirt, then he picked up the receiver saying in a very officious voice, 'Hello, this is Alan here. We're sorry but Kelly Ann can't come to the phone right now as she's about to be shagged by the finest stud in all of England.' I giggled but then his face went all serious. He handed the phone to me and said, 'Kelly Ann, I think your dad would like a word with you.'

Had a horrible conversation with my dad while Alan sat on the bed pretending to read a tourist leaflet that had been lying around. Then, in order to stop my dad getting on the next flight here and dragging me home, I had to put him on to Alan. Of course my dad told Alan, among other things, that I was not nineteen and a student but sixteen and at school. It was all too humiliating. Eventually I couldn't take any more so went out and sat on the balcony.

Alan joined me after about, oh, half an hour. He said sixteen was OK – at least it was legal, thank God, and I wouldn't happen to have packed a school uniform, had I? He said not to worry about him. While the conversation with my dad had been a bit awkward there were worse things. Just last week he'd picked up a girl in a club here, assuming she was single, and went back to her hotel room. He said the heart-shaped bed, champagne on ice and confetti scattered on the floor should have alerted him. Turned out the girl was on her honeymoon but had fallen out with the groom on their wedding night (too much booze). Alan said the conversation he'd had with the girl's new husband on his return had been a lot more awkward than the one with my dad, I was to trust him on that.

Not sure this story was really true but it did make me smile, which was probably the point of it. Decided to tell Alan the whole truth about me. It was a relief really not having to pretend any more. Alan said, God, a virgin, he hadn't seen one of those in years. Bit of an endangered species. Then he said I shouldn't have sex just to please my friends or piss off an ex but only if it really was what I wanted to do. He kissed me and said it had been a long night, he was going back to think things over and he'd see me tomorrow.

Stephanie said there was no chance I'd see Alan again but she was wrong. In fact had an amazing day with him. We went scuba diving in the morning and hired a boat to explore the island in the afternoon. What a beautiful place this was – sparkling clear waters teeming with fish, cloudless azure skies, mountains and beaches, vines and fruit trees. *So* romantic. Only trouble was, Alan seemed to have morphed into some sort of perfect English gentleman instead of the totally up for it Londoner he'd been yesterday. He didn't make a single pass and only massaged sunscreen on the bits of my body I really couldn't reach by myself. It was so frustrating, especially as I was starting to fancy him more and more.

Oh God, Stephanie was right: I should never have admitted to being a virgin, especially with my dad telling him my real age. She said I should cut my losses and start over, maybe with a Greek who spoke no English at all so even I couldn't mess things up by saying exactly the wrong thing. But I didn't want to. The truth is, Alan is the only guy I've felt even remotely attracted to since Chris.

In the evening Alan went out with his pals while Stephanie, Liz and I went to a pool party with Kostas. Stephanie tried to get me off with Kostas's cousin Nicholas, who did look really hot, but I found it too difficult to get involved as he hardly spoke a word of English and I don't know any Greek.

Stephanie said what had talking got to do with it for God's sake – she despaired of me, she really did.

SUNDAY JULY 22ND

Spent the entire time with Alan, who told me he'd missed me last night and sod his mates, he'd see enough of them back home.

But still he didn't snog me once, just gave me a kiss on the forehead when he finally left me at the apartment at the end of the night. Yes, on the forehead! Almost slapped him but stopped myself as I suppose it's a bit weird to slap a guy for not making a pass, much as I'd like to.

MONDAY JULY 23RD

Yet another very nice but completely frustrating day with Alan. He'd hired a car and suggested touring the island, then invited Stephanie and Liz along too. Despite my scowling at them they agreed.

We did have a good time though, and now I know what it would be like to have a really attentive and generous big brother. But what I really want to know is what it would be like to do it for the first time with a totally hot English guy.

Last night of the holiday so last chance with Alan. Was determined he wouldn't be able to think of me as some kind of wee sister tonight. Borrowed an outfit from Stephanie: see-through black top worn over a black lace Wonderbra and teamed up with a very short tight red skirt which had slits on either side. Used the rest of my holiday money to buy red stilettos and even wore stockings despite the heat and the awful memories they brought back. Finally painted my fingernails, toenails and lips scarlet. If this didn't do it, nothing would.

Alan was pretty impressed, I think. He said I looked 'bloody arresting' but still only gave me a quick kiss before setting out for the restaurant. He also started calling me his 'little Lolita', which annoyed me because I knew this had something to do with me being too young.

At the restaurant Alan perused the menu carefully, making suggestions about what I might like to try, but I wasn't paying attention. I was totally determined not to be fobbed off with another very nice but totally platonic evening. Interrupted him to say that I wanted to have sex with him tonight and it wasn't to please my friends or annoy Chris but just because I really fancied him. Told him that it wasn't fair of him to turn me down just because I didn't have any experience. I mean what if everyone did that? No one would ever have sex at all.

Besides, I wasn't just sixteen, I would be seventeen really soon. October 14th in fact.

Alan said, 'Cheers, mate, but I don't think we're ready to order yet.'

Glanced up to see the waiter, whose expression was one of total envy. Don't think I'd have had any trouble if it had been him I'd been talking to. Was a bit embarrassed at being overheard but I suppose it would be a while before I'd be back here anyway.

When he'd gone Alan said look, this had been an amazing week and I was something else, I really was, and so, er, direct. He hadn't had this much fun with a girl he wasn't sleeping with, well . . . ever. But it wouldn't be right for us to have sex now. This couldn't be what I really wanted, a one-night stand for my first experience?

Reassured him that of course it wasn't. Told him that I really liked him as well as fancying him. London wasn't that far away. It wasn't as though he lived in New Zealand or anything. I could come down and visit and he could come up and see me. If we got on really well maybe one or other of us could move permanently. We should just do what we wanted to. Then I handed him a post-card, on the back of which I'd written my address and phone number.

I babbled on for a bit more but Alan stopped me. His expression was grim. He said that it wouldn't be a good idea for us to see each other again after the holiday. The thing was – and OK, he knew he should have told me this before – but . . . er, he was getting married the week after he got back.

I said nothing.

Alan said, 'Please don't look at me like that, Kelly Ann. The last thing I wanted to do was hurt you.'

Then he went on to explain that the holiday had just been a kind of 'last fortnight of freedom' fling before settling down. And no, he wasn't cheating on his fiancée. Wendy was in Spain with her pals, probably shagging for England as we spoke. It was a mutual thing that I was too young and naïve to understand. Another reason he should probably not have gone on seeing me this week.

I thought about this. I really did. But no, I couldn't accept it. And it wouldn't matter what age or how experienced I was. Told Alan that if I loved someone enough to marry them then I could never do what he and Wendy had done. It just wasn't and never would be me. Then I said goodbye and walked away. Alan didn't attempt to stop me. On my way out I saw our waiter looking at Alan and shaking his head in disbelief.

Wandered around for a bit, not wanting to go back to an empty apartment just yet as Stephanie and Liz were both out partying. It was still very hot so I soon got tired and sat down on a bench by the road.

Even in my miserable state couldn't help noticing a gorgeous sleek silver Mercedes which was travelling very slowly. The driver was probably a tourist who'd got lost. Sure enough, he stopped, opened the door and beckoned me over. Most likely I'd got so tanned he'd mistaken me for a local Greek girl and was going to ask me for directions. Made my way over, mentally rehearsing my 'sorry, but I'm not from here either' spiel. I bent down to the driver, who was an expensively dressed man maybe a bit younger than my dad.

Got a shock when he took a wad of notes from his wallet and asked in a foreign accent, 'How much for the whole night, please?'

Bloody hell! Obviously Liz was right and I'd overdone the vamp look tonight. Told him I was very sorry but I wasn't a prostitute – in fact I'd no experience at all and was just a sixteen-year-old virgin. This didn't seem to put him off: he offered me double. What a sleazer – and he'd looked so respectable in his nice suit too! Told him what to do with his cash, threatened to report him to the police, then stomped off.

Liz and Stephanie were very sympathetic when I told them about my night up until the part about being mistaken for a prostitute. Stephanie in particular seemed to find the whole thing hilarious but said she'd definitely wear that outfit for Dave when he came back.

WEDNESDAY JULY 25TH

Saw Alan at the airport tonight. His flight was leaving a half-hour before mine. He came over and asked for a goodbye kiss but I slapped him instead, then turned my back on him. He didn't try to talk to me again but spoke to Stephanie for a while, handed her a note then left. Stephanie said the note just said sorry but also had his address, email (home and work) and phone number (home, work and mobile). Great, just what I needed, a long-distance affair with a married English tosser. Told her to bin it.

THURSDAY JULY 26TH

Dad met us at the airport. He dropped Stephanie and Liz off first. He hadn't spoken a word to me the whole journey but that changed as soon as we got home.

He was really disappointed in me and I'd betrayed his trust. What in God's name had I been up to on holiday – but no, don't answer that, he didn't think he could stand hearing that his youngest daughter had turned into a cheap tart. How could I have been so irresponsible and who was this English chancer anyway? At least I wouldn't be having any more to do with him or anyone else either. That was it, I wasn't to have any more boyfriends ever and I was grounded until further notice.

Told Dad I was too old to ground and this was ridiculous but he said I wasn't and while I lived under his roof I'd abide by his rules.

Used to like my dad but I hate him now. Actually I hate all males so Dad needn't have bothered ranting on about how I wasn't to have any more to do with them. As far as I can see, if they're not liars like Alan, they're control freaks like Dad or, worse, a bit of both like Chris. The only male I really like is Danny. Hope he doesn't grow up to be a useless tosser like the rest of them.

SATURDAY AUGUST 4TH

Thought things couldn't get any worse but they have. As further punishment Dad has docked my allowance so that I am no longer just existing on a pittance but am actually destitute. Even my mum and Angela say he can't leave me with absolutely no money but Dad is being totally mental about it and says if I need anything he'll buy it for me – I'm getting nothing on my own as I can't be trusted.

Phoned Stephanie who was outraged on my behalf and said she'd be right over to 'sort this thing out' and not to worry. Sure enough, ten minutes later she swept in and tackled my dad immediately. Kelly Ann needed to do some shopping so she supposed he'd have to come along and wouldn't be able to work at the garage this afternoon as he'd planned. It wouldn't take long. Where were his car keys and don't forget the wallet.

First stop was La Senza, where Stephanie waved

wispy bras and a selection of barely-there knickers about two centimetres from Dad's face, saying stuff like what did he think would suit Kelly Ann, the black lace balcony or the strapless peekaboo? Should she get the matching thongs or should she go for the see-through strings or these cute scanty panties?

Dad was mortified and mumbled something about Stephanie and me deciding and he'd meet us at the check-out. Then he walked off and stood just by the door, trying not to look at anyone or anything.

Stephanie grinned and set to work helping me pick out loads of really nice stuff. Great fun. About half an hour later we were ready and Dad was so relieved to be leaving he didn't even comment on the £150 bill.

On the way back Stephanie told Dad to stop off at the chemist. Dad said it had better not be as expensive as the last shop or we could forget it but Stephanie reassured him it would just come to a few pounds so he agreed. Of course she made straight for the feminine hygiene counter. What did he think we should go for – light, medium or super absorbency tampons? Plastic or cardboard applicators? Were they really leak-proof and – oh, this one was interesting: *expands to fit the female form exactly*. Sounds good.

Maybe we should get some pads too, just in case, for heavier days. Ultra thin or night-time maxis? Wings or no wings? What did he think?

Even I was mortified by Stephanie now, but as she

later told me, this was war. Dad was challenging a girl's most basic freedom: the Right to Shop. It couldn't be tolerated in a civilized country.

SUNDAY AUGUST 5TH

Dad has reinstated my allowance.

MONDAY AUGUST 6TH

Got my results today. Failed maths and English of course – only the two most vital subjects in the curriculum – but didn't do too badly with the rest, getting two Bs and a C. Stephanie got As for art and French and will go to art college this year. She's quite looking forward to it but says it'll be full of girls and gays and it was a pity she wasn't good at engineering – all the fittest guys did engineering. Also she'd heard my so-called friend Shelly was going there too this year, just her luck. Liz did well in English and biology but will do a sixth year before starting psychology at Glasgow Uni.

Chris came over this evening to boast about his six straight As. Suppose that's not fair – he never boasts about exam results – but I don't feel like being fair. Mum answered the door so I shouted down to her to tell Chris to sod off but she said to tell him to sod off myself, she was watching telly. But she kept him waiting on the doorstep. Asked my dad to tell him that I wasn't allowed to talk to boys any more but Dad just shrugged and said it was only Chris and that he trusted him. *Trusted him!!!*

Stomped off to the door. Chris asked how was I and how did my holiday go?

None of his business.

Chris said Gary, Ian and he would definitely be going to university this year and would be moving to a flat in the West End along with another Glasgow medic come September. He asked if I would visit them sometimes and maybe go to some of the uni social stuff with them. After all, just because he and I weren't going out any more didn't mean we should lose all contact. Surely we could at least be friends again.

Said that was a great idea and smiled but then told him there was one tiny flaw in the plan, a small but important little glitch. The thing was – 'call me picky' – but I preferred to make friends with people I actually liked. Now the truth was, if I was feeling a trifle lonesome one night and had the choice between spending an evening with him and a pack of scavenging jackals, well, I'd have to go for the scavenging jackals option.

In fact, I went on, if I found myself really stuck for a bit of companionship and fancied meeting up with a pal for pizza and a bit of a chat, and I had the choice between him and a bubonic plague-carrying sewer rat, well, there were worse things than rodents after all, even disease-carrying ones.

Finally, imagine I was bored one afternoon and had a notion to see a movie with a friend but, as luck would have it, only he and a pile of maggots were available. Well . . .

Chris said he got the message.

Told him, 'Don't call me,' and slammed the door shut feeling really pleased with myself. Then I went up to my room and cried. God, when will I ever get over him?

FRIDAY AUGUST 10TH

Gary invited loads of people over to his place this afternoon because it wasn't raining and he wanted to try out the new barbecue his parents recently bought. I'm supposed to be grounded but Mum and Dad are at work and there's no way Angela would tell. She's a lot better that way these days. She does owe me, after all.

Everyone was to bring something to cook. Gary would do all the barbecuing. Oh, and maybe we girls could do some salads and desserts. And, erm, also prepare the meat for barbecuing first – he'd seen his mum do it once but wasn't quite sure about it. What was a marinade exactly? Also could we come over a bit early and help him set up the buffet tables?

Sounded like too much hard work to me and I wasn't

going to go but he bribed us with offers of free drinks and assured me that Chris wouldn't be there as he is working at the hospital all day.

In the end we all had a good time, although Gary's only contribution to organizing things was to stand self-importantly by the barbecue, waving a pair of tongs about and chatting, while Liz, Stephanie and I got conned into doing everything else as he didn't have a clue.

However, afterwards it was nice to lie about in the sun getting mildly drunk. Gary joined us, complaining about being knackered after all his hard work. Yeah, right. Then he was talking about Chris's job at the hospital. Apparently the consultant surgeon there has taken a liking to Chris and lets him observe some of his and other surgeons' operations. Chris has seen open heart surgery and even observed the removal of a bit of someone's brain and he was totally cool about it, but when the surgeon performed a circumcision Chris fainted in the operating theatre.

Huh, Chris may think he's so smart and logical but as Stephanie said, he's just a typical guy and we all know what *they* think is their most important organ.

SATURDAY AUGUST 11TH

Offered to look after Danny today so Angela could go out with Graham as he was up this weekend but she surprised me by refusing, saying that she and Graham wanted to spend time with Danny.

I suppose it's only right and I know I should be pleased that she's coping so much better with Danny now but I can't help feeling a bit, well, jealous, I suppose. Just feels like it's one more male I'm going to lose to another girl . . . even if she is his mum.

SUNDAY AUGUST 12TH

Mum and Aunt Kate were discussing mortgages and flats with Graham and Angela today. Dad was working even though it was Sunday. Tuned out at first as all that financial stuff is a total bore but then suddenly realized that Angela must be planning to move out once she gets married and I nearly freaked.

Found myself saying totally mad stuff like why on earth would she want to leave home, it was really nice here? But then, OK, right, if she had to go, fine, but she should leave Danny here and I'd take care of him. She could visit on weekends.

Trailed off as I saw everyone looking at me, shocked into silence. Realized just how stupid I must have sounded. Of course Graham and Angela would move out. Who wanted to stay with parents or in-laws once they were married? Also, I couldn't look after Danny during the week because I had to go to school. Anyway,

Danny would go with them because he was *their* baby. Not mine. No matter how much he felt like mine. Oh God, what an idiot I'd made of myself yet again. Felt my face flush and tears start to well but I forced them back.

Finally Mum broke the silence and said, 'Never mind, Kelly Ann, love. One day you'll probably have kids just like I've done and wished you'd never bothered.' She laughed but then gave me a hug, handed me twenty pounds and told me to away out and enjoy myself with my pals. I was too young to be stuck here talking about mortgages and babies. Also I wasn't to worry about my eejit of a father and his grounding rubbish. What did he think this was, the Middle bloody Ages? Someone needed to tell him the days when a man could lock up his daughters were long past whether he liked it or not. Might as well be her.

Went to Liz's and Stephanie joined us. For once Liz listened to how upset I was without offering any psychological counselling rubbish. And Stephanie didn't say what was I bothering about Danny for, babies were disgusting drooling creatures, like she usually did when I talked about Danny.

We bought pizza and I got to pick the DVD I wanted to see. So we didn't watch a movie about a psychotic serial killer who chopped up his victims with nail scissors (Liz's choice). Nor did we watch *Lucky Lucy*, a film about a girl who becomes the mascot for an American football team and has to go everywhere with them. And I mean everywhere (great plot, Stephanie).

Instead we saw a movie about a girl whose sister and brother-in-law tragically die in skiing accident so she has to give up her ambitions to be an actress in order to bring up her sister's children. Later she meets this fantastic-looking rich guy who's well impressed by her beauty and goodness and falls in love with her. Luckily he also turns out to be movie producer so she becomes a famous actress anyway.

When the film was finished it was still early so we decided to watch *Lucky Lucy* after all, which turned out to be really good. Especially the scene in the locker rooms. Mmmm. American footballers. Maybe Mum is right and I'm too young to be tied down with babies and mortgages.

MONDaY AUGUST 13TH

First day back at school. Seemed really weird to be there without so many people I'm used to, like Stephanie, Ian, Gary and – OK, yes, Chris.

The big news is Mr Dunn has left to join a biker's gang in America who call themselves Satins Angles (now renamed Satan's Angels after Ms Conner helpfully pointed out their error, although this was a problem because they'd all had the name of the gang tattooed on their knuckles). She doesn't seem too upset by Mr Dunn's departure. She admitted to us for the first time today that – 'and this will come as a surprise to all of you, I know' – she had got to know Mr Dunn personally as well as professionally. Indeed he had asked her to join him abroad but she had been unable to bring herself to relinquish her pedagogic responsibilities. How could she abandon the students who relied so much on her for insightful instruction, moral direction and indefatigable advocacy on their behalf?

Johnny (one of Gerry's best friends) annoyed her then by calling out, 'Och, you should just have gone, miss. English teachers are ten a penny these days. We'd have been fine.'

We've now got a sixth year common room where we can study (ha ha) or sit around chatting and playing cards, chess or (last year's sixth year) strip poker. All of us are prefects, which means we wear braid on our blazers, get to boss younger pupils about a bit and have to hand round tea and biscuits at parents' nights. Power has already gone to Liz's head and she's been going round all day telling first and second years to pick up rubbish and straighten their ties. She's got a nerve telling anyone off for not being tidy.

MONDAY AUGUST 20TH

Have noticed that teachers aren't as formal with us any more and chat to us about stuff other than lessons. Mostly they moan about how much they hate teaching now and how discipline has gone down the pan while paper work is drowning them. Have also noticed that when we flirt with the younger teachers they flirt back, except for our register teacher, who blushes and is great fun to wind up. Mr Simmons hasn't changed any though. He still treats us all like first years and gave me a punishment exercise today for eating in class. Honestly.

TUESDAY AUGUST 21ST

Used to like English but all the stuff we have to read about now is so depressing. Every novel, play and poem seems to be about people falling madly in love, only to top themselves when they are dumped or cheated on. I mean, why can't they just get over it? And why can't we read a book that has a happy ending, like *Black Beauty* or something?

WEDNESDAY AUGUST 22ND

Am in so much trouble. Today in English we were reading a Robert Burns poem called 'Ae Fond Kiss', which is about a couple who've split up. It has the lines:

> Had we never lov'd sae kindly,
> Had we never lov'd sae blindly,
> Never met – or never parted –
> We had ne'er been broken-hearted.

Ms Conner talked about it for a bit, then asked us to write a short story based on the lines. Can't believe what I did. Stood up and shouted that I was sick of this depressing stuff, it was all rubbish and I wasn't doing this stupid exercise, then threw down my textbook and rushed out crying.

Oh my God. Ms Conner of all people. She's not a teacher to cross. I'm dead. Totally finished.

Had to go see her at the break in her office in the English base. Said I was really sorry, I didn't know why I'd done that and it would never happen again. Honestly. And to please not report me to Mr Smith or tell my parents, I'd already been in so much trouble this year.

Thought Ms Conner would rant on at me at the very least but she didn't. Instead she said that I must miss Chris a lot and she was sorry I was so unhappy. She added that I wouldn't have to do that particular essay but not to make a habit of refusing set work. And that was that. No rant, no referral, no suspension. I couldn't have been more surprised if a rottweiler had started to purr at me. Conner is all right sometimes.

THURSDAY AUGUST 23RD

Spoke too soon. In English today Ms Conner gave me a 3000-word essay for homework based on a quote from Tennyson: ' 'Tis better to have loved and lost than never to have loved at all. Discuss.'

Actually, if you ask me, I think Burns was right and Tennyson talks bollocks but I don't suppose I'll get away with saying that in my essay.

MONDAY AUGUST 27TH

Although English is still depressing, with Ms Conner insisting that all great literature is about love, sex and death, am really enjoying drama this year. We've got a new young drama teacher, Miss Kennedy, who's brilliant. She does really fun stuff – not 'pretend you're a daffodil' like the last one or stupid gritty reality plays like Ms Conner but real drama with music, dance and happy endings. I love it. It's cool pretending to be someone else, especially as being me isn't that great just now, what with my dad still on my case, the certain knowledge I made a total idiot of myself on holiday plus, worst of all, Chris, which still hurts actually, I must admit.

Miss Kennedy says I'm really good, particularly at dance and imitating accents, so despite my parents' total lack in faith in me, and my agreement to go to university first to get a degree, have decided I'm definitely going to be an actress. Gerry is one of the few boys in the drama class. Liz said he only joined so he could hit on all the girls but actually he's good too, and Miss Kennedy has selected us for the lead male and female parts in a play we'll be performing this term. It's a kind of modern *Romeo and Juliet* where both sets of parents disapprove of the relationship because they support different football teams – i.e. Celtic and Rangers. It's got a happy ending, however: the young couple tell their parents to stuff it, they're both Partick Thistle supporters, and run off together. They live happily ever after – except presumably for the poor performance in the league of Partick Thistle.

THURSDAY AUGUST 30TH

Gerry said that we needed to practise our lines for the play and he's right. There are lots of long scenes with just the two of us and it's difficult to memorize our lines properly and really get into character. Agreed to meet him tomorrow at his house after school.

Liz said I shouldn't go. She said Gerry is still a sleazer and is just asking me back to hit on me. Honestly, Liz is getting nearly as cynical as Stephanie these days. My relationship with Gerry is totally professional and he feels the same.

FRIDAY AUGUST 31ST

Practice went OK until Gerry put his tongue in my mouth while rehearsing a love scene. Hadn't liked this when I used to date him and liked it even less now. Gerry tried to excuse himself by saying that this was all part of method acting and getting right inside the mindset of the character. Then he went on to tell me that the new trend in acting was for total realism and that performers now even had full real sex on stage and screen to make things more authentic.

Yeah, right. Like the pensioners at the day centre where we're going to perform the play are going to really appreciate that, I don't think.

Then Gerry tried a different tack. OK, he admitted it, he really was just trying to cheer me up now that Chris and I were finished. He thought I might be missing a bit of affection.

Told him to keep his affection and his tongue to

himself and he was OK after that. He even offered to walk me home – something he had never bothered to do when we were dating – and suggested we go by the fish and chip shop and get something to eat. I was famished, so agreed. Big mistake.

It was drizzling so Gerry shared my umbrella, putting an arm round my waist as we walked. When we got to the fish and chip shop I spotted Chris and Gary just coming out with open fish suppers which they were starting to eat. I said 'Hi' to Gary but pointedly ignored Chris. Chris ignored me too but said to Gerry, 'What the **** do you think you're doing?'

Gerry's body tensed and he moved away from me but then he just smiled coolly and said, 'Relax, Chris. I'm just taking good care of one of your exes. The one that isn't pregnant. Yet.'

Was surprised when Chris dropped his fish supper on the ground as he'd only just started it and it wasn't like him to drop litter. Soon realized the reason for this odd behaviour: next second Chris hit Gerry so hard that it split his lip and sent him sprawling onto the wet pavement.

I hunched down to help Gerry but Chris pulled me away so I hit him with my open umbrella. This proved to be a pretty useless weapon and I only succeeded in breaking two of the spokes, which made me mad as it wasn't one of those cheap £1 umbrellas that always break on the first day but a proper one which cost me a tenner and had lasted for two months. Now I would have to throw it away. Meanwhile Gerry had got to his feet again and pushed me away from Chris, presumably to hit him, but Gary got in between them both – still trying to hold onto his fish supper – and got on at the two of them, not for fighting as such, but for being stupid enough to do it right in front of the CCTV camera positioned outside the chippy, and warned them that the manager of the shop had called the cops.

This cooled them both down a little and they agreed to settle things another time, much to the disappointment of the nosy crowd who'd gathered around us. One wee skinny drunk with scars on his face said: 'Which wan o' these clowns is yer man, doll? Thought I was in for a bit of entertainment the night but it seems noo like the pair of them couldnae fight their way oot a paper bag.'

Gary told the drunk to shove it and mind his own business, then said we should get going before the police came. This made sense and I turned to go, only for Chris to grab my arm again and say he'd take me home.

Told him no way but he wouldn't let go, insisting that I should come with him. This was the bloody last straw. It was bad enough being bossed around by parents and teachers all my life, I certainly wasn't going to be told what to do by a psycho ex-boyfriend. Slapped Chris about the head and face with my free hand, which seemed to cheer up our audience who were looking for a bit of violence (and couldn't wait until the pubs and clubs came out later). The skinny nyaff commented: 'Gaun yersel', hen, bet ye could knock lumps oot o' the two o' them an' aw.'

But then Chris caught my other hand and so I was stuck.

Gerry said he didn't know Chris had so much difficulty getting a girl these days that he had to force them to go with him, while Gary tried to reason with Chris, saying that he was out of line this time as, like it or not, I wasn't his girlfriend any more. Or I think that's what he was saying as he was still trying to finish off his fish and chips while they were at least warm so his speech was a bit indistinct at times.

But Chris still wouldn't let me go. The worst thing about the whole episode was everyone gawping at us and it didn't help that all the while I could feel my hair frizzing in the rain and knew I must look awful.

At last, thank God, people must have got bored with us because the crowd suddenly melted away. But it turned out it was the police rather than boredom that had caused them to push off. Brilliant.

There were four of them in all, one young police-woman and three men. Two got out of a police car and the other two from a van and made their way towards us. Thought the van was totally over the top. God, it wasn't as if we were having a riot or anything; it was just two idiot guys spoiling for a fight. One of the policemen was older and obviously in charge as he did all the talking.

Seeing Gerry's bloodied lip he said: 'Right, son, what's your name and who did this to you?'

Gerry said that he wasn't the policeman's son, that his name was Donald Duck and that a lamppost had walked into him, not that it was any of the police's business.

The policeman said, 'Don't get cheeky with me, son, or I'll have you down the station faster than you can say "I didnae dae nothing."'

He told the policewoman to get Gerry's details and not to take any nonsense from him, then turned to Chris and said, 'There's no point in turning your face away from me now, Chris, I recognized you even before I got out the car.' Then he looked at Gary as well and said, 'Right, which one of you is the lamppost? And don't waste my time now or I'll arrest the pair of you.'

Chris said he hit Gerry and Gary had nothing to do with it. When asked why he muttered something about it being a private disagreement.

The policeman looked about him at the crowded street, CCTV camera and heavy traffic, then said sarcastically, 'Aye, right, about as private as a streak at Hampden during an Old Firm match. And your dad's always boasting about how brilliant you are as well. Wait till I tell him about this.' However, he did add that as 'Donald Duck over there' didn't seem keen to press charges he'd let Chris off this time and to bugger off home before he changed his mind but clear up the fish and chip mess on the pavement first.

Finally the policeman turned to me and said, 'You. In the car!'

What had I done?

Nothing he could arrest me for apparently, more's the bloody pity given that I was probably the cause of this whole pantomime. They were just going to take me home to make sure I didn't cause any more trouble.

Didn't want to be taken home in a police car but didn't want to argue either as he sounded annoyed enough already so I decided just to get in the back of the car. As I passed, heard Gerry chatting up the policewoman. He was admiring her handcuffs and telling her that he liked girls in uniform. She could take him into custody any time.

Honestly, with his dying breath Gerry would be trying to pull his hospice care nurse. Don't know how Shelly puts up with him.

I waited in the car while the police made sure Gerry and Chris went off in different directions then they finally drove me home.

Another awful night and it's all Chris's fault.

SaTURDaY SEPTEMBER 1ST

Chris rang and asked how I was.

I told him I'd never forgive him or talk to him again for making a show of us last night and for breaking my umbrella, but he just said I don't talk to him anyway so how was he to tell the difference and I wasn't seriously trying to blame him for the broken umbrella, was I? It wasn't his idea to be hit with it after all.

He said he was sorry for upsetting me but refused to promise never to hit Gerry again unless he stayed away from me. He told me that Gerry wasn't just a tosser but really bad news and that he had issues with him that weren't only to do with me. He warned me to stay away from Gerry.

Shelly rang. She hadn't contacted me for ages and I was so looking forward to moaning to her about Chris's awful behaviour, especially as Liz and Stephanie weren't very sympathetic (tosser deserved it and to tell them again how hard Chris had punched him), but she wasn't very nice at all. Instead of going on about Chris she started going on at me. What had I been doing over at Gerry's place? Why was he walking me home, he never did that with her, and I'd better not be making a play for Gerry just because I didn't have a boyfriend now and was probably desperate.

Think Liz and Stephanie must be right after all and Shelly is a queen bitch who's never really liked me.

Began to wonder too about the way Shelly was always bad-mouthing Chris to me while pretending to be my friend. Was it just possible that maybe it was all lies and Chris really hadn't cheated on me? Oh God, how I wish that could be true.

But no. There was no point in fooling myself. Shelly wasn't the only person who believed Chris had got Linda pregnant. Linda's best friend for a start. Plus I *know* Chris was lying when he told me he'd no idea who the dad was. No, the truth was, neither Linda nor Chris had ever really cared about me. Hated both of them.

MONDAY SEPTEMBER 3RD

Gerry was nice to me this morning when I talked to him as we were both waiting outside the main staff room. We'd been sent there with messages from our register teachers. His face was still all bruised but somehow it looked quite romantic and attractive on him. I thought he'd be really annoyed with me for all the hassle and I apologized to him but he said it wasn't my fault I'd a psycho ex. He said it wasn't the first and wouldn't be the last time he'd got into a fight over a girl, and besides, he and Chris had stuff between them that wasn't all to do with me. Then he said if I still wanted to make up for it I could give him a kiss. He promised no tongues so I agreed.

Although he kept his 'no tongues' promise, the kiss did last for a lot longer than I'd intended but to be fair I hadn't specified any particular time limit and I didn't want to seem awkward after all the trouble I'd caused him. However, his hands suddenly wandered down to my bum and I was about to push him away when Mr Simmons came out the door.

We broke apart and Gerry just smiled at Simmons but I was embarrassed as it must have looked like we'd been snogging. Mr Simmons didn't say anything at first – just looked at Gerry's bruised face then back at me, and I thought I saw an expression of, well, respect, I suppose, certainly not the way Mr Simmons usually looks at me anyway. Finally he just said that he hoped this wasn't another young lad I'd been assaulting, at least not on school premises anyway, then moved on.

TUESDAY SEPTEMBER 4TH

Gerry has been pestering me to see him. He says there's
no need for Chris or Shelly to know anything about it.
Yeah, right. My life is bad enough without dating a serial
cheater like Gerry. Have resolved to have nothing to do
with guys any more and to throw myself into my work. I
have a maths test tomorrow and for once I'm really going
to be sensible and study hard for it.

THURSDAY SEPTEMBER 6TH

Got 5 out of 25 for my test. Can't believe I'm repeating
a year and my maths seems to have got worse instead of
better. Neither can Mr Simmons. It's so depressing.

Stephanie says never mind, maths is rubbish anyway
and who ever got rich and famous for being good at
maths? She says I should concentrate on my acting career
instead and – fantastic news – she's got me an audition
for a part as a murder victim in a real TV show. She was
dating a guy who hauls sets about in TV studios and he
told her about it. She's going to be my agent now. Of
course, as my agent she'll get 45 per cent of all my
earnings if I'm successful.

Thought 45 per cent was a bit steep but was too excited
and grateful to say so. Other than a date and time
(Saturday 3 pm) she didn't seem to have much more

information about the part – no script or plot details, not even how I died. It was going to be very difficult to practise before the audition but Stephanie says not to worry. As long as I looked good and offered to have sex with whoever was in charge of the audition I should be OK. Well, unless the person in charge was male and gay, which was an all-too-common problem in this line of business. I'd have to play it by ear.

FRIDAY SEPTEMBER 7TH

Practised being murdered by different methods in front of the mirror in my room tonight. Had done being stabbed, shot and battered to death. Finally tried being strangled. Had got to the end bit where I'm lying on the floor with my tongue hanging out and my eyes bulging when my mum walked in (without knocking as usual) and screamed.

She fell to her knees clutching me and saying stuff like, oh, my God, her baby, please, please don't be dead, please say I'm not dead, and before I could get a word in she had screeched to Dad downstairs to phone an ambulance.

Finally managed to say, 'I'm not dead, Mum, just pretending,' but she didn't let me go right away but carried on hugging me and saying embarrassing but quite nice stuff like, oh thank God, she couldn't have stood it if she'd lost me, she wouldn't want to live if her baby had died.

But suddenly she stopped being nice and screeched, what did I mean *just bloody pretending*? How could I have worried her like that? She was going to kill me for this, so help her, she would swing for me. Then she started slapping me about the head and face, and Dad, who fortunately hadn't phoned an ambulance but had come up to see what was the matter, had to drag her off me.

Wish Mum would learn to control her temper. Imagine if everyone just slapped people about every time they got annoyed.

SATURDAY SEPTEMBER 8TH

It's the big day and am feeling very nervous. This could be the day my acting career is launched. Stephanie came round to check on me an hour before my audition. She was horrified to find me dressed in a smart skirt and blouse I'd borrowed from my sister.

These people were artists for God's sake, not civil servants. I wasn't attending an interview for a job as a data-entry clerk, I was auditioning for a *part* in a *TV drama*. Honestly, what was she to do with me?

She picked out a pair of my very lowest low-rise jeans and a black T-shirt, added some dramatic jewellery of her own, then did my make-up with lots of blusher and fake tan (all successful actresses have a tan all year round unless they're deliberately going for pale and interesting, in which case you have to be really famous first to get away with bucking the trend).

Arrived on time but was made to wait, stomach churning, for over an hour before it was my turn to go into the audition room. There was a man and woman sitting behind a desk plus another guy with a camera standing behind what looked like a hospital gurney.

The man behind the desk introduced himself as Jason and, I suppose to make conversation, asked if I'd just got back from holiday as I looked so tanned. Blurted out that no, it was fake tan as I wasn't famous enough to be pale. He said, er, right, then, let's just get started, and asked me to take off my shoes and socks and lie down on the gurney.

Worried for a moment that this was some odd casting couch thing but he'd only asked me to bare my feet, not take off all my clothes, so supposed it must be all right. I did as he told me and at the same time asked him if he had a script for the part and if so could I have a look at it before we started.

Jason laughed and said, 'No, love, no script. You're supposed to be a corpse in the morgue so it's not a speaking part as such. To be honest we were surprised when your audition was organized through an agent. They don't usually get involved in this kind of stuff. And who is your agent, by the way? We've never heard of her before.'

Was disappointed to know it wouldn't be a speaking part. Still, I suppose loads of successful actors had to start off with quite minor roles at first. Offered to go clean my fake tan make-up off so I'd look a bit more realistically pale for the corpse character but Jason said no, not to worry about it, they were only going to film the soles of my feet in any case. Then he put a white sheet over me, just leaving my feet exposed.

Really gutted that my face wouldn't be seen on TV but Jason made me feel a bit better by saying that I'd nice dainty feet, not like the previous candidate who, to put it kindly, had a good grip of Scotland (size tens at least and nearly as broad as they were long). Everything was OK until they tried to attach a tag to my toe. I have *very* tickly feet. Started giggling and couldn't stop. Was scared they'd touch my feet again so pulled the sheet down from my face and tried to look at what was going on, squirming and giggling when the cameraman tried to get near me.

Eventually fed up, Jason told me to put my shoes and socks back on. He said they wouldn't be able to use me as I was too fidgety and giggly for a corpse.

Am so humiliated. Have just realized that I have auditioned for the role of a corpse – or, to be more exact, a corpse's feet – and have been rejected. This doesn't augur well for my future career as an actress.

MONDAY SEPTEMBER 10TH

Mr Simmons says I've to join his remedial maths class after school. He says if I don't I'm liable to embarrass both of us by getting a lower grade after repeating the year than I got first time around. No excuses, no arguments, be there at four o'clock tomorrow.

TUESDAY SEPTEMBER 11TH

There were about fifteen of us in all, from all different year groups, our only common factor being how useless we all were at maths. To be fair, can't be much fun for Mr Simmons to take a duff class like us.

He'd set us all different remedial exercises and was going round helping people who were stuck (all of us) when the door opened and a skinny red-headed woman burst into the room carrying a large laundry bag.

So here he was, she might have known. Wasting his time trying to teach the unteachable and for what? Not an extra halfpenny earned. This wasn't going to get her the new three-piece suite she wanted, not to mention her washing machine, which had just packed in and who could blame it, it was ten years old for God's sake and a total embarrassment. And don't even talk to her about the cooker. Theirs was so ancient Noah's wife would have laughed at it.

When he was promoted this was all supposed to change. Her arse. The only thing that changed was he was too tired out to have sex any more, which used to be the only thing he was any good at. Not any longer. Now he was useless for that too. Well, she was sick of it – and here she threw the laundry bag at Mr Simmons, scattering the contents, including embarrassing stuff like underpants, across the floor – he could take himself and his laundry to his mother's. Let her wash, cook and skivvy for him for a while. And he wasn't to come back until he'd the time and the bloody money to sort his marriage out.

Mr Simmons was mortified. He tried to get her to shut up and leave but she ranted on anyway. After an initial stunned silence most of the class were starting to titter or giggle at poor Mr Simmons. That was it. Mr Simmons might not be my favourite teacher but he didn't deserve this. I got up and confronted her.

Told her she'd no right barging into our school like this and slagging off our teacher. Mr Simmons might not earn a lot of money and, erm, be not very good at other things but he was a really first-rate maths teacher. Well, I'd failed my maths actually but that's because I'm really lousy at maths and didn't do any work, not because Mr Simmons was a bad teacher. She was probably just being horrible to him because of that fling he'd had with Mrs Valentine on the school trip to Paris last year, and I must say I hadn't approved of that at the time, but now that I saw what Mr Simmons had to put up with at home I could understand he was probably driven to it.

Oops. Apparently Mrs Simmons hadn't known about that. But she does now and is seeing her lawyer.

Mr Simmons has told me never *ever* to try and defend him again.

WEDNESDAY SEPTEMBER 12TH

Feel so guilty about Mr Simmons. His marriage has ended and it's all my fault. What if he gets so upset that he kills himself – then I'll be like a murderer.

Maths was just before break so told Mr Simmons I needed to talk to him after class about an important matter and he said OK. As soon as the class had filed out I asked him how he was feeling and begged him not to do anything rash but he didn't reply and just looked puzzled.

Told him that things were never as bad as they might seem, that there was light at the end of the tunnel, and that the darkest hour is just before the dawn. Well, actually the darkest hour isn't really just before the dawn and the sky gets gradually lighter in the hours before-hand but what I meant was there was always hope so he shouldn't ever, erm, take things into his own hands. Just think of all the people who would miss him. OK, so maybe he wasn't the most popular teacher in the school and probably people like Stuart Thompson, who'd been given ten punishment exercises by Mr Simmons so far this term, would be glad to see the back of him, but loads of other pupils who hoped to pass their exams this year would be gutted as all the other maths teachers were rubbish.

Mr Simmons interrupted, 'Kelly Ann, what on earth are you on about?'

I blurted out, 'Please don't kill yourself, sir. I couldn't stand the guilt.'

Mr Simmons was silent for a while then said slowly and carefully, as though speaking to an imbecile, 'Kelly Ann, your maths grades this year are a disgrace, it's true, but I assure you I've no intention of committing suicide because of them.'

Told him I wasn't talking about my maths grades, which I agreed weren't exactly brilliant but I wouldn't expect anyone to top themselves over them exactly. Said I was really meaning about my ruining his marriage.

He said, 'Kelly Ann, your appalling performance in maths is your own fault because you have simply not worked hard enough at something you find very difficult.' Then he paused, sighed and continued, 'The collapse of my marriage is *my* fault – for much the same reasons, as it happens – but I've no intention of giving Stuart Thompson the satisfaction of seeing me quit this mortal coil just yet.'

Was so relieved not to feel guilty any more I wasn't

even annoyed when he gave me a punishment exercise for not handing in my maths homework on time.

THURSDAY SEPTEMBER 13TH

Actually Mr Simmons doesn't seem to be any grumpier than usual. Maybe a bit less so in fact. Until third period today anyway, when he had to 'observe and participate in' our English class. It's part of a 'cross-curricular development initiative', which means that teachers are supposed to know and get involved with what goes on in other subjects. Ms Conner and Mr Simmons are meant to shadow each other. While Ms Conner is all for it – 'it's so important that English language is part of every lesson' – Mr Simmons thinks it's all crap. Not that he actually says that of course, but everybody knows from his bored expression and sarcastic comments what he really thinks.

Today Ms Conner had given us an essay to do in class: 'To what extent have Shakespeare's plays influenced modern English drama?' and invited Mr Simmons to have a go. After about one minute he ostentatiously put his pen down and sat back. Ms Conner marched over to his desk, heels clicking. She glanced at his sheet of paper and read out his answer between gritted teeth: 'Seventy per cent.' A little brief, perhaps – would Mr Simmons care to elaborate on this?

Mr Simmons did, but after only another thirty seconds he put his pen down again and folded his arms in front of him. *Clackety clack.* Ms Conner read out his expanded essay: 'Seventy per cent plus or minus five.'

Well, Mr Simmons challenged, was he right or wrong?

It wasn't a matter of right or wrong as such. It was a matter of marshalling reasoned argument to support a position.

So, Mr Simmons said, shaking his head incredulously, he could have said zero per cent or one hundred per cent and have been right either way, could he?

Precisely.

Mr Simmons muttered something that sounded a lot like 'logic of the Mad Hatter's tea party' and I'm sure Ms Conner would have loved to issue him with a punishment exercise and a referral to Mr Smith but instead had to content herself by saying how much she was looking forward to attending Mr Smith's maths class tomorrow. It was said in such a menacing tone, however, that if I'd been Mr Simmons I'd have much preferred the exercise and referral options.

FRIDAY SEPTEMBER 14TH

Mr Simmons asked in maths today for the definition of a prime number. This was easy so everyone had their hand up but Mr Simmons chose Ms Conner to answer.

Ms Conner said a prime number was a lonely but at the same time strangely beautiful concept that could be viewed as symbolizing the essential existential isolation of the human condition while celebrating the uniqueness of the human spirit and the achievement of individual independence.

Mr Simmons said, 'Wrong answer. Can anyone else tell us what a prime number is?'

But Ms Conner cut in that of course, viewed simplistically, a prime number is one that can only be divided by itself or one but that this narrow definition is only one possible interpretation of a range of meanings, the richness of which would probably take her at least several months to explore in any depth. Oh yes, at least that.

The perception of the meaning of a prime number could be considered as a metaphor . . .

On and on she went for the entire period. We all just tuned her out and played hangman but poor Mr Simmons was invited repeatedly to comment and expand on her ravings.

MONDAY SEPTEMBER 17TH

Mr Simmons behaved himself in English this morning and made a real attempt at a short story, for which Ms Conner gave him 39 per cent. Almost a pass.

The truce continued this afternoon and Ms Conner attempted some maths. Mr Simmons told her that though none of her answers were correct they were not totally and completely wrong as such.

In a further spirit of 'compromise' Mr Simmons has agreed to call their joint policy document 'Curriculum Integration: the Importance of English Language in Maths' and not 'Curriculum Integration: Educational Theory Gone Mad' as he'd originally intended.

TUESDAY SEPTEMBER 18TH

Stephanie and Liz were over at my place tonight when Gary and Ian called round. They say they moved into their flat last week and have invited us to lunch there on Saturday, and no, Chris wouldn't be there, he was on holiday and wouldn't move in until next week along with the other medic.

We agreed but Stephanie warned Gary it had better not be like the barbecue where we had to do all the work but he promised he would cook so we said OK.

It was a tenement flat on the fourth floor with four bedrooms, a kitchen, living room and bathroom. The place was Baltic as the rooms were all large with high ceilings and there was no central heating. Every room was painted magnolia and had mingin' brown carpets. Still, it must be cool to live in a place with no parents to annoy you.

Of course the boys had done their best, so they said, to 'brighten up the place' with posters. Don't ask. At least they were just put up with Blutack so will be easy to remove if their mums visit.

Lunch on offer turned out to be a selection of pot noodles of almost every variety except the only flavour we liked – i.e. chicken and mushroom. Had a look in the fridge to see if there was anything else we fancied but all it contained was around three dozen cans of beer and one small carton of sour milk.

In the end Liz and Stephanie went off to the deli we'd spotted on the way here with Gary while I stayed behind with Ian to set the table. Easier said than done. There were no clean dishes, cutlery or glasses, just a week's worth of greasy crockery left in the sink, so I had to wash it all up. Also had to clean the table and other surfaces plus mop the floor, which was so filthy my shoes were sticking to it. Don't know how they managed to get the kitchen that dirty in just a week. Only the unused cooker was spotless. Ian was useless, so slow and clumsy I eventually ordered him out just to get him out of my way. He didn't argue and switched on the TV to watch sport.

By the time they came back I was furious and so were Liz and Stephanie as they'd had to pay for the shopping. Didn't they realize how expensive keeping a flat was?

But Ian and Gary did produce some quite nice wine they'd stashed away secretly for use with future girl-friends. Ian said he'd given up hope of finding one tall enough in Glasgow so we might as well have it and Gary knew he was in serious trouble if he didn't do something to put us in a better mood.

By the end of the afternoon we were feeling quite happy but when Gary invited us to an end of freshers week party at the flat next Saturday, I refused at first because of Chris but Gary says I'll hardly see him. Chris is working a double shift at the hospital that day and won't get back until midnight, when he intends just to say hello then pack it in for the night. Honestly, it's all Chris does these days: either work at the hospital or haunt the library looking up medical books. He'd become a total bore and Gary blames me by the way.

I was still wary but Gary pleaded, saying there weren't nearly enough girls at the party and he needed us to come, so I gave in. After all, 'not nearly enough girls' meant . . . Besides, it was a fancy dress theme party where everyone had to come dressed as Action Man or Barbie so it might be a laugh.

SaTURDay SePTeMBeR 29TH

Not nearly enough girls my arse. Like every other party organized by guys the place was hoaching with good-looking girls but despite that things started off quite well. Felt really cool to be in a student flat and have no bother with parents and the like, although several neighbours complained about the noise and were ignored. They were just told that it was Saturday night, for God's sake, and to get a life.

Jamie the medical student appeared to be interested in me and made a point of chatting me up. He seemed like a good laugh, although it was difficult to know whether he was fanciable or not as I'd never met him before and he was wearing a blond wig and pink dress with matching high heels. I was in camouflage combat trousers and vest.

He invited me to sit on his knee and gave me a paper cup with a strange-looking fruit punch drink in it. I took a sip; it tasted odd – very sweet, but quite nice really.

At this point Chris came back from his shift in the hospital. Hadn't seen him for a while and he looked different somehow ... older and tired but annoyingly enough just as sexy as ever, and I felt myself briefly longing to go over and kiss him. It's awful the way you can still fancy a lying cheat you basically hate. Maybe that's why horrible people like Stalin and Hitler still managed to get wives and girlfriends.

I decided to ignore Chris and concentrated on flirting with Jamie but Chris came over anyway. He said nothing to me but took my drink away and spoke to Jamie. He advised Jamie not to give me any more of the punch as I'd only throw it up on his lap later.

Jamie must have noticed the hostility of Chris's tone and asked whether there was 'a problem here' – he was under the impression we'd split up a while ago.

Chris told him there wasn't a problem, it was cool, but warned him that I spat in corridors, had a vicious right hook and he wouldn't get any sex from me until Valentine's day, if then – and he moved off to get a beer.

Jamie seemed to go off me after that. I stormed over to Chris, who was sitting on the floor next to Gary. Both of them were drinking beer from cans and discussing whether the redhead with the hopefully fake rifle or the blonde in the silver stilettos with combats was the sexiest. Gary took one look at my face and made himself scarce. Chris just asked me to sit down and shout at him quietly if I had to shout as he was tired.

Demanded my drink back but he offered me wine instead, telling me that the punch was lethal. He said it was made from a mixture of pure ethanol Gary had stolen from the chemistry department combined with, on Jamie's recommendation, corn syrup and sparkling wine. The fizzy wine and sugar were designed to rush alcohol into the bloodstream in the fastest possible time, resulting in almost instant drunkenness. The plan was to use it to seduce girls as quickly as possible. He said that in my case the likely result would be throwing up in the bathroom rather than getting amorous in the bedroom, or God knows he might have tried it with me himself in the past, but anyway it wasn't a good idea for me to drink it tonight. Then he said he was tired and was going to bed and did I want to come with him? He thought not. Then he left.

Later on I told Stephanie and Liz about the punch and we decided to try it. Found Gary in the kitchen hitting on the redhead, whom he was plying with the punch. We asked for some too. Gary looked uncomfortable and avoided our gaze, saying he couldn't give us any. He said Chris had told him the three of us were mad enough without it and had threatened to break his legs if he so much as offered us a drop of the stuff. We just *looked* at him for a bit then Liz spoke. She said he had to ask himself who he was more afraid of – Chris or us? He said he'd get us our drinks right away.

The punch was amazing. One minute I was almost totally sober; the next I was completely flying. Remember winning a pole-dancing competition and being really pleased to have beaten Stephanie – although the vote had been unanimous as I was the only entrant to pole-dance upside down, but almost nothing after that until I woke up next morning starkers in Chris's bed.

SUNDAY SEPTEMBER 30TH

Chris was already up, sitting on the armchair opposite me drinking coffee and reading a thick textbook. He said, 'Good morning, Kelly Ann,' quite formally and asked how I was feeling.

Oh. My. God. How had this happened? I searched my memory, frantically trying to figure out how on earth I'd got here, but huge chunks of the night were totally missing. But, oh no, I did vaguely remember Chris carrying me to bed and undressing me. God, he was right about that stupid punch, I shouldn't have touched it. Now I'd lost my virginity to Chris of all people and I didn't even remember it.

Chris offered to get me a cup of tea. When he'd gone out I got up and dressed. He'd hung my clothes neatly over the radiator nearest to the bed. Trust Chris to be organized even in the middle of a sex session. Noticed that my thighs felt very sore and had to hobble about when getting dressed. What *had* I been doing?

When he returned I saw that he looked totally shattered but decided not to comment on this. Certainly didn't want him to tell me any details about how he'd got so tired. I wanted to go right away but Chris insisted I drink the hot, sweet tea first, and I must admit it did make me feel less shaky. He asked if my thighs were sore and I said warily that they were a bit. He told me I'd probably pulled a muscle with my 'performance' last night but it wasn't serious. Would I like him to massage them? No way!

He drove me back mostly in silence but as we got near home I told him that last night didn't change anything between us; in fact I hated and despised him more than ever.

He said, 'That's nice, Kelly Ann,' but – get this – he'd hoped I might be *grateful* to him. Didn't I see how exhausted he was taking care of me last night and he could do without the abuse at least.

Grateful! What a nerve, arrogant tosser. I got out, slamming the car door without a backward glance, and hobbled to my door. He waited until I got in before driving off. Nice of him to see me home safely. Wouldn't do if some other callous chancer took advantage of me.

I was so knackered I went straight back to bed again but then suddenly had an awful thought. I wasn't on the pill any more and I didn't know whether Chris had used a condom last night. Bollocks! But surely someone as smart as Chris with ambitions to be a top doctor wouldn't be stupid enough to have got me pregnant. Then I remembered Linda. I'd have to ask.

Called his mobile and asked in what I hoped was a calm matter-of-fact voice whether he'd used a condom last night. He laughed. Yes, *laughed,* and said he hadn't. Hurled my phone at the wall in terror and rage then threw myself face down on my bed and screamed into my pillow.

Quick panic calculation. Thirteen days since my last period. Exactly mid cycle. Brilliant. Oh my God!

Had heard somewhere that sperm can take ages to swim up fallopian tubes which, given their size, is like swimming the English Channel, and anyway they might have to hang around for a while waiting for an egg so maybe I wasn't pregnant yet. On the other hand I could be getting fertilized right now just lying here. Got up immediately. OK, I *know* you can still get pregnant even if you do it standing up but it *must* be harder to swim upstream.

As I was pacing (hobbling) up and down I remembered a programme about people who had serious diseases like cancer being asked to visualize the invading cells being killed off by body defences or treatment and wondered desperately if this might work for sperm. Maybe I should try imagining the millions of tadpole cells as enemy invaders, like SEALS or something, and picture them getting knackered and demoralized then giving up or heading back to base camp. But then the depressing idea occurred to me that since they were Chris's sperm they would probably be totally stubborn, determined, 'failure is not an option' types who wouldn't give up until their mission was accomplished.

What was I doing? This was totally mad, talking to and pleading with sperm. Even giving them personalities! Decided instead to bargain with God. Got down on my knees like a Catholic – but was careful to keep my torso vertical, so sperm would still be swimming upstream – and promised God if He would please, *please* not make me pregnant this time I would never *ever* have unprotected sex again. In fact, if God was a Catholic, I would never have sex again ever but would become a nun and do good works for the rest of my life. Please God. Please. Let me off with it just this once. It was a first offence after all.

Must be something in this religious stuff: a wonderful thought occurred to me out of the blue. Morning after pill. Hallelujah! Must get to a chemist straight away.

Except, of course, it was Sunday and nearly all the chemists were shut. Didn't know which ones would be open so decided to phone Stephanie and see if she knew. Had to use the land line because of broken phone. She took ages to answer and sounded terrible but eventually did give me some good advice.

She said it was great I'd had sex at last but it was annoying I couldn't remember any of it and that Liz would be *so* disappointed. She said it was a pity about the no condom stuff and agreed with me that all guys were selfish scum. But she said the morning after pill didn't have to be the morning after and would work up to seventy-two hours after shagging so I could deal with it tomorrow.

Spent the rest of the day and much of night fantasizing about what I'd do to Chris next time I saw him. Particularly enjoyed the roasting-on-a-spit-over-an-open-fire scenario but settled eventually for him being obliged to endure a lifetime of counselling from Liz on what a selfish worthless person he really was.

MONDAY OCTOBER 1ST

Decided to go to the chemist this lunch time. Wasn't looking forward to asking the pharmacist for the morning after pill. I mean, you might as well just come out with it and say, 'I am a stupid slut-girl, too thick, drunk or slapperish to make sensible choices about contraceptives and sexual partners.' Oh God. Maybe I could persuade Stephanie to go for me but she wasn't there and I couldn't see Liz doing it. Just had to comfort myself with the thought that at least asking for the pill was more sensible than not asking under the circumstances.

Spoke to Liz at the break. Hadn't been able to contact her all yesterday as she'd been ill. She gobsmacked me by saying she was sure I hadn't done it with Chris that night and filled me in on what I'd been up to at the party. She said that after the pole-dancing stuff – which by the way I'd won partly because Ian had been my 'pole' and had caught me several times before I landed on my head (he says to tell me I'm heavier than I look, especially when I wriggle) – I decided to show off to everyone how I could do the splits, which I did easily. Not content with that I boasted that I could do a vertical splits up a wall! Everyone was well impressed and applauded wildly when, keeping my left leg on the floor, I stretched my right leg up flush with the wall. However, just afterwards I collapsed, moaning in pain. Jamie rushed up shouting, 'Everyone out of the way, I'm a doctor,' and rubbed my thighs for me but I'd recovered enough to tell him to 'get lost, sleazer', especially since his hands had wandered *very* far up my thighs.

After that I felt unwell and crawled to the bathroom to be sick. I didn't come out for ages, wouldn't answer Liz when she called and had locked the door so she got worried and woke Chris up. He forced open the door, only to find me unconscious and damp in the bath. He lifted me up and took me to his bed even though I came round and protested that the bath was really very comfortable, especially as I could just turn on the taps any time I wanted and enjoy a good warm soak if I got cold during the night.

He told Liz he would have to stay awake to watch me in case I was sick when I was asleep and choked to death. He added that having his girlfriend choke to death in his bedroom probably wouldn't have looked good in his cv.

Ex-girlfriend, I corrected. And why had she let him undress me?

Liz said my clothes were damp from the bath and I'd spilled some of the punch down my front.

Oh God, what an idiot I'd made of myself! How could I have been so stupid? And why just me? Why hadn't Liz and Stephanie made arses of themselves?

Oh, but they had. Learned later that Liz had promised to marry some guy at the party she doesn't fancy at all. Seems he's bought the ring and wants her to meet his parents tonight.

Stephanie got very friendly with a drunk engineer from Ian's course. Apparently they thought it would be laugh to go to an all-night tattoo shop and declare their love for each other by having their bums tattooed with complementary messages. Unfortunately Stephanie now has inscribed inside a heart shape on her left buttock 'I LOVE WILLIE'. She says next time she decides to go off to a tattoo shop in the middle of the night with some guy she's picked up she'll ask his name first.

TUESDAY OCTOBER 2ND

Chris has insisted on seeing me today. He says it's important and won't take no for an answer. Thought it was probably just to lecture me about how I can't handle alcohol but I decided to get it over with and arranged to meet him at lunch time, so at most I had an hour not to listen to him banging on.

It was a nice frosty autumn day so we went for a walk in the park. He started off by saying he'd been talking to Stephanie and wanted to make it clear to me that, call him picky, he preferred to have sex with girls who were at least semi-conscious at the time. Then he went on about what a state I'd been in, didn't I know how dangerous it was to binge-drink like that?

Told him of course I didn't think he'd do anything with an unconscious person, it was just that I thought I might have been drunk enough to forget how much I hated him and so it was just possible we might have had sex but I'd forgotten.

I added that I was so glad we hadn't as he was the last person in the world I'd want to do anything with.

Chris ignored the insults, instead pointing out that obviously this meant I'd also had memory blackouts and how could I be so totally irresponsible?

He was right of course. Not that I'd tell him that. Although I hadn't behaved as badly as I'd imagined – at least I hadn't had sex with anyone while plastered – it was scary not remembering everything and I never wanted to get that drunk again.

Refused to give Chris the satisfaction of admitting this so I interrupted his rant to say that I'd rather be called irresponsible than a pompous bore who lives in the library. But actually I wasn't really up for a serious argument with Chris. Couldn't help thinking about all the happy times he and I had playing as kids in this park, so wasn't really spoiling for a fight. Remembered how we used to fish for tadpoles and minnows in the pond and how Chris would always give me some of his if I couldn't find any.

Also remember playing five-a-side football with Chris and his friends and how he would force his pals to let me play even though no one wanted a girl in the team (well, until Ian fell on me anyway). He used to be really nice to me before I fell in love with him and we started dating; now it was too late to go back.

Felt tired so sat down on a bench by the pond but then I was shivering. Though I'd a coat on I'd no gloves or scarf and it was freezing when I stopped moving.

Chris took off his own scarf and wrapped it around my neck then took my hands in his to warm them. He was going on again about his conversation with Stephanie – why hadn't I spoken to him if I thought I was pregnant? Surely it would have been more his business than Stephanie's if that were true. Why did I have such a low opinion of him? All he'd done was try to take care of me.

Told him to stop acting all innocent and injured. He'd no need to undress me completely on Saturday night and he knew it. Chris laughed and said he thought he'd deserved some fun for his troubles, and by the way my breasts had definitely grown a little.

Was secretly pleased by this remark but slapped him anyway. He accepted this without a fuss. Suppose he's used to it. But then he started going on about how this was the longest fall-out we'd ever had and when was I going to come to my senses? He didn't know why I wouldn't trust him. He'd told me a hundred times that he hadn't cheated on me with Linda: why wouldn't I believe him? Then he tried another tack. So, OK, he gave in. Let's suppose, just for argument's sake, that he was guilty of cheating on me, and let's say he was really, really sorry about it. Would I forgive him and take him back?

Yeah, right. So I said, let's suppose, for argument's sake, that I'd cheated on him – with Gerry, for example – and I was now six months pregnant – but hey, never mind all that, I was now really, really sorry. Would he forgive me and take me back?

The look on Chris's face only confirmed what Stephanie has always said: all guys are hypocritical tossers.

We walked back mostly in silence but as we got to the park exit Chris asked me 'one last time' if I'd go back with him and I said hell would freeze over. Then he told me that there was a girl called Amy he'd met at freshers week whom he liked and intended to ask out. He was pretty sure she'd say yes. He didn't want me hearing about it from anyone else. It was only right that I should be the first to know.

For a moment I could hardly breathe with the shock and pain of it. Strange really, since I thought that after finding out about Linda, Chris would never be able to hurt me again. Just shows how wrong you can be.

Wanted to sit down right there and cry but Chris was looking at me and there was no way I would ever let him know how I really felt. In the end just said, 'Makes a change from the last person.'

He asked me for a final goodbye kiss and stupidly I agreed. So now I remember why I couldn't stay just friends with him for ever and how much I used to love him. Brilliant. Watched Chris walk away and determined never to see him again.

WEDNESDAY OCTOBER 3RD

Stephanie was saying last night that it wouldn't be long until her boyfriend Dave got back. Not that she'd really missed him all that much of course, but still, it would be nice to see him again and catch up with things. She supposed she'd have to try and do something about the tattoo.

Liz'd had a long phone call from Julian saying he didn't think he'd be able to last out until Christmas to see her and was trying to arrange an earlier trip over.

I know I shouldn't feel jealous and obviously I do want my best friends to be happy but I didn't feel like talking about boyfriends to anyone today so decided to spend lunch time with Ayesha since she was guaranteed never to raise such a topic.

As it so happened though, she was talking about

romance, sort of, as she told me her brother had got engaged yesterday. She's warned his fiancée that he's a useless lazy slob and advised her against marrying him but the girl wouldn't listen – she was in love. What can you do? This stupid Western notion of romantic love was getting everywhere.

I asked Ayesha if it was an arranged marriage (a totally gross idea in my opinion) but she said not: they met at college so they'd only themselves to blame. According to her, arranged marriages could be quite a good idea, if you were into getting married, that is, as it saved all the hard work of looking for someone. You just get your family to sift out some of the rubbish and send round a selection of possibles to choose from. If the selection turns out to be dross as well you simply knock them back and tell your mum and dad to try again. It was a bit like having a free dating agency.

The thought of my mum or dad picking out boyfriends for me filled me with horror and I told her so, but as Ayesha said I hadn't exactly had much luck picking out my own, had I?

Gerry, Chris and Alan. Cheats and liars, all of them. Ayesha had a point.

Imran came over to me later but before he opened his mouth told him that no, Ayesha hadn't mentioned him.

Happened to be sitting next to Imran at dinner today when he started on at me again, asking if I'd any idea how he could get Ayesha to like him. I suggested that he should get friendly with her family but he said he'd already tried that.

He's spoken to her older brothers, who say they're totally cool about him seeing her, anything to take her off their hands. However, when they tried to put in a good word for him with Ayesha she told them to shove it – the day she listened to their advice on who she should or shouldn't like would be the day she'd ask to be sectioned under the mental health act.

Imran had also asked his dad to speak to Mr Hassan (Ayesha's dad) about his interest in her but Imran's dad had refused. He said that Mr Hassan was a lifelong friend whom he trusted, respected and admired. Imran on the other hand was a lazy, feckless and sometimes immoral (don't think he hadn't heard about it) son who was a huge and continuing disappointment to him. Nevertheless blood was thicker than water and this was why he couldn't bring himself to do something that might lead to Imran having to endure a life of misery with Mr Hassan's vile-tongued harpy of a daughter.

Found myself saying weird stuff like maybe Imran should listen to his dad and that sometimes parents might actually be right after all, but Imran said he couldn't. He said that without Ayesha life would have no meaning for him.

I got quite choked up at that and couldn't finish my lunch. Honestly, it was so sad and romantic.

Imran asked if he could have the rest of my chips since I didn't want them, then turned round and started discussing cricket with his pals. When will I ever learn that all guys are devious, two-faced tossers.

FRIDAY OCTOBER 12TH

Gary has invited Liz, Stephanie and me to Glasgow Students' Union and we are all interested in checking out the talent but I didn't want to bump into Chris and especially *not Amy*. Gary swore blind that there was no chance of that as Chris hardly ever socializes there – he spends most of his time either at the flat or round at his girlfriend's place, and please would we go with him as he was trying to get off with someone there who'd be impressed if he turned up with three girls.

Gary signed us in. The place was heaving but he soon spotted the girl he was interested in – a pretty blonde with a very large chest – and homed in on her. We put on our act for him, all pretending to fancy him while he knocked us back, and soon the girl was all over him like a rash. Gary bought us all a drink then told us to push off with a 'thanks, girls'.

We had another drink and checked out the talent – not bad – when a tall guy in a blue shirt called over to me, 'Kelly Ann,' and gestured for us to join his group of about six other guys, some of whom looked quite hot. Didn't recognize the one who called my name but we went over anyway while I tried to figure out who he was.

He introduced us to the group: 'This is Kelly Ann. She spits in corridors, can do the splits up a wall and only has sex on Valentine's day. And her two lovely friends are Stephanie (can we see your tattoo?) and Liz, who holds something of a record for the shortest engagement in history.'

On closer inspection I could see it was Jamie, who looked better without the wig and pink frock, but I wasn't interested in anyone right now, far less someone who lived with Chris. The others in the group were all medical students too and were quite a laugh if a bit crude, so I was quite enjoying myself until Chris walked up to us with a girl I presumed must be Amy. Honestly, I would kill Gary for this!

She had light caramel-coloured hair, swingy and straight, a clear complexion and perfect white teeth. Like Stephanie's her clothes were obviously expensive, but unlike Stephanie's not expensive-slutty, more classy, I suppose.

Chris said, 'Hi, Kelly Ann.'

Amy said to me, 'Oh, hi there. I'm so pleased to meet you. I've heard *such* a lot about you and, oh yes, you're just as pretty as everyone says you are. You and Chris used to be childhood sweethearts, didn't you – how lovely . . .' She gushed on, being insufferably nice in a very posh voice, and all the time she was touching him constantly. Not snogging or anything, nothing so obvious, but stroking his hand with hers, or brushing his elbow, or running her fingers through his hair. I wanted to slap her hand away and say leave him alone, he's mine, but of course I couldn't because he wasn't. Felt tears start to sting my eyes and heard Chris say in a concerned, kind voice, 'Are you OK, Kelly Ann?'

Oh God, the total humiliation of it. He was feeling sorry for me. Heard myself say, 'Fine, thanks, but must be going now, I'm off to a party.'

Of course all the medic guys were asking what party where and could they come so I said no it was just me and, er, Gary who'd been invited.

Everyone looked over at Gary, who was contentedly sucking the face off the blonde in the corner of the bar, but I marched over anyway, conscious of being watched all the time, and prised them apart before asking her for her phone number. She was so astonished she gave it to me without thinking. I wrote it on Gary's hand using an eye pencil which I'd fished out of my bag, told the blonde he'd ring her and marched Gary out.

Gary pleaded with me not to hit him. Honestly, Chris hardly ever came to the Union – well, not very often any-way – and he really, really thought, er, hoped he wouldn't be there tonight and that the blonde was so hot I could hardly blame him for telling a few white lies, and yes, he'd pay my taxi home.

SATURDAY OCTOBER 13TH

Seventeen tomorrow. If Julian hadn't given me the fake ID it would be another year before I could go to the pub to celebrate.

SUNDAY OCTOBER 14TH

Mum and Dad were working and Angela had gone to Aunt Kate's so I was alone until Stephanie and Liz came over around eleven with my prezzies. A book on coping with being a failure in love from Liz, the gist of which was there are winners and losers in life (guess which category I belonged to), and thermal underwear from Stephanie – but no, she hadn't given up on me, some guys were turned on by this, honest. Then they gave me the make-up and DVDs that were my real presents.

Had just settled down to gossip when the doorbell rang. It was for me. A delivery of seventeen long-stemmed red roses. There was no message with them but I knew who they were from and dropped them in the large bin in the kitchen.

Stephanie retrieved them and gave me a lecture about never discarding gifts from ex-boyfriends. Carry on this way and I could turn into one of those stupid women who gave back expensive diamond rings just because their engagement happened to have ended or, worse, let their husbands keep the BMW and second home in the country when they got divorced.

She went on at me for some time – this was *very* important – so I was glad when the doorbell went again and interrupted her.

Couldn't believe my eyes at first when I saw who it was. Alan. He was standing on the doorstep holding out a bunch of flowers and a fancy box of chocolates. He said, 'Happy birthday, Kelly Ann.'

He wasn't tanned but still looked good. So did the Porsche he'd parked at our front gate. He saw me glancing at it and said that unfortunately the Porsche wasn't his, he was delivering it to a client, but he didn't need to hand it over until tomorrow morning so did I fancy going for a drive while I ate the Belgian chocolates and we talked things over?

Was about to tell him to stuff it, go back home to his wife and shut the door on him when Liz and Stephanie pushed past me, saying, 'mmm, Belgian chocolates' and 'gorgeous Porsche'.

Stephanie draped herself over the bonnet of the car and asked Liz to take a photograph of her with her camera phone but Liz had already grabbed the chocolates and was too busy unwrapping them to comply.

Alan said, 'Er, maybe you'd all like to come then.'

At Stephanie's suggestion we drove up to a restaurant by Loch Lomond. On the way there Alan was saying how lucky we were to have such wonderful mountains and lakes so close to the city and how beautiful Scotland was. He added that some of the inhabitants were not bad either but I just scowled at him and he shut up.

The restaurant was right on the loch beside a nice jetty thing with ducks swimming underneath. Everyone had been well impressed by his Porsche as we arrived and he got some envious looks from other guests, particularly males, who seemed to think we were all his girlfriends. Alan offered to buy us lunch but we were stuffed with chocolate so just had Coke and dessert. Alan ordered steak (didn't girls ever eat any protein at all?) and then we talked, mostly about the holiday in Greece – no one mentioned Wendy so as not to spoil the occasion, I suppose. But after we'd finished eating Alan said why didn't Liz and Stephanie go outside and feed the ducks while he settled the bill and talked to me. And he didn't care that neither of them had brought jackets or coats and it was Baltic outside, he was sure Scottish girls were a hardy lot. Just go feed the ducks.

When they left Alan said he hadn't got married when he got back to London. Sex was one thing but dating a girl for a week and really enjoying her company was something else and he'd decided he shouldn't marry Wendy.

He said he'd thought about me a lot since the holiday so when this delivery job had come up just at my birthday he'd decided to look me up. Well, OK, he wanted to be honest with me – the car should have been delivered last week by a mate of his but he'd, er, ensured the paperwork was 'mislaid' until now. All's fair and all that. Anyway, he hoped to persuade me to visit him in London sometime. I'd love London.

I was surprised Alan remembered my birthday as I'd only mentioned it in passing and told him so. Alan said he remembered every detail about me, especially the little red skirt. When I confessed that it was Stephanie's skirt he just shrugged. 'Your legs, your bum. We'll buy the skirt from Stephanie.'

On the way home Alan asked to take me out to dinner in the evening but I said I'd have to have dinner and birthday cake with my family so he said could he come. He'd like to meet my family anyway. Told him he wouldn't want to meet my family if he'd met my family but he said he'd risk it.

Alan turned out to be a charmer and a big hit with everyone except Dad. He complimented Aunt Kate on her superb cake decoration (a figure of me, made with pink icing, with my hair in bunches and wearing skates – she'd been doing the same one every birthday since I was six) and listened patiently to Uncle Jack droning on about golf.

He told Mum he could certainly see where I got my good looks from but he found it hard to believe she was my mum. We looked more like sisters.

As for Angela, Graham was a lucky man to be marrying her and what a fantastic kid Danny was. Angela liked him so much she invited him to her wedding and he accepted. He told her (with a wink at me) that it had been a long time since he'd attended a wedding and he'd be honoured.

Only Dad was chilly with him, which annoyed me, but Alan said not to worry. He'd expected Dad to be a bit cautious, that's what dads were for, and anyway he'd hardly made a good first impression with the phone call from Rhodes. Before he left Alan handed me an open return rail ticket from Glasgow to London to be used before November. He said there would be no pressure and I could sleep in the spare bedroom. He knew it would take a while before I trusted him again and he was willing to wait. What did I say?

I said, 'Maybe.'

After he'd gone Dad started on about how Alan was too old for me and I shouldn't have any more to do with him.

Oh really. Pointed out that Dad had dated Mum when she was seventeen and he was five years older, which would have made him, let's see now . . . oh yes, twenty-two. One year older than Alan. Dad blustered something about how that was entirely different and he had been totally trustworthy but Mum just laughed and said that's not what she remembered. Mum said that Alan was a very nice, discerning young man and was welcome back any time.

MONDAY OCTOBER 15TH

Mum is totally stressing about her Open University exam on Wednesday. She's been wandering round the house chanting stuff she's memorized, then stopping and cursing because she's forgotten something before lighting another fag, seemingly not realizing she's already smoking one, then stubbing it out and cursing again.

Have told her not to worry, she could only do her best and that's all anyone could ask for, and besides, I was sure she'd do fine.

She told me I just didn't understand and rushed out sobbing, banging the door on her way.

TUESDAY OCTOBER 16TH

Everyone is trying to stay out of Mum's way. She was studying in the living room, her books and notes spread all over the floor, so we all cowered in the kitchen, only going in to bring her cups of tea and empty her ashtrays. Even Danny was quiet and subdued, making no protest when we put him to bed at seven. Can't wait for it all to be over tomorrow.

WEDNESDAY OCTOBER 17TH

Finally mum is herself again. Well, not quite herself. The exam was in the morning and she went to the pub at lunch time to celebrate with some of the other 'mature' (i.e. ancient) students so she rolled in totally pissed at five in the afternoon. Wouldn't have been so bad if she hadn't done a bit of shopping on her way home. I mean just what were we supposed to do with a hubble-bubble pipe, a prayer mat and pair of incontinence pants?

THURSDAY OCTOBER 18TH

Have decided, sort of, to go and see Alan in London tomorrow so have told Dad that I'm going to stay in Edinburgh with friends of Stephanie. This is half true as Stephanie is going to Edinburgh to stay with friends and also to look for a flat for Dave, who says he'll be back next week and he can't wait to see her. He was actually due back two weeks ago but got delayed. Stephanie was disappointed, but at least it gave her some more time to try and get her tattoo removed.

FRIDAY OCTOBER 26TH

Feel a bit nervous about going to see Alan in London.
After all, I hardly know him, but Liz and Stephanie say it
would be mad to turn down the offer of a free weekend
in London, and besides, it wasn't as though Alan was the
Ripper or anything. Probably not, anyway.

Alan met me at Euston Station, kissed me on the mouth,
then took my bag. He said we'd go get something to eat
first as it was the rush-hour still and I wouldn't want to
travel on the tube at this time. Trust him.

   He wanted to take me to a proper restaurant but I just
wanted a burger and a Coke so that's what we had. Alan
said he was really happy I'd come as he thought I might
have chickened out at the last minute. Didn't tell him that
I had but Stephanie and Liz threatened to tell everyone
about my airport humiliation with Chris and (horrors!)
release the picture they'd secretly taken of me on my
knees if I didn't go, so had no choice.

   The journey to Ealing took a really long time – London
is a lot bigger and more sprawly than Glasgow. There
were still loads of people on the tube for most of the time
but none of them paid any attention to us. Honestly,
London people are great. *So un-nosy.* No one remarked
on my accent and asked where I was from, why I'd
come down, and what I intended to see and do
while I was visiting. It was fabulous to be so anonymous

and free from cheeky questions.

When we got to Ealing Station we took a bus to Alan's place, which was in a row of redbrick houses all turned into flats. Felt quite shy all of a sudden but Alan took my hand, said this wasn't Rillington Place (whatever that meant) and ushered me in.

It was quite tidy for a guy's place – two bedrooms, a lounge and kitchen. The bathroom and my bedroom were done in pink, which surprised me until Alan said he and Wendy used to live here together. He supposed he should really look for a smaller place as the rent was high for one but he'd got used to it now so just worked more overtime.

I asked if Wendy wasn't mad about the cancelled wedding and he said beyond mad. She'd spray-painted insults on his car and posted unflattering comments about him on a website before finally going to live with one of his best friends in Acton. And yes, he knew how sexist this sounded but he really did miss his best friend.

He got a beer for himself and asked if I wanted anything to drink. Decided to be honest and asked for red wine with lemonade. He said that was an awful way to drink wine but got me it anyway, which reminded me of Chris, who I really did not want to think about. It was quite late so we just chatted and watched a movie and I felt comfortable until it was time to go to bed. I'd never stayed overnight in a guy's flat before, unless you count the awful night at Chris's and I certainly didn't want to think about that.

But Alan just kissed me goodnight, said he'd see me in the morning and left me to get ready. The kiss wasn't just a friendly peck but wasn't a snog either – sometimes I can't work out whether he actually fancies me or not.

The bedroom was bare and absolutely Baltic. I put on a long-sleeved shirt and a cardigan over my pyjamas, plus thick fluffy socks and finally a woolly hat, but I was still cold. I'd never sleep like this. Decided to go and see if Alan was still awake. If he was I would ask him if he had a hot-water bottle. If not, I'd have a hunt around on my own. Crept into his room. The light was off. Didn't turn it on but, using just the light from the hall, tiptoed right up to his bed and whispered, 'Alan?'

He said, 'Kelly Ann,' then kissed me and pulled me into bed with him. He was murmuring stuff like he was so pleased I'd decided to sleep with him after all because he couldn't think straight just imagining me naked in bed right next door to him and being unable to touch me. And all the while he was kissing and caressing me frantically but then he stopped abruptly. What on earth was I wearing? He sat up and put on the bedside light then pulled the bedcovers away. Bloody hell! Was this what I always wore to bed?

Explained to him that I was freezing and that I'd come to ask him for a hot-water bottle. He sighed and said yeah, Wendy had left one here – he'd go get it for me. He added that at least he wouldn't be tormented any more with tempting visions of me lying naked in the room next door to him, then he got up. He was starkers so I turned my head away, embarrassed, but noticing this he said that no, he was the normal one, I was the freak. Most people took off their clothes when they went to bed rather than put more on. What did I wear in the shower? Gloves and scarf?

But he pulled on boxers and told me to stay in his bed to keep warm while he got the hot-water bottle. His bed was nicely warmed up so was quite pleased when he returned with the bottle and said I could stay where I was. He'd sleep in the spare room as he didn't feel the cold.

Dad is wrong about Alan. He's really nice. Wendy must have been gutted to have lost him but while I don't really feel that's my fault I did feel guilty about using her hot-water bottle, which does, or should anyway, still belong to her.

SATURDAY OCTOBER 27TH

Went to Oxford Street and shopped (mainly requests from Stephanie). Also went to Harrods and bought sweets just to get a bag. There were some really posh boutiques near Harrods with totally snobby assistants who scowled at me and Alan when we walked in. I wanted to slink out but Alan got bolshie and insisted I tried on several thousand-pounds-plus outfits before saying we'd think about it.

Went to St James's Park, which was really nice, and saw Buckingham Palace. Although the flag was up, which means the queen was in, I didn't see her. Also went to Downing Street but couldn't get very near as it was all fenced off. It looked quite small for an important place. If I were prime minister I'd expect to live somewhere a lot bigger, like a mansion or something. Didn't see the prime minister either.

We had hot dogs for lunch but went to Covent Garden for dinner, which was *so* nice although very expensive. Alan paid for everything, which was just as well as I couldn't have afforded it, but this did make me feel a bit bad. Thought maybe I should have sex with him after all to make up for all the expense but decided just to let him sleep next to me instead. Whatever happened, I didn't want to have to sleep in the cold guest room.

Really loved Covent Garden. It's just so cool, and though I didn't see anyone famous there it's definitely the type of place where you might. But the most fantastic bit of the evening was still to come. Alan had booked for us to see a musical in the West End, which was fabulous. I know for sure now what I want to do. I want to be on stage dressed in gorgeous clothes belting out songs and dancing, then having everyone applaud me. Just wish I'd chosen an easier ambition. Like being an astronaut or nuclear physicist maybe.

When we got back to Alan's flat I suggested to him that we should just sleep together and not have sex but he said no, he really couldn't sleep with me and not have sex, even in my very unattractive night gear, but I could have his room again.

SUNDAY OCTOBER 28TH

Last day. Alan's friend Paul from the holiday turned up this morning. He asked how my blonde friend with the great knockers was doing. Was she still stuck on that computer geek?

Told him her name was Liz and yes. We went for a pub lunch, where we met more of Alan's friends who were all older than me. Stupidly I'd forgotten my fake ID and I was refused alcohol, which embarrassed me, but Alan said not to worry, he had plenty of drinking mates, and just ordered orange juice for both of us. Most of his friends were really nice and didn't talk down to me, except for one girl who must have been friends with Wendy because she was quite bitchy and asked Alan if this was 'the little schoolgirl' he'd dumped Wendy for.

But Alan just said, 'Yeah, she's great, isn't she,' which shut her up.

After lunch Alan took me back to Euston. He asked if I liked London and I said I did. Then he asked if I would consider coming to live here when I'd finished school and I said, 'Maybe.'

MONDaY OCTOBeR 29TH

Helped Angela do the last of the wedding invitations tonight. She's decided to invite Stephanie as she'd helped so much with the arrangements, advising her on everything from flowers and table decorations to hair and make-up for the Big Day. She said that though she was a bit nervous she was really looking forward to her wedding now and felt so much happier than she'd been at the beginning of the year. She doesn't know whether it was the pills or just being able to admit that she was miserable and needed help that had done it. Either way, it was all thanks to Chris really. Of course maybe she shouldn't mention Chris. I must be very upset about the break-up still, especially as he was now seeing someone else.

Told her it was cool and that I was totally over him now so she said she was glad to hear it as she really wanted to invite him to her wedding. She'd known Chris for so long now he seemed just like a brother to her. So if it wouldn't upset me . . .

TUeSDaY OCTOBeR 30TH

Linda is back home in Glasgow. Her baby girl arrived a week early – she's going to call her Morgan. She still won't say who the father is. Don't know why she's still protecting Chris. He doesn't deserve it.

THURSDAY NOVEMBER 1ST

Refused to go to Gary's Halloween party last night. Told him I didn't fancy dressing up as pole-dancer, wasn't worried about retaining my title, and didn't see how his fancy dress theme fitted in with scary Halloween traditions at all. And no, it had nothing to do with me not wanting to see Chris with Amy – why should I care if Chris was dating the most boring student in, like, the entire universe – that was just his bad luck.

Called Chris tonight. He seemed pleased as well as surprised at first. However, his tone soon got frostier when he realized why I'd rung. Told him he'd probably received an invite to the wedding by now but he'd better not accept it and to stay out of my life.

Chris said that he wouldn't be told by me what to do and he'd come if he wanted to.

Told him over my dead body and he said fine by him. Then he said to tell my sister he'd definitely be there, he was looking forward to it, and hung up on me.

Liz wasn't very sympathetic later when I moaned to her about my phone call to Chris. She just gave me a paperback called *Basic Psychology for Complete Dummies* and advised me to read it.

FRIDAY NOVEMBER 2ND

Stephanie has invited Liz and me to Edinburgh for the weekend to stay with her and Dave in his flat. We declined. We didn't think we'd actually see much of Stephanie, who'd most likely spend the whole weekend in bed with Dave, and neither of us has any money for socializing.

Have moaned about always being broke to my mum. She says I'm old enough to get a part-time job and not rely on her and Dad any more to finance what she calls 'my social life'. *As if.* She says I'm nothing but a lazy article and when she was my age she had a full-time job as well as a part-time job and still had energy left over to date three boyfriends at once, yet here I was looking to her and Dad for handouts and couldn't even manage to keep the one sodding boyfriend. It was a disgrace, wasn't it, Tom?

However, Dad wasn't that pleased with Mum as apparently he'd been one of the three boyfriends and hadn't known about the other two. Although he does now.

MONDAY NOVEMBER 5TH

It's not that easy to get a job. You can't work in bars or most restaurants until you're eighteen, and anyway, every job they advertise always asks for experience. I mean how am I ever going to get experience if no one will give me a job without it?

Was moaning about this to people at school when Ayesha said she thought she'd be able to help. Ayesha's dad owns a newsagent's-come-grocery shop. She says she's sick of working in it and has told her dad she won't do it any longer even if he pays her to, which he never has. She says if he tries to make her work there she'll totally embarrass him by going to the police and telling them that he's intending to force her into marriage with an ancient toothless goatherd from Pakistan.

Her dad has told Ayesha that after five minutes with her the police would know it was the ancient toothless goatherd who'd need to be forced into marriage but that OK, if she could find a replacement she didn't need to work there any more.

WEDNESDAY NOVEMBER 7TH

Met Ayesha's dad, Mr Hassan, at his shop after school today. He was really nice to me and thinks I'll do fine after a bit of training. He told me it will be a relief to have someone pleasant and polite working in the shop as his harridan of a daughter was putting off his customers. Then he left Ayesha to mind the shop and show me how to work the till while he went to collect some supplies.

After a few hours watching Ayesha serving in the shop I could see what her dad meant. For example, she told one man that the newspaper he was buying only required a reading age of seven and was full of rubbish anyway. Next, when one lady asked her whether she thought the pilchards and salmon flavour Whiskas or the chicken and turkey was better, Ayesha shrugged and said how was she to know, she wasn't a cat, and advised the woman to 'get a life'. Likewise when Imran came round and spent a long time deciding what to buy she asked him if he was 'browsing or stalking' and to get a move on. He bought a chocolate heart and offered it to her. She unwrapped it from its pink foil, snapped it in two in front of him and gave me half. Then she told him he'd better push off or she'd throw him out. My mum calls Ayesha a 'nippy sweetie' (although Dad says Mum's got some nerve calling anyone else nippy), but whatever, I don't think I'm going to learn much in the way of good customer relations from her.

SATURDAY NOVEMBER 10TH

First day at the shop by myself. It was busy in the morning but I coped fine, not making a single mistake with change or anything. Things had quietened down a bit by the afternoon and come three o'clock I hadn't had a single customer for over half an hour when Billy the Bam, a total ned I've known since primary, walked in wearing a pair of tights over his head. He took a baseball bat from inside his anorak, brandished it at me and demanded in a stupid false menacing voice that I fill a bag with cigarettes and the money from the till.

Was absolutely furious with Billy trying to cause trouble on my very first day working by myself. Told him he wouldn't be getting anything and if he didn't clear off right away I would beat him to a pulp with his own baseball bat and tell his granny on him. Billy's parents are hopeless junkies who don't have much to do with him but he's terrified of his granny, who would give him real trouble if she knew about this.

Billy's shoulders slumped and he asked how I knew it was him. Honestly, he's such an idiot. Who else wears those awful lime-green trackies, and anyway the tights were only about ten denier, sheer enough to see every feature clearly even if his face was a bit squashed.

Anyway, realizing I was on to him he gave in and just asked to buy ten Kensitas Club but I told him we only sell twenties and I would need proof of age. Billy said he hadn't brought any ID as he didn't think he needed any, but 'C'mon, Kelly Ann,' I knew fine well he was over sixteen.

However, Billy had really pissed me off so I refused to sell him the cigarettes and we settled instead for him buying a Bounty bar and a packet of prawn cocktail flavoured crisps. Had just rung up the sale when four policemen burst in. They were not very nice to Billy at all. Two of them grappled him to the ground and handcuffed his wrists behind his back. Then they hauled him up and marched him off. They even refused to let him take the Bounty bar and crisps even though I told them he'd paid for them.

The other two policemen told me they'd received reports of a 'masked man' entering the premises and asked me for a statement.

Masked man? Honestly, it was ludicrous. Tried to tell the police that it was just Billy and he was harmless but they were taking the whole thing totally seriously. Before leaving they said they would be charging him with attempted armed robbery and would be in touch with me again. The rest of the afternoon was pretty quiet except for a visit by a woman PC, who gave me the contact number for Victim Support. *As if!*

Hoped to have a long lie-in this morning but no such luck. Was woken at eight by Mum screeching at some people who'd come to the front door. Heard her scream at them to bugger off and shove their camera up where the sun doesn't shine. Then she banged the door shut, raced up the stairs and stormed into my room.

What the hell had I been up to? There had been two reporters at the door asking to speak to me. I hadn't been talking to reporters, had I, like that eejit of a father of mine did last year? I'd better not have been because if there were people she bloody despised more than lawyers and politicians it had to be bloody reporters, slimy two-faced sewer rats, the lot of them.

Then she told me to get dressed and go and buy her cigarettes, she was out, and to never mind putting on bloody make-up and doing my hair, I was only going fifty yards to the shop, not attending an Oscar bloody awards night.

Stumbled out of bed, pulled on my jeans, an old bobbled woollen jumper and a pair of grey-looking trainers, then grabbed the tenner she was holding out for me and hurried out. From bitter experience I know just how bad-tempered Mum can be if she's forced to go for more than ten bloody minutes without a fag when she wants one.

Met the sodding reporters on the way. They shouted,

'Kelly Ann!' at me like they really knew me or something and stupidly I answered. So then they were taking photos and asking for my story on the armed robbery. Told them to push off, but they kept on at me – had to run through one close and back through another to shake them. This meant that even though I ran all the way to the shop and back I was about two minutes late delivering my mum's fags so she was in a foul mood with me. Brilliant.

MONDAY NOVEMBER 12TH

Oh my God. Am mortified. My photo is in the front page of our local newspaper and I look a fright. There are at least sixteen naked spots on my chin and forehead, un-disguised by foundation or concealer, and my unbrushed hair is flat on the side I slept on and sticking up madly on the other. Not to mention my bobbly jumper and furious expression which makes me look like an escaped lunatic from Carstairs. Bollocks.

The caption read: '*Plucky schoolgirl sees off alleged would-be armed robber.*' Then followed a load of rubbish about Billy being some kind of ferocious scary criminal. There was a 'quote' from me. 'Modest heroine Kelly Ann just said, "I was only doing my duty. It's what anyone would do." '

Have to agree with Mum about one thing anyway. Reporters really are scum.

More good news. Not. Dad says I can't work in the shop any more. It's too dangerous. He wouldn't budge, no matter how much I argued and pleaded. That's it, I'm going to kill Billy for this.

Mr Hassan is in agreement too. He was horrified by the whole thing and said ridiculous stuff like I should have just handed all the money and cigarettes over to Billy. (*As if!*) He said that from now on only he or his sons will work in the shop.

It's so unfair and totally sexist as well but Ayesha is fine about it. She says it's about time her lazy good-for-nothing brothers did something for a change. But I'm gutted. Totally.

The only good piece of news is that reporters have stopped hassling me: there is now a new leading story about a seventy-eight-year-old grandmother from Govan who rugby-tackled a burglar to the floor and tied him up with her support tights until the police arrived to arrest him.

Her photograph looked a lot more attractive than mine.

WEDNESDAY NOVEMBER 14TH

Ayesha's mum invited me round for dinner on Saturday to thank me for having worked in the shop (however briefly) and cheer me up now that I've lost the job. She's promised to make a curry from scratch and show me how to cook it.

Imran overheard Ayesha inviting me and has pleaded with me to put in a good word for him and try to find out why she won't show any interest in him. He's tried everything to get her to like him but nothing works.

SATURDAY NOVEMBER 17TH

Went over to Ayesha's house at six. Mrs Hassan usually wears normal stuff but tonight she'd put on a gorgeous blue and gold silk sari. She frowned at my brown sweater and dark blue jeans then advised me to wear bright colours. She said I was such a pretty girl but I'd never get a husband wearing dull colours like that.

Couldn't help glancing at Ayesha, who was dressed entirely in black. Her mum saw me and sighed. She said that Ayesha would never get a husband anyway because she'd a tongue sharper than a poisoned dart. After four sons she and her husband had prayed for a daughter and this was what they got.

The meal was delicious so I don't know why Ayesha's four older brothers passed on it and had lasagne instead. Ayesha got annoyed with them for being awkward, especially as they didn't help with anything like setting the table or taking the dishes out, never mind cooking, but they just ignored her 'nagging'.

However, when dinner was over and they refused to help clear up Ayesha went mental. She emptied a large jug of water over one of their heads – the one who was in the process of gelling his hair prior to going out – and threatened to put curry powder in the fuel tank of another's new Audi sports car if he didn't move his lazy selfish backside. This drew a reproof from her dad – not for the threat but her language. She ignored him and continued to hurl abuse until they gave in, cleared the table and stacked the dishes before going out.

Didn't seem a good time to talk to her about Imran but I'd promised so eventually asked her why she kept knocking him back.

Ayesha said it was nothing personal but all Asian guys were the same. They were all spoiled and used to their mothers and sisters doing everything for them. Honestly, her mum still put out clothes for her brothers in the morning and she'd only just given up squeezing the toothpaste on their toothbrushes for them. That's why they were all lazy slobs.

Imran would be no different. He was nice enough at the moment but as soon as he got some girl hooked he'd expect her to cook and clean for him just like his mum. Ayesha wasn't interested in any of it. She was going to concentrate on her career, become a rich lawyer, then hire servants to do the cooking and housework.

Personally I didn't think Asian boys were any worse than others. I know for a fact that Gary still takes his laundry home for his mum to do every week and he says all the others at the flat do too. Even Jamie, whose mum lives on the isle of Arran. Still, there's no arguing with Ayesha.

When I got back phoned Stephanie and told her about my night and what Ayesha had said about Asian boys. This started her off musing on which boys were the most spoiled in the world. She eventually decided on Italians, which she said was a pity really as some Italians were just so hot. Had she ever told me about Guido?

To shut her up I asked her how plans were going for her eighteenth birthday party, which was next Saturday.

Was furious when she told me she'd invited Chris and Amy to the celebrations – some friend she was. She defended her decision by saying she'd invited all her *own* ex-boyfriends – gosh, there would hardly be any males at the party if she hadn't – so she felt justified in inviting Chris, whom she really liked even though he was my ex. Amy was with him at the time and had assumed, wrongly as it happened, that she was included in the invite and what can you do?

But then she cheered me up by saying that she'd invited Alan, who said he'd come – he could stay at her place until the wedding as she'd loads of spare rooms in her house. What a fantastic friend she is.

Liz had great news too. Julian was coming back for Stephanie's birthday and staying until after New Year. They're going to let him more or less work from home until then bar a few trips.

So that will be the three of us with boyfriends again. Was so happy I decided to see what I could do to make Imran happy too.

MONDAY NOVEMBER 19TH

Imran cornered me in computing today. Had I spoken to Ayesha? What did she say?

Told him he should show some interest in cooking and housework then Ayesha might, just might, thaw a bit.

Imran was aghast. Cooking? Housework? That was girls' stuff.

I just shrugged and told him to suit himself then and don't say I hadn't tried.

TUESDAY NOVEMBER 20TH

Instead of sweets, Imran offered Ayesha a piece of chocolate cake which he said he'd baked himself. She let him sit with her at break while she ate it and he wrote out the recipe for her.

At lunch time he was sitting with Ayesha again. Overheard him talking about ironing. He was saying that most people thought ironing was boring but that he personally got a lot of satisfaction from turning a crumpled heap of clothes into a nice, neat pile of pressed garments.

He sounded quite convincing and Ayesha was smiling admiringly at him, but when I checked with Yasmin she laughed and said Imran was a lazy slob at home. She knows his big sister, who says all Imran ever does is veg out in front of the TV or play computer games. He has never so much as made a cup of tea at home and is totally spoiled by his mum, who dotes on him. He's probably just pumping his mum and sister for information on cooking and housework to fool Ayesha.

I hoped Ayesha would be smart enough to work this out eventually but I didn't have time to worry about it now. Tonight I was going shopping with Stephanie to look for an outfit for the party so that I looked absolutely fantastic for Alan and, more to the point, tons better than Chris's Amy.

* * *

We found a gorgeous simple but sexy cashmere skirt and teamed it with a shocking-pink silk camisole. Looked fantastic. Only problem was they were both very expensive so I couldn't buy them right then and had to beg my parents for more money.

Mum was OK about it – 'We're in so much bloody debt already, what's the odds? You'll have to speak to your skinflint of a father as well though.'

Dad said, 'What do you need more clothes for – you've a wardrobe full of clothes.'

Yeah, right. Pointed out that the last time I'd got any new clothes was in the summer and it was all underwear. But hey, great idea. It was the fashion now to wear underwear as outerwear and I'm sure I'd find something sensational for the party.

Dad forked out the money.

FRIDAY NOVEMBER 23RD

Imran and Ayesha spent the break and lunch time together again. It looked like Imran's tactics were working and Ayesha couldn't see through him. Talked to Yasmin about it and suggested we tell Ayesha that Imran was lying but she disagreed. Didn't I remember how arrogant and superior Ayesha always was about us stupid girls falling for useless guys? Wouldn't it be fun to see her all gooey about Imran?

Er, yes and yes . . . but still.

Despite Yasmin's objections felt I had to try. Just hoped I wasn't too late. Managed to catch Ayesha as she was going home after school. She said she was in a bit of a hurry as Imran was coming round to her house for dinner with the family and she wanted time to get ready.

I said, 'Erm, about Imran—'

But Ayesha interrupted me. Oh yes, he was fantastic, wasn't he? He wasn't like other guys; he was intelligent, sensitive and special.

Bollocks, looked like I was too late. Way too late.

SATURDAY NOVEMBER 24TH

Night of the party. Stephanie's parents had of course spared no expense to ensure that the party was a fantastic affair, although like last year the best thing about it was that no parents would be there.

Liz and I, plus Dave of course, were the first to get to Stephanie's but soon loads of other people crowded in, lured by the promise of unlimited free drink and the total absence of responsible adults (except for the security guards her parents had hired – but they'd been plied with booze by Stephanie earlier and were sleeping it off upstairs).

Unfortunately Alan had been delayed by traffic on the M6 and phoned to say he wouldn't get up until nearly midnight so had to endure the arrival of Chris and Amy without him.

Amy thanked Stephanie profusely for inviting 'them', complimented her on her 'fabulous' outfit and asked who her caterers were as she was so impressed with Stephanie's choice. On and on she trilled, tediously pleasant. When she and Chris had moved on I hissed to Stephanie and Liz what an awful bore she was, but they just said that they thought she was 'very nice actually, Kelly Ann'.

So much for loyal friends.

Liz and Julian disappeared upstairs to 'catch up with news' – yeah, right – and Stephanie was busy circulating so I spent most of the time chatting to Gary and Ian.

Tried not to pay too much attention to Chris and to concentrate on enjoying myself but somehow I couldn't help being aware all the time of exactly where he was, who he was talking to and what he was doing. Or I should say where he and Amy were because she never left him for an instant. Honestly, I wouldn't have been surprised if she'd accompanied him to the toilet. Only a tapeworm infestation could have been closer to him. Mentioned this to Ian and Gary but they just shrugged and said yeah, she was quite keen on Chris but was 'very nice really, Kelly Ann'.

At last around eleven thirty Alan arrived. He kissed me, said hi to Stephanie and was introduced to Dave, who got him a pint of beer. After taking just one swallow

Alan asked Stephanie if the band could play 'Zorba the Greek'. He'd something to show us.

The band did a passable impression of the number, which starts very slow and gradually gets faster and faster. Alan had asked for the dance area to be cleared so he could perform the party piece he'd been practising for Stephanie's birthday as she'd said she liked Greek dancing.

Putting the pint of beer on his head and holding his arms out for balance, Alan performed a Greek dance, not spilling a drop until the music got too fast and the whole pint slopped over him, to wild applause from the audience.

I took him to the shower room and turned it on for him. He took off his shoes and socks then stepped in fully clothed – he could wash the beer off his clothes and body at the same time, he said. When I laughed at him and called him an idiot he dragged me in with him and kissed me in the shower, which might have been sexy if I hadn't been thinking about my new skirt, which was dry clean only, and the hour and a half at least it would take me to straighten my hair.

Much later we returned to the party. Stephanie had lent me a skirt and top which I thought really suited me although Alan said I'd looked better in the towel.

Alan asked me to point out Chris, who was standing by the buffet table with his limpet, then he made his way towards him with me following reluctantly. Alan shook Chris's hand, introduced himself then said he'd heard that Chris and I used to go out together. Glancing at Amy he added that Chris had obviously moved on and said that I had too. In fact he intended to persuade me to join him in London next year and he was a very persuasive bloke.

All the while he was talking I'd been mostly staring at the design of Stephanie's carpet. Well, actually it was plain so didn't really have a design but anyway it had an interesting texture which I was studying.

Chris said nothing to Alan. Instead he cupped his hand under my chin, tilting my face up to look at him, then asked me if this was what I really wanted. Forced myself to stare right back at him and say, 'Yeah, absolutely.' When I turned away noticed that, for once, Amy didn't look too pleased and was frowning at Chris. Alan looked a bit annoyed too. I went back to examining the carpet again.

No one said anything for a while, which was a bit awkward, but fortunately Amy recovered her usual annoyingly friendly manners and started prattling on again and for once I was grateful. Oh, London was marvellous. Daddy went there loads of times on business and sometimes she went with him. Wasn't Westminster Abbey beautiful? And St Paul's. Lovely. Maybe we could all meet up there one day. Perhaps go to the theatre together.

But Alan interrupted her, and lapsing into very pronounced estuary English (which I've noticed he does when surprised or incredulous) said, 'Nah, sweet'art, you're 'avin' a laugh.' He went on to explain a bit more politely that it wouldn't be a good idea. In his experience it was better to keep exes where they belonged. In the past. Then he kissed me on the mouth in front of the pair of them and, hooking an arm round my waist, steered me away.

I was annoyed and embarrassed by the whole thing and later tackled Alan about it but he wouldn't apologize. He said it was better to lay your cards on the table in these types of situation. My ex was maybe an OK bloke but he'd already knocked up one girl, was definitely knocking off another but still hadn't taken his eyes off me all evening. Bit greedy, if you asked him.

Most people, including Chris and his limpet, had left by about three o'clock but Alan, Stephanie and I plus Liz, who'd returned with Julian, all stayed up until breakfast time, when Alan cooked bacon and eggs while I fried potato scones and square sausages. Alan was well impressed with the scones and sausages. He says I have to bring a supply down with me next time I come to London, which he hopes will be soon.

MONDAY NOVEMBER 26TH

Alan said he'd like to go to some of the pubs and clubs in town tonight as he'd heard Glasgow was great for that sort of thing. Unfortunately I had a wedding rehearsal at the church to go to, after which we had to visit Graham's awful parents. Wasn't looking forward to it. Especially the visit. Graham's dad is a sad hen-pecked loser but his mum is worse. She's a nasty snob who terrifies Angela and is the sort of person you'd like to punch on sight. Dad says she has a face like a well-skelped bum, partly due to all the gin she drinks, and has some nerve looking down on us but we've to try and be nice to her for Angela's sake.

Alan said it was a pity about tonight but OK, he'd just explore Glasgow's night life on his own. I was worried about this so rang Ian and told him to go with Alan and make sure he didn't wander into any dodgy areas.

Ian was probably the best person to take care of Alan for a lot of reasons. Although he's just turned eighteen he's always been big for his age so he's been getting into pubs and clubs since he was fourteen and knows them all pretty well. (Not that, as he constantly moans to anyone who'll listen – not many – he's managed in all that time to find a girlfriend tall enough for him.) Also, because of his size, stupid neds don't usually bother him, although in actual fact he's a really gentle guy and, Gary tells me, so slow and clumsy that he's not much good in a fight unless he happens to accidentally fall on his opponent.

Alan laughed at my plans for a 'chaperone', saying he'd lived three years in Hackney and didn't need protecting, but I insisted and warned Ian he'd be in *so* much trouble if anything happened to Alan.

The wedding rehearsal was awful at first. The ancient wrinkly priest, who looked like a skinny tortoise in his robes, was obviously not pleased to be conducting a mixed marriage service and made it plain he disapproved of our side of the family. He said since Angela wasn't Catholic we wouldn't be getting the full proper ceremony but some shortened version, which he made obvious he considered totally inferior but still too good for the likes of us.

Even the shortened version turned out to be quite complex though, with people sitting, standing and kneeling at odd times with no clue as to when to do what. Dad was annoyed about the kneeling thing, which Catholics seem to be into. When the priest had shuffled off to get some hymn books Dad hissed at Mum that he was an atheist, thank God, and he wasn't kneeling down for any eejit of a priest or priest's imaginary friend, but Mum said he'd kneel when he was supposed to kneel all right and not affront her or she'd cut his legs off if necessary. But he didn't kneel at the rehearsal, which infuriated Mum and drew scowls from the priest.

Eventually the priest finished and said he would be

going now but we had to stay there. He'd send someone back out to us with some pamphlets about the duties of non-Catholic participants in mixed marriages. He left us sitting bleakly in a side room, with Angela looking cowed and my dad furious. Must say I'm glad I'm not Catholic if this is what they have to put up with.

Spoke too soon. Just then the most gorgeous man I've ever seen – even though he was wearing a black frock – came in and smiled at us. Speaking in a soft Irish accent he said that from our glum faces he'd take a wild guess and say we'd just been talking with that miserable old coffin-dodger Canon Murray. Honestly, the canon could suck the joy from a saved soul in paradise and there should be a papal edict forbidding him to take any services except for funerals but unfortunately the Holy Father hadn't got around to it yet.

He turned to Graham and Angela. So this was the happy couple, was it – or before the canon had got to them anyway. By God, Graham was a lucky man. How had he managed to persuade this lovely young woman – whose beauty would tempt the saints themselves – to marry him? The lads of this parish were growing more cunning by the day.

He added that Angela wouldn't need the pamphlets about non-Catholic participants in mixed marriages and he tossed them in a bin. If she loved Graham and their children and looked after them even when they drove her mad, then even the Good Lord couldn't ask for more. All the while he was talking I couldn't take my eyes off him. He was tall with jet-black hair, deep blue eyes which crinkled at the sides, and a dazzling smile. Bet loads of girls go to mass when he takes it. Just a pity priests are still not supposed to have girlfriends – it's a sinful waste, if you ask me, but no one does.

TUESDAY NOVEMBER 27TH

Ian called to say that was the last time he'd be taking care of Alan until he learned some sense. He said that for a start Alan had arranged to meet him at this 'great pub' he'd found where the people were 'so friendly and generous'. Ian had been obliged to tell him that it was a well-known gay bar and not to accept any more free drinks until he got there. Alan had been embarrassed by his mistake, saying that he could usually tell but that the Scottish accent had confused him. It sounded so, well, straight.

After that Alan told him he wanted to see the 'real Glasgow' and insisted on going into a very rough pub in the East End. And when Ian said rough he meant rough; absolutely everyone had at least one scar on their face. It didn't help that at one point Alan had gone on about how Celtic had deserved their two–nil victory against Rangers. And this despite all the Rangers paraphernalia displayed on the pub wall. It's a wonder the two of them hadn't been lynched and their bodies dumped in the Clyde. I was to tell Alan for future reference that Hackney wasn't Glasgow, and if he didn't listen to advice he was on his own.

THURSDAY NOVEMBER 29TH

Ian and Gary invited Alan and me over to watch football at the flat. Gary said Chris and his girlfriend plus a bunch of other people would be there but so what? I wasn't still hung up on Chris, was I?

No way could I refuse after that. Of course I was over Chris. Totally.

Alan was pleased at first to have some male company to watch the England v. Germany match with but got a bit depressed when he realized that everyone bar him was supporting Germany. How come we hated the English so much we'd take the Germans' side?

Gary tried to reassure him by saying that we didn't hate the English players, just the biased commentators and, er, some of the thuggish fans.

Ian said that, look, everyone loved Scottish fans, who were welcome everywhere in Europe (except England), but our team was rubbish and which would he rather?

Eventually I got them to invite round an English guy who lived downstairs (and had been suffering from the same lack of support from his flatmates) to keep Alan company.

Amy hardly watched the football, just stuck close to Chris all night except when she went to make sandwiches and pass them round. When everyone (barring Alan and his newfound English friend) leaped up, punching the air as Germany scored a goal, she clapped her hands politely. When the ref disallowed a blatant foul and (almost) everyone else swore, Amy just said, 'Oh dear, that doesn't seem fair.' Honestly, what an embarrassing girly bore she was – though when I remarked on this to Alan he just shrugged and said that she seemed OK – 'a nice bit of toff tottie, if you like that kind of thing' – but added, 'Your ex drinks a lot though.'

I'd been avoiding looking directly at Chris but glanced over then and was surprised to see he was drinking whisky straight from a bottle. Had never seen him drink spirits before, never mind swigging the stuff like that. Huh, so much for all his lectures to me about the dangers of too much alcohol. A hypocrite as well as a lying cheat. I'm so glad we're finished. I really am. Am just so over Chris it's not true.

FRIDAY NOVEMBER 30TH

The night before the wedding and everyone was tense. Alan came round for a while and really helped by amusing Danny for hours on end. He played peekaboo about one million times, then when he (and I mean Danny!) tired of the game, Alan got down on his hands and knees and chased him around the living room pretending to be a fearsome monster, growling and roaring while Danny toddled and crawled away from him, squealing with delight.

When I commented on how fantastic he was with kids Alan told me he loved kids and that was another reason he hadn't married Wendy. She'd made it plain she wasn't interested in children. Ever.

Everything was fine until Alan was just getting ready to go back to Stephanie's. He said his goodbyes to Mum and Dad, then wished Angela good luck for tomorrow. Finally he kissed me on the cheek, said don't bother to see him out but, oh yes, before he forgot, I'd left this in his place last time I was down. He fished out my woolly hat from his jacket pocket. Then he added he'd had the central heating upgraded so hopefully I wouldn't have to go to bed with a woolly hat next time I visited.

That was it. Now Dad knew I'd lied to him about being with Stephanie the weekend I went to Alan's and he went mental, shouting at me in front of Alan and saying he'd never trust me again. Alan tried to calm Dad down but that just made him worse and he ordered Alan out of his home. Alan said OK, he'd go but Dad was making a big mistake – I was seventeen, not seven, and if he wasn't careful he'd lose me altogether.

I said nothing but inside I'd made up my mind. I had no reason to stay in Glasgow any more. Mum was too busy to notice me and Dad was always on my case. Even Stephanie and Liz would be too happy and preoccupied with Dave and Julian to spare much time for me any more. And Chris – well, let's not go there. It might just have been bearable if I'd still had Danny to love but he was going to be looked after mainly by Aunt Kate and Mum until Angela and Graham got back from honeymoon, then he'd go and live with his parents for good.

Later I called round to Stephanie's and spoke to Alan. As soon as the wedding was over, the very next day, I would go with him to London. Alan tried to talk me out of it at first, saying I shouldn't be in such a hurry or leave in a temper just because I'd had a disagreement with my 'old man'. But I was adamant. Said I was going anyway, with or without him – would he take me? Eventually Alan said yes. Told him to keep quiet about it until after the wedding so as not to cause any hassle for Angela and he agreed.

Went back home and started to secretly pack some stuff so as to save time the day after tomorrow. Felt sad and a bit scared leaving home, but who would really miss me much? Oddly enough the only person I could think of was Gerry, who'd now have to make do with a last-minute stand-in for our play in December, and there was so little time, whoever it was would probably be rubbish.

SaTURDaY DeCeMBeR 1ST

Finally it has arrived. I put on the stupid tangerine dress and instantly felt and looked like an under-developed eleven-year-old. Hope this doesn't put Alan off the idea of going away with me. Can't help remembering how he used to think I was too young for him.

Then Mum, Stephanie and I spent ages getting Angela ready. Told her she couldn't put her dress on until the last minute as I wasn't going to hold it for her if she needed to go to the toilet. Must say she did look gorgeous when she was all done, but yes, then she needed to go to the toilet.

Just before the wedding cars arrived saw Mum looking at me oddly then she said: 'Are you all right, Kelly Ann, love. You look a bit pale.'

Told her I was OK, just a bit nervous with all the carry-on, so she gave me a hug and said not to worry, everything would be fine. Trust Mum to be all nice and loving just when I'd definitely decided to leave home, so now I feel guilty as well as upset. Typical.

Graham was waiting for Angela at the front of the church and I must say he looked not too bad. He'd on a full kilt outfit thing and I saw that he'd really quite good sturdy footballers' legs. Absolutely essential if a guy is to look right in a kilt. We'd had what I thought was going to be good news earlier: the miserable old canon couldn't make it and I was hoping to see the gorgeous young priest but no such luck. Turned out they'd dug up someone even more ancient than the canon and so senile, in fact, that he kept trying to marry me off to Graham during the ceremony. No, I wouldn't take this man and – here's a clue – the bride is the one in the white dress.

Finally it was over and then there was just the reception thing and I'd be free. It was a five-course sit-down meal and the longest, most boring of my life. I was sat at the top table sandwiched between my dad, whom I refused to talk to, and the best man, probably the most boring best man in the world, whose speech would get into *The Guinness Book of Records* as the dullest speech at a wedding ever. My dad's wasn't bad – at least it was short even if it did have stupid jokes like he wasn't 'losing a daughter but gaining an eejit', which annoyed Graham's parents. Graham's speech was surprisingly good but I was mortified when he talked about how he used to bribe me with a fiver to push off to a friend's house so that he and Angela could be alone (and I'm sure we all knew what that meant) together.

At last the meal and speeches were over and the cake cut. Angela and Graham got up to dance a waltz thing, then me and the best man plus the parents had to join them on the floor. After that I was free and immediately went in search of Alan but got ambushed on the way by Amy, who came up to me trailing Chris behind her. Oh, it had been a wonderful service, the bride was so beautiful and I looked fantastic too. Wasn't this a lovely venue and the band was *so* good. On and on, relentlessly nice. Chris said nothing.

Spotted Alan chatting with one of Angela's friends so made my excuses and practically ran into his arms. Spent the rest of the time with him until Angela and Graham went off to get changed in the hotel room they'd booked for the purpose then came back to say goodbye to everyone. Angela threw her bouquet, which was caught by Stephanie of all people. Apparently the one to catch the bride's bouquet is supposed to be the next girl to get married. Huh, so much for that superstition.

Afterwards I went up to the same room to ditch the awful bridesmaid dress for normal party clothes. Had changed and was sitting at the dressing table putting on my make-up when there was a knock at the door. Thought it might be Stephanie looking for our secret stash of vodka or maybe Alan looking for me but it was Chris. What did he want? Before I could say get lost and where's your barnacle anyway he'd barged in and shut the door. I went back to putting on my make-up and ignored him.

He simply stood by the door and watched me. He said why was I putting all that muck on my face, I'd a beautiful face. Honestly, Chris is so old fashioned sometimes he makes my dad look modern. Still, not my problem any more. I applied another coat of mascara, lipstick and eye shadow, putting on twice as much as normal just to make my point, then I got up and told him to shift it, he was blocking my way, but he didn't budge. Instead he said in what I now noticed was a slightly slurred voice that he'd let me past if I gave him a kiss.

Told him in his dreams and he said he did dream about it in fact. Then he started going on about Alan. Did I love this English guy? Was I sleeping with him?

As if it was any of his business. Was getting fed up with Chris's nosy questions but thought it best to humour him as he was obviously a bit pissed. Told him OK, if he moved away from the door now I'd give him a kiss. He moved and I grabbed for the door handle, intending to make a quick exit, but unfortunately alcohol had not slowed Chris's reactions enough and he caught me before I escaped.

He turned me round to face him, held my arms behind my back, pushed me up against the door and kissed me hard on the mouth. For an inebriated person he had a grip as tight as a giant sea squid. The door handle was pressing against my back and his lips tasted of whisky (a drink I hate) so any normal, sane person would have found the whole thing an uncomfortable ordeal and a total affront to their civil liberties. Not me. Next thing I knew I was snogging him back, trying to free my arms – not to slap him but to pull him closer – and totally enjoying the first passionate kiss with him I'd had in months, all the time conscious of the fact that no other guy ever made me feel this good. Not nearly this good.

After a long time we stopped for air and I noticed the expression on Chris's face. It wasn't love or even lust but triumph. He said there was no way I loved Alan, not after the way I'd just kissed him. He said I still wanted him, still belonged to him, and we'd both have to tell our current partners. This was stupid. Neither of us really wanted anyone else.

He went on, his voice urgent and earnest, with no trace of the drunkenness I noticed earlier. He wanted me to come back with him 'now, tonight'. Just say I'd come right away and he'd show me how much he loved me. We'd never be apart again, never let anyone or anything come between us. This moment was so important. He knew it. 'Please, Kelly Ann, please say yes. It's now or never.'

Almost *did* say yes – can you imagine? Fine, so he was a liar who'd no conscience about cheating on me or abandoning his pregnant girlfriend, but hey, that was OK, I'd like him back, thanks, because I'm a person with no self-respect at all.

No, no matter how much I still wanted him I'd never forgive him or take him back. Told him I hated him, that he disgusted me and to shove off, then dashed out the room and back to the reception, determined not to cry.

But he was right about Alan. I would need to talk to him. Alan deserved better than a stupid girl who was still hung up on her arrogant tosser of an ex-boyfriend. I couldn't go with him to London until I was free of this horrible obsession with Chris and I'd no idea when, if ever, that would be.

The rest of the evening was awful. Alan argued with me for a bit but in the end said that, OK, right, if that was how I felt he certainly didn't want to play second fiddle to some tosser who couldn't handle his drink. He said if I changed my mind to let him know. I knew where he was.

He was right about Chris not handling his drink because he got totally pissed later. Might have been funny if I hadn't felt so miserable. For a start he insulted just about everybody at the reception. When Graham's horrible mother made some comment about it being a bit rich Angela getting married in white and her already with a baby, Chris ignored her but spoke to her husband, saying why didn't he take control *for once* and tell his wife to shut her nasty mouth? When Dad, although secretly pleased, said, 'Now then, Chris, that's out of order,' and suggested that he should leave the whisky alone – not that he should have been drinking anyway – Chris told him he'd some nerve to talk, having been paralytic drunk for almost the whole of last year when Mum ran off with her toy boy – and while he was on the subject, if Dad and Mum had been more responsible parents and paid proper attention to me I might not have turned out the impossible brat I had.

Charming. And it got worse. At one point Chris decided to get up on stage with the band and sing 'Flower of Scotland'. There's only one thing in the world Chris is not good at and that's singing. He couldn't hold a tune even if his life depended on it. It was *so* embarrassing. Not content with that he did an awful impression of Elvis singing 'It's Now or Never' and dedicated it to me. This totally pissed off Amy, who ran out crying.

Eventually Dad and Uncle Jack phoned Chris's dad, who sent a cop car that had just gone off duty to collect him. The police 'arrested' Chris on a charge of 'murder' (that is murdering one of Elvis's best songs – ha ha). They took him home despite the protests of one tone-deaf guest who'd requested him to sing 'Hound Dog'.

SUNDAY DECEMBER 2ND

Alan came round this morning to say goodbye. I managed not to cry in front of him but I am so depressed. Although he said to 'keep in touch, darling' I know I'll never see him again and it's all Chris's fault. Hate him.

Wish Chris would just go away. Maybe if I didn't keep seeing and hearing about him I'd have a chance to get over him. It would be too late for Alan of course. By that time I would already have lost him, no doubt to some blonde English girl. Still, for the next Alan that comes along, it would be great to be free of all these stupid longings for Chris.

Dad has noticed how unhappy I am and keeps asking what the matter is but I just snap, 'Nothing.' He said he wanted to talk to me and I said to talk away but he'd be wasting his breath because I wasn't going to listen anyway, I was watching Mum's *EastEnders* omnibus.

Dad said, 'Fair enough.' Then he told me it was really hard for him losing Angela as well as Danny but it was going to be even harder when I left. He'd always felt so close to me. He knew he'd made a lot of mistakes as a dad but he'd just been trying to protect me and he'd do anything to make me happy. So if this Alan character was who I really wanted then OK, he'd accept it. All right, he was maybe a bit old for me and his accent took a lot of getting used to but he seemed like a nice enough lad. If I wanted to visit him in London then OK, he'd let me go.

Told Dad I wasn't going anywhere but could I come and help out in the garage next Saturday and he said yes. Could I have a ten pound a week increase in my allowance? Dad said, 'No.'

Chris called round. He didn't look as mortified as I would have been (maybe he doesn't know how awful his singing is), just depressed. He said his dad 'after extensive enquiries' had given him a list of all the people he needed to apologize to at the wedding reception. He said it was a very long list but all he really remembered about was me, although he knows for sure that he must have upset Amy a lot as she'd phoned him to say she'd never forgive him and they were finished.

So he'd been having memory blackouts then – didn't he realize how dangerous this was? How could he be so irresponsible? Revenge at last. Couldn't help smiling with satisfaction.

Chris said it was nice to see me smile, even if it was *at* him rather than with him. All he wanted, all he'd ever wanted, was to make me happy but all he seemed to succeed in doing was making me miserable. He would do anything, absolutely anything that would make me happy. Just tell him what he could do and he'd do it.

This was too good an opportunity to miss. Told him I wanted him to leave Glasgow and never come back. He said did I really mean that and I said I did. He said this was really, really serious: was I absolutely sure that's what I wanted and I said it was. Chris didn't say any more after that except goodbye, then he left.

Don't suppose there's much chance of him really leaving Glasgow given that a medical degree takes at least five years. Still, he did ask.

TUESDAY DECEMBER 4TH

Can't believe it. Stephanie has got engaged to Dave. Couldn't have been more shocked if the pope had just announced he was getting married, yet it's true. Stephanie *did* seem embarrassed telling me and Liz about it. She tried to justify herself by saying Dave had a great body and the sex was the best she'd ever had – well, except for the Nigerian construction worker who'd dumped her for the limbo dancer – but anyway, the best regular sex she's ever had and . . . erm (and here she blushed scarlet) she quite liked him.

Liz and I were horrified. Stephanie of all people respectably engaged. We felt so betrayed, totally let down. Was our most fun friend going to become a bore? But we needn't have worried. In the next breath she was talking about the arrangements she was making for her hen do. First we'd spend a weekend shopping in New York followed by a ten-day beach holiday in the South of France before finally topping it off with a totally out-rageous party in Glasgow to which she was inviting all the young single off-duty firemen, but only if they wore their work gear. Her dad had already agreed to pay for everything, including our travel and accommodation. What did we say?

We said, 'Congratulations.'

WEDNESDAY DECEMBER 5TH

Performed the play for the old people at the day care centre. They really liked it but some old ladies complained that it was a bit tame. They said they'd heard that performers these days were a bit more daring and some even did it for real on stage. We really needed to move with the times – there hadn't been a single nude scene in the whole play.

THURSDAY DECEMBER 6TH

Chris's mum called me. Had I heard Chris was quitting medicine and had applied to the RAF? He was to go down to Cranwell in England after the New Year to undergo selection procedures in order to train as a fighter pilot. She says the minimum enlistment period is twelve years and I have to stop him. Chris would never be happy if he quit medicine and would probably get killed. Being a fighter pilot was such a dangerous job.

After I'd recovered from the shock of the news I told her this had nothing to do with me but she said it had bloody everything to do with me and I knew it. She argued with me for a while and even cried over the phone, which was awful, but there was no way I was going to try to stop Chris going away. I really needed him to get out of my life. All Chris's mum cared about was him. Someone had to care about me and it looked like that someone would have to be me. Eventually I hung up on her.

Liz and Stephanie came over to discuss the news about Chris.

Liz thought it was so romantic Chris running off to be a fighter pilot but tragic too. Obviously now that he's accepted he's lost me for ever his life has become worthless to him. Probably one day, after single-handedly saving his whole squadron without thought for his personal safety, he'll fly straight into a mountainside because the pain of living without me would finally become too much to bear. It was fascinating really how depression due to emotional trauma could override the basic survival instinct.

Told Liz this was rubbish. Chris was the most careful and least suicidal person I knew. Obviously I wasn't going to get a sensible opinion from Liz so I asked Stephanie what she thought. Should have known better.

Stephanie said Chris would look great in an RAF uniform and mmm pilot's flight gear. Did I think he could get us invites to parties at the base?

Told Stephanie to 'try to concentrate' – the whole idea of Chris joining the RAF is that we won't see each other, and besides, she was engaged now and she shouldn't be thinking about parties at the base.

Stephanie said she was planning to get married next year not interred and had no intention of giving up partying.

MONDAY DECEMBER 10TH

Linda visited the school today with her baby. Everyone, pupils and staff, cooed over it but I tried to keep a distance. I know it isn't the baby's fault but somehow I just didn't want to be holding a baby Chris had had with another girl.

Linda had taken Morgan to the common room, and after showing her off to everyone there except me (I was pretending to do maths homework) she looked for someone to mind her baby while she talked to Mr Smith and her guidance teacher about doing Highers at college. None of Linda's close friends are at school any more, as they all left after fifth year, so she asked Yasmin to take care of her.

However, after Linda left, the baby started to cry and Yasmin couldn't soothe it so she handed her to me. She'd heard I was really good with babies. Couldn't really say no.

Must admit I studied her face to see if there was a resemblance to Chris but I couldn't see any. Gerry was there and I was chatting to him about the next play we were going to do when he surprised me by asking if he could hold the baby and then seemed to take a real interest in her. When she started to cry he didn't hand her back but instead asked if he could feed her. I made sure the bottle that Linda had left was at the right temperature and showed him how to hold it so the baby wouldn't get any air bubbles and he just sat there patiently feeding her and gazing at her face.

Before he'd finished Linda came back and she went mental at Gerry. She screeched at him to give her back her baby and got on at Yasmin for not looking after her. Thought she was going totally over the top myself. She might not like Gerry but it wasn't as though he was some paedophile or anything and he was doing a good job with Morgan. Tried to point this out to Linda but she wouldn't listen, just kept demanding Gerry hand over her baby.

Gerry said nothing at first, just ignored her and kept feeding the baby, but when she tried to grab Morgan off him he told her to stop getting her knickers in a twist and that she was only upsetting the baby. Then he said he'd give Morgan back to her in a while but right now he wanted to hold her for a bit. After all, she was his baby too.

Oh. My. God.

Yesterday was awful and today even worse. I was furious with Gerry at first but he pointed out that he'd never said Chris was Morgan's dad, I'd just assumed it, and besides, I couldn't hit him while he was holding the baby. He admitted that when Linda told him she was pregnant he'd asked her to keep quiet about him but then later he'd changed his mind, saying he wanted to see Morgan – though Linda had refused.

My anger turned to Linda then, who must have known all the trouble her secret had caused me. I took her aside and demanded to know everything.

Linda told me she'd been upset after the break-up with Chris and had a one-night stand with Gerry when they'd both got very drunk at a party. She'd hoped to 'get away with it' and ignored all the signs of pregnancy until she couldn't ignore them any longer. Chris was the first person she'd told and he'd been fantastic, letting her talk and cry and just being there for her while she made up her mind what to do. She'd decided she was keeping the baby but didn't want anything to do with Gerry so she'd told no one about him, not even her parents, and that had suited Gerry. Until now anyway. Linda said she'd told Chris he could talk to me about Gerry but he refused. Chris had said the only sure way to keep a secret was to tell no one, and besides, it was important to him that I learned to trust him.

Great, so this was some sort of stupid test and I'd failed. As usual.

Phoned, texted and emailed Chris almost constantly after that, but except for one text message which said '2 l8' he'd blocked me. Obviously Chris didn't believe in test re-sits or appeals. Why would he? Finally went up to his flat tonight but he wasn't in and Gary said he'd no idea when Chris would be back as quite often these days he stayed out really late. This suited everyone else in the flat as they all had end of semester exams to revise for and Chris was annoying everyone when he was in by watching sport, or playing loud music, and on one occasion bringing some giggly drunk girl back when they were studying. He said he'd call me when Chris was in next time and promised not to tell him.

When I got home it occurred to me that maybe I was worrying too much. After all, Chris might not be accepted for the RAF – perhaps they wouldn't want him, in which case I'd have plenty of time to win him back.

Searched on Google and discovered that to be a pilot you had to be fit and have perfect eyesight. Tick. Also candidates needed to pass problem-solving tests mostly based on maths and logic. Chris could pass stuff like that even if he was as drunk as he'd been at the wedding. Bollocks.

Still, maybe there was other stuff you needed to be a pilot that the RAF site hadn't mentioned. Spoke to my dad about it.

Dad said to be fighter pilot you had to be able to fly fifty million pounds worth of equipment two centimetres from the ground at six hundred miles an hour over mountainous terrain in the dead of night. He said if any-one was capable of doing stuff like that it was Chris . . . just so long as the RAF didn't expect him to sing in tune at the same time.

WEDNESDAY DECEMBER 12TH

Was in the shower when mum banged on the bathroom door and told me that my idiot of an ex-boyfriend was on the phone and desperate to speak to me right away.

Jumped out with shampoo still in, threw on a towel and grabbed the phone from her.

It was Gerry! Could have killed my mum but she just said that she couldn't be expected to keep track of all my idiot ex-boyfriends.

Gerry told me that Linda had agreed to him seeing Morgan but still wanted nothing to do with him. However, she'd just dumped the baby on him while she went out with her pals. He said he hadn't a clue how to look after a baby and his mum wasn't not in the house. Could I help him?

Was in a bad mood with Gerry for not being Chris and because soap suds from my hair were dripping into my eyes, but he sounded pretty desperate and I could hear Morgan crying in the background so in the end I agreed 'this once'.

Went over to find him struggling to change a nappy – 'the bloody sticky tabs don't stick'. No wonder – he hadn't peeled back the protective plastic covers. Honestly!

Sorted things out and handed Morgan back to him. He sat on the sofa holding her in his lap until she fell asleep. Asked him what Shelly thought of his being Morgan's dad. He told me that she had known for a while about it but said it was OK as long as he'd nothing to do with Linda or the baby. Now that he wanted to see Morgan she'd dumped him for some guy called Steve who was doing engineering in the same classes as Ian.

I said, 'What a bitch,' but Gerry shrugged. It was fair enough – he could understand her not wanting to be bothered with, as she'd put it, 'all that baby baggage'.

Gerry didn't seem at all upset by the split. In fact as I watched him gazing at Morgan I saw an expression on his face I'd never seen before. He was genuinely in love with a girl at last. Didn't stop him pinching my bum as I left, however. He apologized, saying force of habit and that he hoped it wouldn't put me off helping him with Morgan again.

Hmmm.

On my way back dropped in on Shelly. Sympathized with her about Gerry and told her I was pleased she'd found someone else who I'd heard was really hot. Also told her that I was sure all the rumours about her new boyfriend being a player and already cheating on her with other girls were lies made up by malicious people to annoy her. However, I said I'd get Ian to keep an eye on things for us and report back to her. Patted her hand as I left and told her she could always count on me.

She seemed grateful but also a bit worried as I left.

THURSDAY DECEMBER 13TH

It was eleven o'clock before Gary called to say Chris was in the flat so had to get out of my comfy bed, leaving a still nicely warm hot-water bottle, get dressed and call a taxi. Was any guy really worth this sacrifice?

When I got there Gary let me in then sloped off to his room. Chris was sitting in the lounge, with his feet up on the coffee table, watching Sky Sport while drinking beer and – bloody hell – smoking a cigarette. Annoyingly he looked perfectly contented and relaxed. I turned the TV off and asked him what on earth he thought he was doing and what kind of example was this, a trainee doctor smoking?

Chris said that he wasn't a trainee doctor any more. He was going to be a fighter pilot. Fighter pilots usually didn't live long enough for smoking to be a problem.

Told him over my dead body he was going to be a fighter pilot and what was the matter with him anyway? I thought he wanted to cure people, not drop bombs on innocent civilians.

Chris said, 'I think the RAF recruitment line is that I will be defending my country, Kelly Ann, not dropping bombs on innocent civilians. Now why don't you just switch the TV back on and run off home?'

So patronizing. Obviously Chris was determined to really annoy me even if he had to ruin his whole life to do it. Honestly, this was beyond stubborn and a lot more like the kind of thing I'd do. There was nothing else for it. Much as I despised crying in front of other people – so girly and pathetic – I didn't hate it nearly as much as Chris hated listening to it. Especially from me. Only trouble was, I was feeling mad instead of weepy so I'd have to put on a good act.

Squeezed out a few tears as a warning shot but Chris wasn't impressed: 'Don't try that one with me, Kelly Ann. It just won't work any more.'

Realized I would have to go the whole way so tried to think of something really sad to help me. Decided to concentrate on a scene from the Disney cartoon *Dumbo*, which upset me so much that I'd never seen the end of the film. Dumbo is a baby circus elephant with these really huge mutant ears. No one will have anything to do with him except for his mum. One day everyone is making fun of Dumbo and being really nasty to him so his mum goes mental and tries to chase them off. Anyway, she ends up being caged up in an elephant jail thing for being a Dangerous Animal, and when Dumbo goes to visit her they can only touch trunks while she sings to him. Honestly, it's so sad.

Soon I was sobbing and wailing hysterically but even so Chris held off for nearly five minutes before finally giving in, putting his arms around me and promising not to leave. But I still couldn't stop crying and blurted out, 'But what about poor Dumbo? He'll be all alone in the world without his mum and everyone will laugh at his ears.'

Chris said, 'So that's it. Not that bloody elephant again. I've told you a hundred times, Kelly Ann. Dumbo's ears turn out to be fantastic *assets* to him because they give him the ability to *fly*. Dumbo's flying circus act is an amazing success and he and his mum become rich and famous. If you'd only watch the film right through you'd see it has a happy ending. It's Disney, for God's sake, not Nietzsche.'

Although Chris must have been feeling a bit conned he didn't stop hugging me which, when I calmed down, felt really nice, but when I tried to kiss him he pushed me away. There was no way he was going back with me. I'd 'messed with his head' for long enough and he couldn't hack it any more. Then he said that if he was going to stick with the medicine course after all he'd need to have a shower and sober up as he'd have to study all through the night for an anatomy exam in the morning. We'd talk again later.

SATURDAY DECEMBER 15TH

Chris and I had a long serious talk about our relationship. Or rather Chris had a long serious talk about it. Chris said that our going out together had been a big mistake. All it had done was cause problems. Almost as soon as we started dating there were constant arguments because of jealousy. To make matters worse the trust I'd always had in him seemed to vanish not long after our first kiss. We'd been much better off as friends. We should go back to being just friends. Totally platonic.

I said OK. Could he help me with a maths exercise tomorrow evening then? After all, you couldn't get much more platonic than maths. Chris said he'd be happy to.

SUNDAY DECEMBER 16TH

Since Chris is now just a totally platonic friend didn't bother to put on any make-up or straighten my hair, although Chris does prefer me without make-up and my hair curly. Did, however, wear a short, tight red dress and scarlet high heels as there's no reason to be dowdy, and besides, red is quite festive looking at this time of year.

When I got round to Chris's he was a bit surprised by my outfit and asked if I was doing anything special later and I said maybe. I suggested we go to his bedroom rather than sit in the living room so we wouldn't be disturbed. He said it was OK, all his flatmates were out that night but I'd already marched into his room and, ignoring the desk, settled myself and my maths stuff on the bed. Chris joined me and soon he was happily absorbed in working out maths problems and talking to me about algebra in a slightly bossy voice. Honestly, it was *so* sexy.

I suggested he take off his sweater – it was hot in here – but he said he was fine and we would just crack on. I told him *I* was too hot and peeled off my dress, then settled back very close to him and pretended interest in the half-finished problem he'd been working on.

Chris told me to stop teasing him – I knew perfectly well he couldn't concentrate on maths with me sitting next to him wearing nothing but a Wonderbra and thong. He said it wasn't too hot in the room and to put my clothes back on. We'd both decided our relationship was going to be totally platonic, hadn't we?

I said he was right about it not being too hot. In fact, look, I'd got goose-bumps and was probably in the first stages of hypothermia. Of course everyone knew the best treatment for hypothermia was close bodily contact followed by full sex and it wouldn't do for his girlfriend to die of hypothermia in his bedroom, would it? That would look just awful in his cv.

Chris closed the maths book, dropped it on the floor then kissed me. He asked me if I loved him and I said, 'Yes.' Then he said did I trust him and I said, 'Absolutely.' Finally he asked me if I wanted to make love, was I sure I was ready, and I said, 'Now or never.'

So now I've actually had sex at last and it was really all right. I mean, it wasn't sore at all and I've never felt so close to anyone – well, I've never been that close to anyone, but to be honest I was just getting all excited, hot and really into the swing of things when everything suddenly just stopped and that was that. Still, at least I'd finally done it and it was OK, even if I couldn't see what all the fuss had been about, which is what I said to Chris.

Chris said that wasn't too flattering and not what I was supposed to say but that tact had never been my strong point. However, he just continued to stroke and caress me for a while, then later we made love again and it was much better this time as Chris had said it would be and now I *do* know what all the fuss is about.

Afterwards neither of us felt like doing any maths so we got dressed and Chris made us each a mug of tea. He asked me if I was OK and I said I was, then he asked if I was happy and I said very.

Later Chris drove me home and we talked on the way, mostly about how great it was to be together again and how awful it had been when we fell out. We both admitted jealousy had been a problem before our split and, oh God, torture afterwards. I said I should have trusted him more and not listened to Shelly. He said he should have trusted me with the truth about Linda. We both vowed that nothing would ever drive us apart again.

When we got to my place Chris walked me to the door and kissed me. Then he joked about the lengths to which some girls will go to avoid a bit of maths homework before kissing me again and saying goodnight.

Mum and Dad were still up but I didn't want to talk to them. Instead I went straight up to my bedroom, sat down in front of the dressing table and stared at my reflection in the mirror. I expected to look different some-how, maybe older and more sophisticated, but I just looked the same except for a small happy smile that I couldn't suppress . . . a bit like the Mona Lisa I'd seen in Paris. So *that* was what she was smiling about.

MONDAY DECEMBER 17TH

In the morning realized that I'd left all my maths stuff at Chris's but I needn't have worried. Chris met me at the school gates. He had done my assignment for me, forging my untidy script, complete with a few errors to make it appear more believable. He said he'd explain the underlying principles to me later and I said I couldn't wait.

Despite having completed my homework I still got into trouble in maths as I just couldn't concentrate on what Mr Simmons was saying. The truth was even the sight of a maths textbook was turning me on. (Liz later told me this was called Association.) Anyway, Mr Smith finally said, 'Kelly Ann, what on earth are you day-dreaming about because your mind is definitely not on this exercise?'

Unfortunately I then just blurted out, 'Sex.'

Mr Simmons was furious and sent me down to Mr Smith's office with a referral that quoted what I'd said and complained that I was insolent and a disruptive influence in the class.

Mr Smith read the referral and said Mr Simmons must be joking and he could deal with this himself so he referred me back to Mr Simmons.

Found Mr Simmons in the maths department at the break. He was sitting down beside Ms Conner explaining some maths proof to her in a slightly bossy voice and was so absorbed and happy that he didn't notice my arrival, but Ms Conner did and removed her hand from his thigh.

Told Mr Simmons that I didn't mean to be insolent or a disruptive influence but that I really had been thinking about sex and it had just sort of come out.

Mr Simmons was not satisfied with this explanation. He said I couldn't just blurt out what I was thinking like that. What if everyone did that? For example, what if he, Mr Simmons, were to talk about sex every time he thought about it? There would be precious little maths teaching done, he could tell me.

Put my hand over my mouth to stop myself giggling about what he'd just said but Ms Conner didn't bother and nearly wet herself laughing while Mr Simmons turned bright red and blustered on for a bit more before giving me a punishment exercise (at my age – I mean for God's sake!) and telling me to behave myself in future.

TUESDAY DECEMBER 18TH

Told everyone I knew what Mr Simmons had said and the story spread throughout the whole school so he was tormented in every class with cheeky comments, even the first years saying stuff like 'Penny for them, sir.'

WEDNESDAY DECEMBER 19TH

Had a lot of bother finding Mr Simmons to give him the punishment exercise, which was a 1000-word essay on 'Responsible and Appropriate Behaviour at School'. Finally found him in the maths store cupboard snogging Ms Conner – and I mean really snogging her with his hands on her bum. They sprang apart guiltily and Mr Simmons muttered something about, 'Yes, Ms Conner, I completely agree with you about the importance of language in maths and we should continue with this interdisciplinary cooperation . . .'

Yeah, right, like I'm totally blind or stupid or something. Honestly, what does he take me for? But I just said: 'Here's your essay on "Responsible and Appropriate Behaviour at School", sir. Oh, and by the way, you have a second-year class waiting for you across the corridor and you might be interested to know that the period bell went ten minutes ago.' Then I turned on my heel and left. Think I made my point.

SATURDAY DECEMBER 22ND

Mum and Dad have had a talk and they have invited Chris to stay the night at our place and say we can sleep together. They recognize that Chris and I must be having sex anyway and they've decided to be more modern, accepting and tolerant parents. Angela is furious as they wouldn't let her and Graham sleep together even after she'd had the baby until they were married. She says it's not fair and it's because she's the oldest that they were so much stricter and old fashioned with her.

But I wish they hadn't bothered. There was no way Chris and I were going to have sex with my parents sleeping right next door. Not only that but we were scared to even move in bed in case they heard bed springs creaking or something and *thought* we were having sex. Was a horribly uncomfortable night, with the pair of us lying rigidly side by side like those statues you see on top of old stone coffins in abbeys. Hope they don't let Chris stay over again.

CHRISTMAS DAY

Chris came over this morning to give me my Christmas present and just spend some time together before joining his family for dinner. Was surprised to get straighteners from Chris as he likes my hair curly but he says since I insist on straightening my curls he hopes that this will save me time – currently almost ten per cent of my life is spent on this single task.

Of course Angela, Graham and Danny came over for Christmas dinner. Noticed Angela didn't stuff herself as usual. Found out she'd just had Christmas dinner at her in-laws. Apparently Graham and she didn't dare disappoint either set of parents. However, Angela *did* say when her mother-in-law criticized her for allowing Danny to eat his pudding with his fingers, the old bag's husband told her to shut her face! Seems he's decided to take Chris's advice after all.

It was great to see Danny again. I'd *so* missed him but couldn't help noticing that though he played with me for a bit he kept going back to Angela, clinging onto her leg and obviously preferring, most of the time, to be with his mum. Must say I felt a bit jealous but I suppose it's only right.

Chris came over in the evening again. I was surprised that Danny took to him straight away and didn't seem shy at all, given it had been so long since he'd seen him. Hmmm.

Chris has confessed that he'd got quite attached to Danny so after our split Angela had let him come round and see him sometimes when I was out. He said I shouldn't be angry with my sister as she'd wanted to tell me about it but he'd asked her not to. He was sorry about keeping this from me and promised never to go behind my back again. He added that a lot of the problems in our relationship had been caused because neither of us were open and honest enough. He said that from now on we should be completely truthful and not keep secrets from each other.

I totally agreed. So much so that I almost told him I'd be going over to Gerry's tomorrow to help with Morgan and that Alan had sent me a Christmas card inviting me down to London at Easter – 'no strings, just as a friend'. However, decided to check with Liz and Stephanie first.

After Chris had gone home I called Liz. She said honesty in relationships was a complex concept. It wasn't her job as a therapist to advise or direct me; rather her role was to offer support and guidance as I struggled with important life-changing decisions. However, she added that on this occasion she would make an exception. She said I should keep my big mouth shut. Could she make it any plainer? And a Merry Christmas to me too.

Talked to Stephanie. She said there was honesty and there was monumental stupidity and I'd better learn the difference quickly if I wanted to keep a boyfriend for more than five minutes. Of all the stupid ideas I'd come up with this had to be the stupidest. Being honest with a boyfriend of all people! She'd never heard of such a thing. Was I insane? She said I should keep my big mouth shut. Could she make it any plainer? And a Merry Christmas to me too.

MONDAY DECEMBER 31ST

Hogmanay – and the first I've spent away from home as we all went to a party in Chris's flat. Was disappointed that Chris would be working at the hospital until after midnight but he said he'd get back as soon as possible. Gary and Jamie had made the punch again, which I'd certainly intended to avoid until they told me that Chris had left word he would break the legs of and bury alive anyone who offered me any of it. Was annoyed by Chris's control freakery tendencies so pleaded with Gary and Jamie and called them spineless wimps but they were adamant about refusing me. However, in the end Gary agreed to one glass in exchange for helping him pull the long-legged girl in the very short pink skirt with the butterfly tattoo on her thigh.

Told him her name was Maria, she had quite a nice face too and she loved Italian guys, so he handed me the punch, put on his best phoney Italian accent and moved in on her. Hadn't told him that she speaks fluent Italian as her mother comes from Milan but I guessed he would find that out soon enough.

At last Ian has found a girlfriend. She is called Valerie and is a six-foot-tall sturdily built giantess with yards of thick red hair tumbling down past her bum. Although she looks like a Valkyrie, Ian calls her his wee carrot-top and treats her like a fragile doll. She in turn is delighted to find a guy who's still taller than her even when she wears high heels, so the pair of them are well loved up.

Phoned Mum and Dad after the bells. Mum said Happy New Year and to tell my father he's a pompous eejit of a man and a totally boring drunk. Dad said Happy New Year and to ask my mother who she was calling drunk – that was a laugh seeing as she'd fallen off her chair twice tonight already and could hardly manage to stagger into the kitchen to pour herself another rum.

Chatted for a while longer before reluctantly putting the phone down. Really missed Mum and Dad – even their stupid fights – so in the end when Chris got back he agreed to drive me home to wish them Happy New Year in person. However, by the time we got there Dad was fast asleep snoring on the sofa and Mum had gone to bed. Typical.

TUESDAY JANUARY 1ST

Was trying to think of New Year Resolutions to write in my diary when Chris asked what I was doing and offered to help. So here are his suggestions:

Chris's New Year Resolutions For Me

1. To stop cheating at Monopoly and to stop trying to cheat at chess.

2. To sleep lying on my own side of the bed with my head on the pillow and my feet pointing towards the bottom of the bed and never ever to sprawl diagonally across the entire bed leaving him about two centimetres of mattress and no duvet.

3. To realize that I have a totally fantastic, perfect boyfriend and therefore I should have no desire to flirt with anyone else, especially the new French foreign exchange student and don't think he hadn't noticed.

4. On a similar topic, when I watch football I should just follow the game without commenting on individual players' bums or thighs. I should also not moan about the fact that they don't take off their shirts any more when they score a goal.

5. I should always love him and stay with him for ever.

Told him I could only manage to keep one of these resolutions and kissed him. Then I asked him if he fancied a game of Monopoly.

Chris hesitated for a moment, then said, 'Only if you cheat, Kelly Ann. Only if you promise me you'll definitely cheat.'

MY desperate LOVE DIARY

by Liz Rettig

There's G. Isn't he gorgeous? I think he just looked at me – well, he looked in my direction anyway. Do you think he'd ask me out if I dyed my hair and got breast implants? KELLY ANN

I think you need **brain** implants, Kelly Ann, then maybe you'd see what a complete idiot G is. STEPHANIE

Stephanie's right. OK, G's not ugly but he's SO up himself! You'd be much better off with Chris. He's really fit and crazy about you, if only you'd open your eyes . . . LIZ

Don't be stupid! Chris is a good friend but that's it. I'd rather snog my brother (if I had one). Now be serious, how do I get G to notice me? A blonde wig and a Wonderbra? KELLY ANN

Navigating her way through teenage embarrassments, sick-filled parties, awful love poetry and green condoms, Kelly Ann is a hilariously endearing character. *My Now or Never Diary* is the eagerly awaited sequel.

Corgi Books 0 552 55332 8   Corgi Books 0 552 55334 4
978 0 552 55332 2 (from January 2007)   978 0 552 55334 6 (from January 2007)

Ros Asquith

LOVE, FIFTEEN

Amy ~~AMARYLLIS~~ BAKER: HER DIARY

In Which Amy's Life Is Over,
And That's Just the Beginning . . .

The pregnancy test is called Herald. Great! Blow the trumpets!
Hang out the flags! Hold the front page! The chicken has come home
to roost! A Little Bundle of Joy is on the way! They should call it
Tenterhooks. Or Tough Luck. Or You Are Not Alone . . .

I blame the Turbo Shaglauncher cocktails – Stanley Maul was helping
me to drown my sorrows after the love of my life emigrated to Japan,
and I have a funny feeling (though I can't seem to remember a thing
about it) that he may have given me more than just a mauling . . .
Tharg! I've betrayed Tom and now my life is over . . .

Isn't it?

From the bestselling author of the hilarious Teenage Worrier
series:

'A female Adrian Mole . . . a mine of
information and fun' *Daily Mail*

'Extremely amusing' *Time Out*

Corgi Books 0 552 14777 X
978 0 552 14777 4 (from January 2007)

Unsuitable for
younger readers

THE BOYFRIEND LIST
EMILY LOCKHART

The Boyfriend List was a homework assignment for my mental health. Doctor Z, my shrink, told me to write down all the boyfriends, kind-of boyfriends, almost-boyfriends, rumoured boyfriends and wished-he-were boyfriends I've ever had. Plus, she recommended I take up knitting.

In the same ten days I: lost my boyfriend (boy #13); lost my best friend; lost all my other friends; learned gory details about my now-ex boyfriend's sexual adventures; did something shockingly advanced with boy #15; did something suspicious with boy #10; had an argument with boy #14; drank my first beer; got caught by my mom; lost a lacrosse game; failed a maths test; became a leper and became a famous slut. Enough to give anyone panic attacks, right? I was so overwhelmed by the horror of the whole debacle that I had to skip school for a day to read mystery novels, cry and eat spearmint jelly candies.

CORGI BOOKS
0 552 55321 2
978 0 552 55321 6